Chapel Field

Paula Hillman

BLOODHOUND
— BOOKS —

www.bloodhoundbooks.com

Print ISBN: 978-1-916978-66-9

Prologue

Walney Island, 1945

Lenny Diamond

A n evening in late summer, with long shadows and crowds of midges. Lenny Diamond pulled his truck onto a patch of shingle at the edge of the wood. No one was about, not even the last stragglers from shipyard kick-out time; he was alone. He rested his forehead on the rim of the steering wheel and tried to contain the joy threatening to punch its way out of his belly like a wild thing. He'd become a father. *A father.* Twenty-four hours of pacing corridors in the maternity home, smoking one roll-up after another, hoping he didn't smell of oil and rust, then she'd done it, his Maisie-Anne: she'd given him a son.

A pail full of barley stout bottles rattled in the footwell. He grabbed one then climbed out of the truck, dropping heavily onto the shingle. From this part of the beach, it was possible to look across the water to the mainland, to a jumble of brick chimneys and the back-end of the shipyard sheds. The new housing estate, too: a place his wife coveted as much as he loathed.

The tide was halfway in, a wide band of glittery blue

cutting into the drab of the mudflats. He knocked the cap of his bottle against a rock and gulped down a first sweet mouthful of the stout. A breath of sea-wind touched his face, and he inhaled deeply. Having a child was the best of things to happen. And the worst. One way or another he would have to get May and the baby a proper home. Living in the caravan didn't bother him; he was a traveller. But she needed more.

The wood caught his eye whenever he drove through this village: Chapel Field, full of old cottages and barns, huddled together at an angle to the sea, as though they were fighting the island weather. Those places would not suit him, even if he did have money. Privacy was what he wanted, and where better than a sea-wood.

His boy had no name yet, but he was thinking something like *Richard*. Richard Leonard Diamond. Perhaps Ritchie for short, Rick for his friends and Rikki for his lovers. Another wash of emotion followed his next glug of beer, and Lenny had to sit for a moment and settle his giddiness. His *son* might have sons: being a granddad in the future was something he hadn't thought about; a new line of Diamonds, children with his height and May's way of smiling.

There had been the opportunity to hold his baby, given grudgingly by a pair of hefty women wearing dark uniforms, eyes like the slits in a post-box. But it had been enough. He'd not felt a rush quite like it, not even when he'd first set eyes on May. With utter certainty, he knew he would kill for this tiny boy, with his head of dark thick hair and angry frown. And he wouldn't let him spend his life dealing scrap metal. An actor, perhaps, or an artist, that would be exactly right for little Richard Diamond.

Further along the shingle, where the borders of beach and wood blurred, were two gigantic boulders, looming upwards, peaks hidden by a mass of tangled branches. Lenny had the urge to climb, to get to the top of the world and shout his victory at the sky. Until this moment, his life had been full of small wins: a good price for copper piping, a winter passed and not gone to his chest. Today felt like he could hold his head up proudly and stand shoulder-to-shoulder with other men.

His boots had a hulking set of treads, and he was up the boulders in a few seconds and thinking he could jump from here and into the wood. He could do anything today, it was his; the universe had his back. With a swing of his arms, he flung himself forward onto a square of bramble and mud, and kept his momentum going until he'd entered the wood proper. What a place it was. The light of evening filtered through a canopy of green, becoming grainy and enveloping in the most comforting way. Lenny liked the feel of it. He knew what happened in wide-open spaces, knew the prying and judging that went on in plain sight.

The trees thinned out once he'd walked a few more paces, muddy paths trodden between them. Hardly being able to read, he had no way of naming anything but holly bushes and stringy nettles reaching for the light. That people used the wood was obvious, and he could smell smoke; woodsmoke.

He picked his way between silvery tree-trunks and shrubby overgrowth, enjoying the way early leaf fall felt like the best kind of carpet. If he could clear an area of thicket, he could build a house. Right here. May would love it. He would give her a garden and the boy could have a bedroom, and no one would stare and judge because there would be trees for protection.

'What you doing here?'

Lenny gasped like he'd been punched. Lost in his little world of playing house, he hadn't seen or heard the man now standing in front of him. He was dressed in the working uniform of a docker: greasy cap and jacket with a string belt, heavy boots. His face was soft and flabby, small features sunk deep. Another man appeared from behind him, the difference being his hard-edged expression.

'All right, fellas.' Lenny scanned around the wood: there were only two of them. Easy. 'Cooking up some supper, are you? Feel like some company?' He pulled the half-drunk bottle of stout from his pocket. 'I've got more of this back in my truck.'

'I asked a question,' the first man said, then hawked up something from the back of his throat and spat on the ground between them.

'And he should answer, shouldn't he, Butch.' The second man shuffled forward, pulling a cigarette from between his lips and grinding it out under his heel.

Whatever pulse of pecking-order excitement Lenny had been feeling was quickly turning into something that burned. 'And I don't feel the need to answer, right now. I'm doing what I'm doing. It's not your business. Unless you're saying this wood is private property, and I don't think it is.'

'Listen to him.' The second man stuck out his chin. 'Not from round here, are you.' He scanned Lenny's overalls and donkey-jacket. 'You're one of them gyppos what's living down the south end. I've seen you. Bloody *offcomers*.'

That word. Offcomer. His life was contained within the sound of it. A flash of hot anger made Lenny bite his teeth together, but he wasn't stupid. Resolution was better with no blood spilt.

'I bet there's good lamping up here,' he said, deliberately relaxing his posture. 'Not that I'm looking for new places. As you say, I live on the south end of the island and the dunes are teeming.'

The men eyeballed each other. Lenny took another swig of beer. He braced himself. He knew how quickly things could turn nasty. And they did.

The first man took two steps towards him and grabbed the lapels of his jacket.

'Teeming with vermin is exactly what them dunes are,' he growled. Lenny was close enough to his face that he could see the dirt ingrained in a spread of enlarged pores, smell the meaty tang of his breath. 'So you'd better get back there. Or better still, piss off out of town altogether.'

Lenny lost his wish for good sense. He swung his fist back then swiped it into the side of the man's head. Boxing had never been his strong point. He liked a dirty fight; temples, not chins. The man released his grip and stumbled sideways. Lenny wasn't going to leave anything to chance. He lunged for the other man, swung his boot to groin-level and connected, bracing himself for an assault launched from behind when the man recovered.

As soon as he felt the weight across his shoulders, he let his knees buckle. His assailant was propelled by personal momentum, then collapsed in a heap of coat and boots. Lenny added a few kicks for good measure. Both men were down now and trying to find their breath. This wasn't how he wanted the atmosphere to be between him and other people. So many times he'd tried to make a good impression, tried to find common ground, but the endings always looked like this one: Lenny Diamond, a line in the sand and the rest of the world crouched on the other side and snarling.

'This isn't what I'd planned, fellas.' He shrugged. 'And wouldn't it be awkward if I turned out to be the owner of this little patch.' When one of the men seemed to be rousing, he added, 'I'm not. But help me out by telling me who is, before I leave you in peace.'

One of the men hauled himself up and for a moment Lenny thought he wasn't done. Then he held up his hands and spoke through gritted teeth.

'I don't know what game you think you're playing, but you

can bugger off. The wood's ours. Belongs to Chapel Field folks, like, and we don't want you and yours anywhere near.' He turned to the other man, now also on his feet. 'Two of us might not be able to give you trouble, but there's plenty more who'll join us next time, believe me.'

'Oh, I do.' Lenny finished the last dregs of his beer, draining the bottle slowly, keeping his eyes on the men. 'Believe you, that is. But you'd be surprised what money can buy. And us *gyppos* have always got plenty.' He threw the bottle, so it landed between them, then turned his back and stalked away, more determined than ever to own a portion of this wood.

Chapter 1

Summer 1996

Laurie

By the time Laurie arrives, evening has closed in enough to cool the air a little. She strides across the field, crows scattering in her wake, cut stalks of grass scratching at her ankles. They'd been the things her mother objected to most about her outfit. *Bare ankles, with those legs,* she'd said, as though Laurie had no right to be offending the world with how she looked. She'd kept quiet about meeting Marcus Butcher: that would have been something real to moan about. With a flick of her pony-tail, Laurie peers up at the tent. It's one of those khaki monstrosities, with a pole poking through the top. A *bell tent,* she'd heard it called. She slaps her hand against the thick canvas of the doorway.

'It's Loz. Can I come in, guys?'

A low mutter of voices, then a hand appears and begins to untie the flap.

'Mummy let you out, did she?'

'Piss off, Butcher.' Laurie rears away as the thick fug of

7

cigarette smoke and sweat creeps from the tent's interior. 'I'm here, aren't I?' She ducks and pushes her way in.

Ruth and Pete and Jamie are sitting cross-legged, with playing-cards fanned out in their hands. From the top of the central tent-pole hangs a torch, splattering the gloom and giving everything a dirty sheen. An empty bottle of cider rolls between them.

'Howdy,' Pete says as Laurie sits beside him. 'You look nice.' His eyes flash across her shoulders and settle on the shadowy hollow at the rim of her vest-top.

'Nowt in there for you.' Jamie laughs.

Marcus joins the circle and picks up his cards. 'You can be her partner for this round, Loz.' He gestures towards Ruth. 'Not that she has any fucking clue what she's doing.'

'Shut your face,' Ruth says. Laurie slips an arm around her friend's soft shoulders; she's made an effort tonight. Her short blonde hair is held back with a pink circular clip and she's wearing a sun-dress rather than her usual denim skirt and tee. Flirtation overlays her insult.

'Now then, now then, ladies.' Pete pouts, and gets a thump on his upper arm from Marcus.

Jamie interrupts, slamming his card-fan down on the polythene groundsheet. 'King, queen, jack, and ace of fucking diamonds. That's the round over before it's even begun.'

No one speaks for a moment, and Laurie suddenly feels out of her depth. This last year of school has been all about pushing boundaries and bending rules to within an inch of their lives. Now the summer of freedom has finally arrived, she feels more like six than sixteen. Marcus Butcher is a roller-coaster of a lad, and she wants to get off. He jumps up from his place next to her and kicks the deck of cards. It scatters. Ruth twitches.

'Talking of diamonds,' he growls, 'who's up for a bit of Diamond-bashing right now?' Silence. 'Petey-boy?'

Laurie pretends to be rubbing at her eye, but whispers *let's go* behind her hand. Ruth doesn't respond, and before she can think any further, Marcus has unfastened the flap of the tent, and they are piling through.

Outside, the heat is beginning to fade and there is the faintest smell of seaweed on the breeze. The sky has a metallic sheen and a tiny sliver of moon, but the ice in Laurie's veins has nothing to do with the change in temperature. When Marcus gets a hunger for tormenting the Diamond family, it never ends well. Not that they don't deserve it, with their complete disregard for the village and its ways, their rough fences blocking public footpaths and their thieving from the shop. She's never seen much of this, but people talk. That's the thing about Chapel Field; everyone knows everyone else, one family keeping an eye out for the next. It feels safe.

Pete slings an arm around Ruth's shoulder. Laurie walks with Jamie and Marcus marches ahead, making a show of lighting up, spitting on the ground a couple of times. He back-heels a loose stone, then taps it with his toe. Jamie responds, running towards him in an exaggerated way.

'And the flanker sets up Butcher,' he calls.

'And Butcher scores.' Marcus hoofs the stone into the air, an arc of glowing cigarette ash following. He dances on the spot, waving to his adoring – and imaginary – fans. Pete moves to join in, but the moment has passed. Marcus has lost his jovial expression.

'What do you think?' He frowns. 'Shall we go to the house? Knock on the windows and stir them up a bit?' He blows a smoke ring into the dusky air. 'Anyone want a drag?'

'Give it here.' Pete takes the cigarette and mimics Marcus in a way that is faintly creepy. While Marcus is slim and golden and intense, Pete has thick arms and legs, heavy dark hair, and stoops to hide his height. Laurie drops behind and links her arm through Ruth's.

'God, I really fancy him. Marcus, I mean,' Ruth whispers. 'What do you think of him, Loz?'

'He's all right, I guess. Don't know him really.'

'Know him? What's that got to do with anything?' Ruth sighs. 'Anyhow, we've known him for ages, if you think about it.'

'Suppose so. He can be a bit nasty though, can't he?'

'You mean he says what he thinks.'

Laurie isn't sure what she means. Only that she doesn't feel easy around Marcus Butcher. He has no interest in or connection with people different to him: parents, kids from other schools, old folk, he hates them all. And that's especially true of the Diamond family. None of them are happy about their concrete monstrosity of a house or the fenced-off land, but Marcus always takes it one step further. Ed Diamond is the same age as them, but he doesn't go to their school – or any other, she doesn't think – and Marcus uses this as an excuse to sling vile comments his way.

Diamond Hall is on the edge of the village, where sea-wood eats into the housing estate. It sits just above the beach and can't be accessed without hammering on one of the two gates in its tattered fencing system. But Marcus knows a way in.

'Let's scoot down to the shore,' he is saying, 'get in the back way. Any bets we can reach the windows before anyone sees us? Fiver says we can, Petey-boy.'

Pete and Jamie set up some rough-and-tumble with him while Laurie and Ruth follow. They leave the field through a gap in the hedge and follow a tarmac path downhill to the first patchy shingle of the beach. The tideline is away in the distance and the sands are deserted. Except they're not. Moving towards them is a dark figure, tall and shambling.

'It's Diamond,' Marcus hisses over his shoulder. 'It's him.

The fucking loony.' Then he charges forward, Pete and Jamie on his tail. Laurie hangs back, tugging at Ruth's arm.

'Don't,' she whispers, but her friend shakes herself free.

'It's a bit of fun. Come on, Loz. It'll be a laugh. You know how Eddie-boy flips out.'

Laurie knows, all right. This isn't the first time they've harassed Ed Diamond. Wherever he goes in Chapel Field, people are ready for him. If he's with his father, silence and ignorance are the weapons of choice, but if he's on his own, anything goes. The cruelty of their torment is something she shouldn't let herself become involved in, but for Laurie, it's the easier choice; better Ed takes the punishment of exclusion than her. Marcus Butcher and his caustic words are lethal.

Up ahead, Ed is surrounded. There are cat-calls and swear-words, demands for him to go back where he came from. There's even a mewling screech from Ruth, words Laurie hasn't ever heard on her friend's lips.

'Lay off,' Ed is pleading as his arms swing randomly. 'Else I'll shout my dad.'

'Daddy, daddy,' Jamie is sneering, while Marcus pushes against Ed's shoulders. Pete takes a swipe at Ed's lower legs, and soon he's down. With his hands on the crown of his head and his spine arched, he begins to scream. Not high-pitched or piercing but a sound that reminds Laurie of a squawking parrot. She hates herself for thinking it. Marcus is howling with laughter and can hardly find breath enough to speak. When he can, there's a new level of cruelty to his words.

'We don't want to find nutters on our beach, making everything filthy. There're girls here. Ladies.' He stretches the word. 'They don't want creepy gits like you lurking in the shadows. And while we're on the subject of ladies, how's that sister of yours? Still dead, is she?'

And that's when Ed breaks. It's like he gets an injection of energy from somewhere, like he's alight. First comes the roar, then he explodes upwards, lashing out and knocking Marcus off his feet. He goes for Pete and Jamie, who fall into each other, then Ruth is flung backwards, winded. Laurie is standing slightly away from them all, and she has time to look Ed square in the face. The dark eyes flash in a way she feels as a blow to her stomach. Then he growls low in his throat and spits at her.

'Fucking brilliant,' howls Marcus, and Laurie realises they are all laughing, clutching at their stomachs and getting up from where they've been floored. 'Look at him run.'

Chapter 2

Summer 2018

Laurie

The painting is startling in its beauty as much as in its quirkiness. Laurie gasps as she pulls back the covering. Across the canvas are sections of yellow and lilac, electric pink and fluorescent green. Some of the sections have a shape, others are random spaces. Everything is edged in rich brown. There is no meaning to it, yet it means everything. She's no idea about art, though she recognises talent. It's not signed, but her mother could never have painted this piece; she must have acquired it. Though Janet Helm once worked in a dressmaker's shop, she had no time for anything creative; Laurie once brought home a felt pincushion made in her school sewing classes, hand-embroidered. It was in the bin before the end of the day.

This room, in a gloomy north-facing part of the house, isn't one Laurie ventured into much. Her mother insisted she kept to her bedroom and didn't get too comfortable in the lounge or kitchen. If they ever found themselves sharing a space, it would end with bickering. Now, she's gone. There won't ever be bickering again.

Clearing the piles of books and magazines, boxed clothing and stacked bedlinen isn't going to be as simple as Laurie thought. Though she'd lost contact with her mother twenty years ago, every item must have meant something to her. How can it be simply thrown away? She covers the painting and walks over to the window. As she pulls back the heavy curtains, the smell is there again: mould and old fish. Below is the back yard with its algae-streaked paving and wheelie bins. There had been a washing line once. In the time before tumble-dryers. She remembers rinsing out her school blouses and letting them drip-dry. Underwear, too. Her mother hadn't been the same as everyone else's. When Laurie went to university, she was already used to fending for herself. While her room-mates sobbed for family and home-comforts, she'd felt real for the first time in her life. It's not nostalgia or grief that's clogging the back of her throat, it's the disconnect of being asked to clear away the possessions of a person she hardly knew.

She needs to get out of the house.

Downstairs, she's managed to create a space tidy enough to live in while she's here. Six weeks, perhaps eight: plenty of time to clear away a life then forget about it. She picks up a sweatshirt, ties it around her waist, then heads out.

Late afternoon sunshine slants along the street. Everywhere is quiet. Laurie has been here for almost two days and the only person she's had contact with is the old gentleman who lives in the house next door, keeper of her mother's spare key. She vaguely remembers him, but he had no knowledge of who he was passing the key to. Only that the estate agents requested it.

There's a closeness to the evening air, and she makes her way to the beach in search of a breeze. She isn't disappointed. As soon as she hits the first patches of shingle, a delicious coolness lifts her hair and runs along her bare arms. The water is golden-green, choppy in places, and she wants nothing more than to sit in the briny shade and watch it ebb towards the estuary. There was once a cluster of boulders along the path. She and her teenage friends used them as a meeting point, a place away from the pry of parental eyes and village gossip.

What those teenage friends are doing now, she has no idea. One of the reasons she chose a university as far away as possible was to leave those friendships behind. When Marcus Butcher died, it was as though the universe decided enough was enough: Laurie received the message loud and clear.

The boulders are still there, not quite how she remembers them, but a great place to sit, nevertheless. Up she climbs.

At the highest point, she takes some deep gulps of air. Though she could never have settled for a life on the island, it has an undeniable beauty, with its coastline and dunes, rural, yet strangely urban. Aside from a hospital, it has every modern requirement, including a road bridge. Laurie's issue with the place has never been about location: it's been about reinvention. She isn't the same person as teenage Laurie Helm, but the island would never have allowed her to shed that skin. People look up to her now; students need her. Her job at a pupil referral unit has forced her to root for the underdog. Something she used to see as a weakness.

Behind her, the sea-wood looms. It's presence presses against her shoulders like a persistent child, desperate to be noticed. And she wonders if somewhere in the gloom, Diamond Hall still stands. Not that it matters much. She never scratches the faceted surface of those particular memories. Much of the wood has been turned over to a new housing estate, as far as she can tell. It stands above her, all orange-brick and brown UPVC, from the edge of the Diamond Hall land to the end of the village. There are more than fifty houses, all with sea views. They must have cost a fortune to build and are probably homes bought by people wanting to live on the island but with no connection to it. Not that she's jealous. She couldn't get away from Chapel Field fast enough. Her curiosity is piqued now though, and she wonders exactly what is left of the Diamonds. The house? Ed and his father? She scrambles across from her perch on the boulder and onto the lower flanks of the wood.

Laurie recognises the look of the place instantly, and her instinct for negotiating it kicks in. Between the tangle of brambles and cow parsley, there is enough space to get small footholds, while clutching at the slender trunks of hawthorn and wild holly. She's done it many times. Not since she was an adult, but the physical aspect of her job means she's had to keep herself fit and flexible.

She is surprised when, no more than a minute into the woodland, a fence appears. It is a monstrosity. Struts of blue metal six-foot high are fastened together with bolted horizontal panels. They almost obscure the view onto the land beyond. Laurie shakes her head. Planning permission is unlikely to have been given, yet the fence is here. Is the house still standing? It's hard to tell.

She peers between the metal struts. There is only more brushwood, dense and catching on itself. Surely no one lives in there now. The main gates of the house would have been somewhere to her right, away from the back gardens of the housing estate, more towards the older part of the village. She could pick her way along the fence for a while and see what's there. Without thinking too much about what she's doing, or why, she moves away, sidestepping clumps of nettle and fleshy thistle. When she'd last been here, the wood had been less dense, less dark, with pathways worn between the thickets and some sky visible.

A shiver creeps across her shoulders, despite the thick heat of the air. There's a suffocating greenness about the place. In the moment she decides to get out, she hears the faintest of sounds from somewhere beyond the fence. Like the snap of a dry twig. She stops and peers through. More sound. It's someone walking. She hides herself as best she can, and waits. A person comes into view, a woman. Tall and long-limbed, dark hair braided down her back. She is wearing a shell-suit jacket, something Laurie remembers from the eighties, and a long floral skirt. She is singing.

Ed

There's someone in the woods. He'll need to get Elissa back inside the house. The time for anger has long passed. What he's left with now is a weary tolerance of this constant interest in his life. The fence has helped him feel safe, so it was worth the money. He calls Elissa, but she doesn't respond, only carries on with her walking and humming. The last thing Ed wants is for her to be seen. Then she'd be one more Diamond for the world to shatter. As if that were possible.

When the person – woman, he thinks – has slunk off back through the undergrowth, he darts from his hiding place and catches hold of his sister's arm. She smiles gently and lets herself be led back towards the house. He could lift her if he wanted to. Though she's tall like him, her bones weigh nothing. There are times when she needs help to get around, especially at the end of the day. Then, he will simply slide an arm under her legs, and let her loop herself around his neck. It takes no effort or strength but can easily reduce him to tears. A life without her would be unimaginable.

Inside the house, he leads his sister along the hallway and gets her settled on the sofa in their living area. He closes the curtains and switches on the lamps. If there are people from the village rubber-necking again, there will be nothing to see. Not that they can get any further than the huge gates at the end of their driveway: some have been known to try. Elissa smiles at his offer of tea, and he kneels in front of her and pulls down the zip of her jacket, then lifts it away. With it comes the smell of laundry powder, and the faintest odour of sweat. His sister isn't fond of bathing, and he can hardly force her. Instead, he suggests, and she responds when she can.

He hangs the jacket up on a peg in the hallway, then comes back in and tucks his sister against the sofa cushions. In the far corner of the room is a metal gate. It is locked to stop her trying to wander upstairs. The staircase is lethal, with high risers and short treads. His grandfather built the house in haste, and with the cheapest materials possible. They live with it as best they can.

Ed walks across the room to their kitchen area and fills the kettle. While he waits for it to boil, he slams in and out of their food cupboards, making a mental list of what he will need to collect from the Chapel Field shop tomorrow. He's heard that people can get deliveries of provisions now, that there is no longer any need to go out to shop in person. He has thought about this but can never see how it would work. He sends away for his books by post and collects parcels from the shop if he needs to, but the logistics of a food delivery baffle him. Besides which, they never need huge amounts of anything.

When the mugs of tea are ready, he tips a few plain biscuits onto a plate and carries everything across to his sister. Her eyes are closed. She's humming.

'There you go,' he whispers, then takes his own drink over to the only other place to sit: his armchair. It's as old as the sofa but has a handle at the side which allows him to lean backwards and have his legs supported. It makes a good bed. Later on, when he's got Ellie to hers, he's going to read one of the new novels that came in his last parcel: the more modern, the better. It's how he finds out about the world.

Ed sips his tea. His sister has stopped humming, and the silence in the room has taken on a life of its own. It presses against his eardrums and whines, taunting him with his lack of conversation. He's not talked to someone who will answer for a long time. From the pit of his stomach, the feeling starts up, all colour and movement: it's grey and wants to be black and carves out a hollow under his ribs. He's tried to hug it away, tried feeding it, stuffing down toast and chocolate. Nothing works. It sits, a lump of solid sorrow that only dissolves if he's busy.

He jumps out of his chair and casts around the room for something to do. Elissa has finished her tea and is cradling the mug with both hands and smiling at him.

He wonders if she ever gets the carved-hollow feeling, or is it reserved for him. More than anything, he wishes he could go out into the world and ask what it feels like to share a joke, have a conversation that turns heated but never morphs into argument, how it is to be held with love. His sister is his life, but she can connect with him only by smiling and if he ever hugs her, nothing is returned.

He takes the mug from her hand and collects his own, and her plate. These things he carries to the sink, then turns on the tap and is thrilled to hear the sound of running water and crockery clinking, to prove he is still alive.

Chapter 3

Summer 2018

Laurie

Though she's not strictly trespassing, Laurie turns away from the fence and scrambles to the edge of the sea-wood. Seeing a woman on the Diamond land has shocked her. A new family must be living there, and she's been caught snooping. Not caught, exactly. The woman hadn't registered Laurie at all. It's more about peeking through someone else's fence, trying to get a glimpse of their home. Like she's a teenager all over again.

On the beach, she stops for a moment. The evening light has faded to grey and only a thin silvery line of tide remains. The quiet of this place is unnerving. London is never quiet. There're always people, traffic, something to be negotiated, something to challenge. It's frenetic but distracting. The past cannot get a foothold when the present is so all-consuming. Which is why she was dreading coming back. She slips her sweatshirt around her shoulders and makes her way along the shingle, to the road.

Just outside her mother's house is a man. He's tall and thickset, with dark hair fading to grey, and he's standing over a small dog, who seems to be rooted to the spot. Laurie slows her pace, and hopes he moves away from the gateposts before she gets there. He doesn't. She's about to negotiate her way around him when he says, 'Laurie? Laurie Helm? Loz? Is that you?'

It's Pete O'Connor. She recognises his voice instantly, with its high-pitched edge of sarcasm and broad northern twang.

'It sure is,' she replies, 'and I don't need to ask if it's Pete.'

They dance around each other. As teenagers, they were hardly close, so hugging doesn't seem appropriate. Laurie steps out of his personal space to make sure.

'God, it's been–' he thinks for a moment, 'twenty years, hasn't it. Last time I saw you was Marcus's–' He leaves the word hanging, like a piece of dirty washing no one wants to touch.

'A lot's happened since then,' she says, thinking up a list of things they could talk about.

'What you doing back here, anyway?' He lunges at her. 'Give us a hug, you daft thing.'

Laurie allows him one squeeze, then frees herself, and makes a show of petting the yapping dog, asking its name, keeping Pete engaged. 'Oh yeah. I heard your mum died.'

'She did. Not that we were close. I've come back to sort out her things. Get the house emptied and sold. It shouldn't take me too long.'

'So sorry about that, Loz. How are you coping?'

'I'm fine. Mum and I weren't close.' She shrugs. 'Sad. But there it is.'

'Still not nice, though, is it?'

'Guess not.'

A stretch of silence hangs between them. Laurie wants to fill it with saying goodbye and getting herself inside the house, but Pete isn't budging.

'What you been doing with yourself, anyways?' he asks. 'You went to uni, didn't you? Always were a clever-clogs.' He laughs at this, and Laurie remembers he loved his own jokes.

'I work in a PRU. In London. A pupil referral unit. It's a kind of secure school for kids who are struggling.'

'Christ.' Pete runs a hand across his face. 'Always did stick up for the underdog, didn't you?'

Laurie wonders why Pete would say something like this. Especially after what happened with Ed Diamond. Perhaps her memory of it isn't as accurate as she thinks. During her time at university, she'd completed an in-depth study into the psychology of trauma-related memory. Seventy per cent reliable is how it's described, but she's pretty sure she wasn't a nice teenager. Definitely not a *champion of underdogs*.

'Maybe. What about you? Did you stay around here?'

Pete needs no more encouragement than this. He tells her about his apprenticeship at a local car dealership, his rise through the ranks of man-and-boy to managerial level, his wife, kids, house, cars, everything. Laurie's face aches with smiling by the time he is finished. She feels no emotional connection with this man, but he might have something of interest to tell her, and his waxing on about himself has given her time to think how to frame her questions.

'Well,' she says when he stops, 'I bet you're a real font of local knowledge. Did you see Mum much?'

'Not much.' He's measuring his words, she can tell. 'The last time I saw her, she looked very frail, but that was quite a while ago.'

Not frail, starving, Laurie thinks. She keeps her expression bland.

'And I guess there are new folk on the Diamond land. Is the house still there?'

Pete tilts his head and narrows his eyes at her. 'The house is still there. And so is Ed. He's totally on his own now though.' He taps his temple. 'Head's gone.'

What is Pete saying? A zip of adrenaline hits Laurie's blood.

She feels it in her stomach first, then as a pounding at the base of her throat. What's happened to Ed? 'I thought I saw a woman up there, in the woods. On the other side of that horrible fence. Is someone living there with him?'

Pete stretches his eyes and snorts. 'Long dark hair and strange clothes?'

Laurie gulps down her alarm. She nods slowly, hoping Pete will tell her something to shut down the fear.

'It's Ed.' He pauses. 'Like I said, his head's gone. He's one of those, you know, *schizo* types. We think he pretends he's his dead sister. It's all very weird.'

'And you know this because–' Laurie's fear turns instantly to anger. She doesn't like Pete's tone. Both of them know exactly how it was for Ed Diamond growing up; she loathes the part she played.

'It's common knowledge around Chapel Field. Some people do see him; he's at the shop quite a lot. Never mentions his sister, though. Funny that. I can't stand the guy, if you want my honest opinion. I always found him creepy. Still do.'

'His sister died, didn't she?' Laurie thinks about timings. 'Never made it to teen-hood, as far as I remember.'

'Exactly.' Pete won't meet her eye.

'Does Ed get any help?'

This comment makes him throw back his head and laugh in a way that transports Laurie to their teenage years. What might have seemed coolly sardonic when they were seventeen, now makes him appear cruel.

'Not in today's market. Might be different for you London types, but we can hardly get a doctor's appointment up here. The wife works in social care, and I still can't. He's past helping, anyway, that guy.' He waves in the direction of the wood.

Laurie doesn't like the way he's calling her a type, doesn't like him much, either. But what's really getting to her is the state

Ed Diamond has been left in. And the thought that it's partly because of her. Pete is asking for them to have a proper catch-up, over a coffee or a drink. It's the last thing she wants but refusing would create more toxicity in her body. There's enough of that, with having to be at her mother's. Eventually, she agrees to call at his house and meet his wife. That way, deep-dives into the past can be limited.

'Great. Gina's not working on Saturday, so pop by in the afternoon. It's sixteen Bankfield.' He tugs on the dog's leash and starts to walk away. 'You remember where that is, don't you?'

'I do remember.' Laurie pulls open her mother's rusted front gate. 'See you then.'

As she watches Pete walk away, something about the set of his shoulders carries her back to their teenage years once again, and she wonders if she should forget about his invitation. Being in Chapel Field, with its beautifully open vistas and closed-up mentality is creating a conflict in her body that feels tangible. She should be mourning her mother, but there's no space for Janet Helm. Instead, Laurie is full of longing for a life she could have had, and scorn for the reality. Which is why she got away as soon as she was able. And now, she's going to be forced to face the past through the lens of Pete O'Connor and a wife she's never met.

Laurie has learnt to deal with a myriad of personalities and backgrounds in her job; she's an expert. Looking outwards at people and their problems is easy. Being forced to look inwards is something completely different. She's never met this Gina, so the woman must be given a fair chance. Even if she is married to Pete. The first thing Laurie decides to do is walk to the village shop and find a gift to take on the visit, something she wouldn't mind receiving herself.

Chapter 4

Winter 1996

Laurie

'I'm not doing it. It's nasty, and that's not me.'

Laurie is sitting at a pub table, head resting against her palms and hiding her expression from Marcus.

'Go on, Loz. It'll be a laugh.' He takes a sip of the caramel-brown liquid in his glass then puts a hand on her shoulder. 'You're not starting to feel sorry for Eduardo fucking Diamond, are you?'

'Why can't *she* do it?' Laurie looks across the table to where Ruth is sitting. She is as close to Marcus as she can be, without being on his knee.

'I can't have that,' he says. 'She's my girlfriend, aren't you, babe.'

Ruth's eyelids flutter and Laurie can't help thinking she's lost touch with her friend. Who allows themselves to be called *babe*? Across the room, a shout goes up. The bandit has been dropped and pound coins are pouring onto the floor. Jamie and Pete are kneeling to catch them. Neither of them is eighteen, and Laurie wonders if they'll get to keep the money. The woman behind the bar lifts her brassy hair for a moment, then catches it in a scrunchie pony-tail. She calls across to Marcus. 'Drinks are on your lads then, matey? Same again?'

Laurie is the youngest in their group. She's not even seventeen until next summer. Alcohol doesn't agree with her. Yet here she is, sitting in a grotty pub on the mainland, drinking Dubonnet and lemonade as though she's some sophisticated woman from London. Not that she knows what it would be like; the furthest she's ever travelled is Preston on a school outing.

Marcus loosens himself from Ruth's embrace and saunters across to the bar. He's almost nineteen and working in the local shipyard, a world of men and machines. Which is why Laurie feels she can't say no to his request.

He brings back five glasses, fingers dipping to hold them all, and drops them onto the middle of the table. 'Get these down you, kids. And I hope you're all coming to watch me play footie on Saturday.' He balls his fists and punches the air. 'Marcus Butcher. Up there with Ferdinand and Fowler.'

Laurie rolls her eyes.

'Don't take the piss, girlie,' he continues, sliding himself into the seat next to her. 'And you are gonna help me wind up that shitty Diamond geezer, aren't you?'

'But he stinks.'

'All the more reason to wipe him off the face of the earth.'

'Why do you hate him so much?' Laurie can't think of anyone in Chapel Field who doesn't, but she's sure most of the bad feeling comes through osmosis. That's a process she's been learning about in biology, when substances move from a high concentration to a lower, without even trying, just because they can. Marcus's concentrated hatred of the Diamonds is spreading to them all.

Later, on the bus back to the island, Laurie stares out of the window and wonders what her mother would say about this secret life she is creating: pubs, cigarettes, kissing boys, sharing bags of chips. The chips she'd find most annoying. Developing the currency of a slim, feminine body is the focus of her mothering, and Laurie has nothing in the bank. Marcus and Ruth are all over each other on the back seat, and she's been left to entertain Jamie and Pete.

As the bus rattles across the road bridge, the lights from Chapel Field come into view. Laurie has never felt so disconnected with the place. If she could pack up her clothes and leave tonight, she would. She's heard of other people being filled with happiness and light: every place in her body is weighted with darkness. And now she's agreed to go along with Marcus Butcher's creepy plan.

'I don't fucking believe it,' Pete shouts suddenly, hauling himself up from his seat. 'Dickhead Diamond is only walking along the prom.' He turns to Marcus. 'Time to get offskie.'

Laurie feels a flash of alarm. It starts in her belly and floods through her body, chasing her blood and banging her heart against the inside of her ribs. She's about to perform the biggest charade of her life.

They jostle their way down the aisle and jump onto the promenade. The tide is high, running just below the level of the road, and the air is raw with seaweed and salt. Ed Diamond is about a minute ahead of them, hunched into a dark duffle coat, and carrying something on his back. A rucksack, perhaps. The poor guy has probably been late-night shopping. As far as she can work out, he does a lot of things at night. She doesn't blame him; Chapel Field hardly welcomes the sight of him in broad daylight.

'Let's run,' whispers Marcus, eyes alight with something Laurie thinks is more sinister than fun. He's not a *fun* kind of person. Fun sounds far too wholesome, though he uses the word a lot. *Persecution* would be better. They set off together, Ruth tottering in high-heeled boots and clinging on to Jamie's arm. When they catch up with Ed, he doesn't register. Instead, he ploughs on, hands shoved in his pockets and neck bent, as though he's carrying something heavy inside his head.

'Ed. Eddie-boy. Wait up.' This is Marcus as Laurie has never seen him. Until he turns back to them all and wafts a hand under his nose. 'How you doing, lad?'

'Get lost.' Ed isn't playing.

Marcus reaches up and tries to slide an arm around Ed's shoulder. He gets an elbow-jab to the middle of his chest. Laurie thinks that will be the end of it, in less than a second they'll be trying to break up a fight. Instead, Marcus laughs and ramps up the charm. 'Don't be like that, my man. I have news. Something you might be interested in.'

'I said get lost.'

Laurie recognises the rise in Ed's voice, the one they often push hard to hear. It's not what Marcus wants tonight. He tilts his head towards her and beckons silently. 'Our Loz wants to talk to you about something,' he tells Ed. 'This is her.'

Laurie has to think quickly. She's supposed to capture Ed's attention and ask him out. How stupid does Marcus think people are? But if she can't achieve some part of the plan, she runs the risk of him turning on her.

'Not talk, exactly,' she says to Ed. 'It's just, well, we're all the same age and living in the same village. I thought we should try and get to know you a bit. We'd like to. I'd like to.' She's using her coy voice, with echoes of her mother.

Ed keeps walking.

'No worries if you're not interested,' Laurie continues. 'Just say the word and we'll go. Promise.' For a moment, she thinks she's lost him, but then he hesitates and slides his eyes sideways, and she knows she's in. 'How come you didn't go to our school, anyway?'

'Didn't go to any school, did I,' he spits.

'Why not?' Laurie notices that Marcus has dropped back. She's on her own with Ed.

He shrugs. 'No need for school, Dad says.'

'It's the law. How come your dad didn't get in trouble for not sending you?' Laurie realises she's sounding preachy. 'I am jealous though. Wish I'd not had to go to school. Bet it was brilliant, all that freedom.' Something about Ed's body language is changing. His shoulders have straightened so that his chin has lifted from his chest. He's turning his head to look at her.

'It's not that good. I get bored, doing stuff around the house all the time.'

Laurie sees her chance. 'Why don't you come and hang out with us, one of the nights? It'd be a laugh. We're not all like him.' She throws a glance in Marcus's direction. 'Would you meet up if it was just me?'

Ed locks eyes with her. She shivers slightly, a cold tingle across her shoulders and the back of her neck. He is quite attractive, in a darkly dangerous kind of way, but she can't let herself think like that. She has to act out.

'Could do,' he mutters. 'Not at the house, though. You could wait at the front gate.'

'When?'

'Tomorrow night?'

She gives a thumbs-up behind her back, and hopes Marcus sees it.

'Tomorrow night it is,' she says. 'About eight?'

'Don't bring that idiot.' Ed attempts a smile. Laurie sees his large, uneven teeth for the first time, and she shivers all over again. Then she drops back and allows him to stride away. Jamie and Pete are at her side immediately, sniggering and guffawing in a way that makes her feel even more grubby than she already does.

'You're in there, Loz.' Pete nudges her. 'Next thing you know, there'll be lots of little Diamond babies.' He turns to Jamie and mimes the act of throwing up. 'How gross would that be.'

Jamie is staring at his feet, hands thrust in the pockets of his parka. Laurie peers at him through the gloom. 'I'd rather have babies with Ed Diamond than you, dickhead.'

'Children, children.' Marcus has come up behind them and is laying an arm across each of their shoulders. 'Play nicely. Did you get an invite to the house, Loz?'

'No I didn't.'

'But we said–'

'I don't care what we said.' There's a build-up of pressure at the back of Laurie's throat and it's propelling her words forward without any control. 'You– we– torment the life out of that guy. He's hardly going to invite us up to Diamond Hall for tea and biscuits, is he?'

Pete snorts at this.

'What were you talking about then? I could see him looking at you.' Marcus has a firm grip on her elbow. Laurie tries to lift herself away with a shoulder shrug, but he doesn't let go. 'Come on, Lozzie. Something's been said. What was it?'

'If you must know,' she hisses, 'I'm meeting him tomorrow night. All right?'

Marcus whoops then jumps up and down, and it doesn't take long for Pete to join the dance.

'She shoots,' he cries. 'She scores.'

'Back of the net.' Marcus can never resist drawing a football parallel. Laurie hates that about him. She wants to run after Ed and tell him the truth. She doesn't want to inflict any more hurt. Now she's met him face to face, he's lost his *non-human* status.

But she must protect herself; the wrong side of Marcus Butcher is not a place she wants to be. Ruth is standing beside her, heels clicking against the pavement.

'What a pair of idiots,' she whispers. 'You'd think they'd won the pools or something. I'd feel sorry for Diamond, if he wasn't so–' She shudders. 'Oh, I don't know: weird? Is that the right word? He gives me the creeps, that's for sure.'

'We don't know him though, do we?'

Ruth huddles herself further into her jacket. 'And we don't want to. Not if what Marcus says is right.'

'And what's that?'

'Stop gossiping, you two.' Jamie has moved in between them. 'It's bloody freezing, standing here. Let's get going.' He grabs Laurie's hand then puts his arm around Ruth's waist. 'We can get warmed up in The Crown, if you like, hide behind Butcher. I've got a pocket full of pound coins that want spending.'

He drags them away from Pete and Marcus and starts chatting about a Christmas disco at the new club opening up in town. As they walk together, Laurie looks across the dark surface of the tide and tries to convince herself that when emotions like shame and fear come into conflict, it's better to let fear have the upper hand.

Ed

Being surrounded by this gang is making Ed jittery. The ring-leader is the blond boy who looks more like a man, despite his lack of height and smooth-skinned face. When he puts a hand on Ed's shoulder, he's in danger of being smashed to the ground, though his father has warned him against getting involved. If

Richard Diamond had heard half the vile things people said about Ed's mother, there might be a different outcome. What puzzles him is that these kids can't have known her; he never knew her himself. There are a couple of photographs of her at home, but that's all. She had the dark hair and eyes he recognises in himself, the same smile, but he never got to hear her speak. That she was Spanish is what his father has told him, that Ed should go back there is something that doesn't make sense; he never came from Spain.

The blond boy is asking for friendship, asking Ed to speak with one of the girls he's seen on the edge of the group. There have been times, since he's grown taller and sprouted a beard, when he's wondered if he'll ever meet girls. This might be his only chance. She doesn't seem like the others, seems kinder, somehow. She's pretty, with her solemn oval face and big eyes. They talk about school for a while then he surprises himself by agreeing to meet up with her.

When they drop back and leave Ed to his business, he finds he is shaking, though whether it is because of the cold, or his anxiety, he doesn't know. What he's got to do is get the shopping home. They'd been short of milk and bread, but the woman in the village shop had stopped serving him a while back. A walk to the Co-op at the other end of the island is the only option now. It's open until late, so he can usually get there without seeing anyone who knows he's a Diamond.

When he reaches Chapel Field, Ed decides to leave the road and follow the line of the shore. He steps away from the promenade and onto a shingle path that will take him past the sea-wood and on to Diamond Hall. The tide is a long way out, visible as the faintest scatter of moonlight.

He stops for a moment and peers towards it, wondering what it would be like to simply ebb away into the evening and have nothing call you back. In the middle of his body is a hollow, a place as dark and empty as the wood on a winter evening. Food doesn't fill it, nor drink, though he's tried. If other people have this feeling, he wouldn't know. Who does he ever talk to? Which is why he'd made the decision to meet with this unknown girl. If she has even a speck of world knowledge, it will be more than he's ever had access to. What he should do is prepare; have lots of questions to ask her, take notes. She might even smile at him. Her smile, it made the hollow hurt a little less.

He turns to look at the sea-wood. In the darkness it sprawls upwards like a cloud of ink squirted into the clearest sea. And in the middle of that chaos lies his home.

Walney Island, 1947
Maisie-Anne Diamond

Two weeks before Maisie-Anne Diamond gave birth to her second son, she thought about wading into the tide until it reached her shoulders, then letting it carry her away. That this act would be murder as well as suicide made her stop at the edge of the water and look back at the island for a moment. Was this how she wanted to be remembered? The young woman with dirty-blonde hair, slim apart from her huge belly, dragged out from some place further along the coast, with Lenny having to identify her and hate her for killing their baby? No one would care about her story, only that she'd taken the life of his second child.

She'd returned home that evening to find him sitting in the yard, with Ritchie in his pyjamas and wellington boots, scratching out a muddy trench for his collection of Matchbox cars.

She loved them both, loved them all, but who loved her back? She was nineteen, still a child herself, confined in a way no child should be. The van, the yard, the sheds, these things held her now. Not the world, just these things. She would live and die never knowing what a life could be.

She'd met Lenny on a night full of promise, when the war was well and truly over. There had been a hint of moonlight and danger in his eyes, as he spun her carriage around on the Waltzer.

While her friend had screamed and covered her eyes, Maisie-Anne kept hers locked onto Lenny's wide shoulders and dark hair. She was seventeen, just out of school. He was a man. That fact alone would have kept her interested. His large hands on her waist had sealed the deal. Though she had parents at home and a bedroom of her own, she'd skipped away when Lenny beckoned, without looking back. And now she had a child, another on the way, and all the excitement of that night had dissolved in a mess of stale bedding and baby-grows.

This afternoon, she'd managed to walk to the nearest shop and spend some of Lenny's money on foods that had come off the ration. Not bread though, and that was what she craved. She taken to wearing boots and thick socks wherever she went, such was the mud around the van, so trekking across the island had taken twice as long. But it had been worth it, if only to have a chat with people who knew nothing about her. Now she was lumbering home, shopping bags cutting into her hands. She was panting like the grizzled dog tied up outside the van next to theirs.

'Mama.' Ritchie was playing in the yard, lining up his cars. He lifted his fist and waved, then ran towards her. 'Dis one gone dirty, Mama. Can you bath it?' This was her; someone who cleaned up.

'You've been a long time, May.' Lenny got up from the old

house-chair where he'd been perched and waiting. 'We're wanting our tea. Let me take those bags.' He turned the tin mug in his hand upside down, shaking out the last of its contents in a slow, deliberate way.

She loved this man, with his dark curls and his height. It was herself she loathed. Marriage had seemed a glamorous thing, made from snatched moments of love and tenderness. The sheer hard work of it, the seep of washing clothes, creating meals, cleaning dirt, she hadn't expected those things. Living in a caravan with no running water hadn't been part of her grand-plan, either. A house by the sea, that's what she thought she was getting. Not a van on an island where the wind never stopped blowing and there was always sand in your nostrils and between your toes.

'I told you where I was going.' Maisie-Anne let him take the bags. She laid one hand on the bulky mass under her winter coat. 'Trying to get this one to shift, aren't I. Took the long way round.'

'Aye, well.' Lenny's lips twisted upwards, not a smile exactly, but something.

'What? Won't be so cocky when there's another one taking up space in the van, will you.' She pushed past him, ignoring Ritchie's pleas and dirty hands, and stepped carefully up the metal steps that would lead her inside. Nothing was different from when she'd left a couple of hours ago. Lenny's overalls were still in a heap in the tiny scullery, the nappy boiler was still full and stinking. A bit like her life.

She slid her arms out of her coat and hung it on a peg in their only cupboard, then lifted the lid of the water bucket. They were never short of things. Her husband had a way of finding whatever she needed; there was always someone who had something or knew a man who did. His travelling days might have been over, but that way of life would forever be part of him.

'What you being all mardy for?' He'd followed her in and was standing behind her, trying to slide his hands around the place where her waist used to be. 'Didn't I say there'd be a palace for you, my May queen.'

Maisie-Anne didn't want to be anyone's queen, she just wanted space enough that her children could grow without feeling their limbs cramped between metal walls or their backs hunched to get through doorways. And bedrooms. They'd be a luxury.

'You'd be mardy if you spent all day dragging this weight around. I've still to clean and cook and entertain the lad, though I'm the size of a house. I can't do it anymore, Len, I really can't. I want it all to stop.' The tears came then. A silent trickle at first, followed by some delicate sobs. By the time Lenny had taken her over to the banquette couch and made her sit, all the despair of the past few months was spewing from her eyes and nose and mouth in the form of panting and gasping and water as salty as the sea itself. She wanted to punch his beaming face. Didn't he know she was at breaking point? Didn't he care?

'Now then, lass.' He pulled a soiled handkerchief from his pocket, then dabbed at her face.

'Is that all you've got to say?' She slapped his hand away. 'I mean it, Len. And I nearly did make it all stop, the other day.' She waited while he processed what she was saying. *Sharp* was how he described himself, but she thought a better word might be *blunt*: human feelings had never been his strong point.

'We don't have a gas-oven.' He grinned and she wanted to thump him.

'I'm being serious, Len. I stood in the tide and wanted to let it carry me – us – away. It wasn't just a whim, there was a pull to it I could hardly resist. What would you have done then, eh?'

Ritchie appeared at the door, still clutching his dirt-covered car. 'Mama, don't cry.'

Lenny picked him up and sat him in his high-chair. 'Mama's not crying, little lad. And I'm going to get you a bowl of water and a cloth so you can clean the car yourself. How about that?'

Maisie-Anne watched while he slammed through cupboards to find a water container, then dip it in the bucket. He put it down in front of Ritchie and gave him the grubby handkerchief, demonstrating how to wet it and rub.

'At least someone's grateful for my help,' he muttered. Then he looked at her and added, 'You need to get yourself together. You were the same in those last few days before this little one came along. The gloom will pass.'

Maisie-Anne couldn't connect with his words, couldn't connect with anything much, like she was watching her life through a pane of glass and not immersed in it at all.

'It's not gloom.' She slammed her hands down on the table, making Ritchie jump. 'Why do you make light of everything? I'm telling you I'm ill, and you make jokes about it.'

Ritchie began to cry. Lenny ran a hand across his soft hair, then lifted him out of the chair. Maisie-Anne saw the situation she'd created and hated herself even more.

'Something has to change, Len,' she wailed. 'I don't even feel anything for my own babies. What's wrong with me?'

'I've a doctor friend who could have a look at you.'

'You've always got a *friend* to help out, haven't you?' Maisie-Anne scrunched up her fists and banged them against her temples. 'It won't be a proper doctor, will it. That's half the problem. We never do anything proper.' But if someone could give her the chance to feel alive again, she'd take it. Better than the shadowy edges where she'd been living. When she looked up again, Lenny was dancing around the caravan, jiggling Ritchie and making him laugh.

'See, this is what I've been trying to tell your mammy, if she'd give me the chance,' he was saying. 'But she's being a silly girl and keeps crying.' He mocks up a sad face and weeps so that Ritchie giggles even more.

'What? What are you trying to say? Tell me, Len.'

'I've got that bit of land. Over Chapel Field. In the middle of the woods, like. D'you remember when we walked there, and you said you'd love to live in a forest. Well, you're going to, now.' He waited for a moment. 'What do you think of that, Maisie-Anne Diamond?'

What she thought of it was that he was lying. Or polishing up the truth, at the very least.

'Why are you saying that?' Her voice was a wet croak. She rubbed the back of her hand under her nose. 'Don't be mean to me. I don't think I can take it.'

'I'm telling you the truth, my darling girl. I've got that land, finally. And I'm going to build the best house you've ever seen. With taps and a bath, and an indoor lavvy.' When she peered at him through watery eyes, he fingered the side of his nose and said, 'My horse came in, didn't it. That's all you need to know.'

Chapter 5

Summer 2018

Laurie

At half-past six on Saturday morning, Laurie is standing in her mother's kitchen, waiting for the gas kettle to boil. The house has electricity so she's no idea why there is no other kind of kettle. Her mother wasn't short of money; a sizeable chunk will come directly to Laurie after probate. More, when the house is finally sold.

She lifts a mug from one of the tatty cupboards and raids her box of essentials for instant coffee and some sugar. A tiny fridge sits on one countertop, and she's plugged it in so she can store her milk and water. It's hardly been used, which doesn't surprise Laurie: her mother hadn't been one for eating and drinking; she saw it as a weakness.

Janet Helm had not been elderly when she'd died, and from what Laurie has been told, her mother had simply faded away. Her own memories were of a woman as small as she was caustic, with wrists and ankles as thin as a child's and a way of glancing at herself in every shiny surface.

When she's made her coffee, she takes it through to the only other downstairs room. It's laid out with a pair of sofas, a dining table and chairs and an assortment of shelving stacks and side tables. Everything is covered with proof of her mother's other mental health issue: hoarding. Clearing away the piles of books and magazines, flattened boxes and threadbare household linen, is a task Laurie hadn't expected to face. Further evidence, if she needed it, that she knew very little about her own parent. Laurie isn't a person who cries, but if she was, she'd be sobbing right now. Being back in Chapel Field has stripped her of an outer shell she hadn't realised she'd developed, and the first thing to be exposed are her feelings about Ed Diamond.

As she sips her coffee, slices of early sunshine push into the room. A Saturday morning like this in London would mean running on the heath, breakfast at her favourite roadside coffee bar, and dozens of conversations with people who hardly knew her, who saw only a youngish and athletic-looking woman with no place in their lives. It's easy to smile at that. Smiling at Pete O'Connor and his wife will require a strength she doesn't know if she has.

Once she's washed and dried her hair, dressed in plain jeans and a T-shirt, and patted on enough make-up so her face looks less blurry, Laurie picks up her handbag and heads outside. The sun is higher now, and along the street, people are emerging onto their forecourts. Some are opening their cars and loading them up with children. This is Chapel Field as she remembers it; villagers living their lives in sync. As a teenager, she'd felt loathing for that. Now she realises it was more about envy than loathing. She'd craved the easy routines of their lives while she had been battling her mother.

The village shop lies along the main road, propped between a pub and a children's nursery. Laurie makes her way past more terraced cottages and some newer housing, built in the 1980s and starting to look scruffy. Her friend Jamie had lived here. She hasn't seen him since she left Chapel Field and has heard nothing about him. She's sure Pete will have all the gossip. Not that she's particularly interested. She knows Ruth married and went to live in Canada; what happened to Marcus Butcher broke her heart.

Inside the shop, Laurie pauses for a moment. The air conditioning is doing its work, and the aisles are spacious and modern. One or two people are wandering around, baskets over their arms and pondering. Near the back of the shop is a stack of tinned biscuits. She grabs one then searches the alcohol section for something light and flowery, a rosé wine, perhaps; whether Pete and his wife are drinkers matters little, and biscuits will always be eaten. At the counter, she is greeted by a huge man with a straggly auburn beard and a head of curly hair to match.

'Hiya, love,' he leers. 'Bonny day.'

Laurie puts down the biscuits and wine, and rummages in her handbag for her purse. 'It is,' she replies. 'Nice and cool in here, though.'

The guy eyes her purchases. 'You having a party, or what?'

'They're gifts, actually.' Laurie stops herself from telling him to mind his own business. This is Chapel Field, after all.

'Nice. Birthday, is it?'

She holds out a twenty-pound-note. 'No, just someone I haven't seen for a long time.'

'In the village, like?'

'Yep. Pete O'Connor. Do you know him?'

'Course I know Pete. He's a good mate of mine.'

Laurie waits while he opens the cash register and counts out her change. She knows he's after more information. 'I haven't seen him for a long, long time, so I thought I'd better arrive bearing gifts.'

The guy nods and slips the biscuits into a flimsy plastic carrier bag. 'Friend of his, are you?' he asks.

41

'I was. Back in the day.' Laurie snorts lightly and hopes the interrogation will stop. She'd never have got in contact with Pete O'Connor had she not met him on the street. Now she's made herself out to be a long-lost friend.

'You from round here, then? I've not seen you in the village, and I see most folk.'

'Janet Helm was my mum.' Laurie arranges her face to match what she thinks his reaction will be. She's not far wrong.

'Oh, my God. You're her daughter. Course you are. I'm so sorry for your loss. I–'

He gets no further. The doors of the shop sweep open and in marches Ed Diamond. Laurie can hardly bear to look. He is much taller than she remembers, his dark hair tied in a knot at the crown of his head. He's carrying a rucksack over one shoulder.

'Look who's here,' mutters the bearded man.

There's a sudden shift in the atmosphere, like there's been an explosion and everyone is standing in the silent aftermath, not knowing how to react. Ed makes his way into the main body of the shop and people scuttle away. Laurie can't believe what she is seeing. How does this poor guy live with the reaction he causes? Heat floods her face when she remembers what happened all those years ago; she's just as bad as the rest of them.

Once she's outside, Laurie decides to stay where she is until Ed emerges. She will try and strike up a conversation with him; he won't have forgotten her. She stands in the canopied shade and watches as people exit the shop. Some nod at her and smile. The sun beats down. Finally, Ed steps through the doorway, rucksack swinging in his hands and a scowl across his face.

'Hi,' Laurie calls as she moves towards him. 'Ed. Hi.'

He doesn't respond, simply strides across the forecourt of the shop as he hauls the rucksack over his shoulder. Laurie follows, trying to get his attention. They pass a woman with a child in tow. She flattens herself against the wall of the pub, pulling the child with her.

Suddenly, Ed stops. 'You're harassing me,' he growls. 'Leave off.' His words are directed at the world. They don't seem personal.

'Ed. It's Laurie Helm. Do you remember me?' She steps in front of him and catches the smell of something that reminds her of turps. There are paint stains around the hem of his T-shirt. He shuffles into the road, then begins to run, but Laurie isn't ready to give up. She chases him, clutching the carrier bag of biscuits and wine to stop them swinging. Running is something she can do.

'Ed. I only wanted to say hi,' she pants. There's an irony to her words and it has the desired effect.

'You must be crazy.' He glowers and slows down, letting her catch up. 'People don't say hi to me.' His gaze runs over her. 'And yes, I do remember you.'

'Sorry to chase you like that.' Laurie puts a hand to her chest. 'I really wanted to talk, that's all.'

Ed peers down at her. The bone structure of his face is visible beneath the taut skin. She glances at his arms. They are the same. He shakes his head. 'Talk? Are you out of your mind?'

'I know it seems crass. I've had to come back to Chapel Field. My mum died and I'm sorting out her estate. Being here has got me thinking about the past.'

'I had heard about your mother. Well, read about it. I'm glad you're having to think about the past. I hope it hurts like hell.' His words come out with a spit of emotion. He isn't the gauche nineteen-year-old Laurie remembers and she realises how stupid she's been. This guy has had a whole lifetime of hurt, yet she's seeking to make herself feel better.

'Oh, God, Ed. I'm so sorry. For everything.'

'Just get lost, will you. Don't come into the wood, snooping, don't try and talk to me. Leave me and my sister alone.'

Then he storms away towards the beach leaving Laurie to her burning cheeks and tattered sense of herself.

Ed

Though this Saturday morning visit to the Chapel Field shop hasn't been as traumatic as some he can remember, Ed is surprised when a woman tries to strike up a conversation with him. She's waited for him outside and calls him by his name. He hasn't heard it on anyone's lips without it being a sneer, for a very long time.

There's something familiar about the woman's voice and then he realises the hairstyle – a low pony-tail trailed over one shoulder – is the same as he saw on the person peering in through his new fence the other day. And worse than that, she's decided to chase him along the main road. Their antics are drawing glances and huffs from local people. He's used to that, but not having someone speak to him directly. The name *Laurie Helm* springs into his mind, and then he remembers. Suddenly she's telling him her mother has died and there is a past they should catch up on.

A pain starts up in his chest. Not a pain, exactly, more like a pressure. This is how it goes: the pressure builds, it makes him struggle for breath, then he feels his heart pounding right at the top of his throat. He will bite his teeth together and clench his fists, then a cold shiver will make its way down his forearms. At this point he'll either run away fast or hit something. He tells the woman to get lost, to leave him alone, then takes off towards Diamond Hall.

The sight of his locked gates and driveway cause Ed to relax a little. He hasn't been followed. There will be no repeat of the incident which resulted in him paying a lot of money for secure fencing and an impenetrable entrance.

Finding a group of teenagers prowling about in Elissa's patch of garden hadn't freaked him out as much as some of the things they'd shouted when he went to chase them off. Though he hadn't been sure what every one of the words meant, the implication had been clear enough: the Diamonds were monstrous people. If they could have seen his sister that day, smiling in her sweet way with no knowledge of what was happening, they might have changed their minds.

Inside the house, the smell of paint is stronger than he expected, and he hopes it hasn't pressed itself into his sister's lungs. He drops his bag onto the kitchen floor and starts opening windows. She must have them closed while he is out.

In the years since his father died, he's felt the responsibility for keeping his sister safe as a weight sitting on the back of his head, never allowing him to straighten up and be free. He loves her, but the worry of it feels overwhelming. He carries the table he's been painting out into the yard. He shouldn't have been working on it indoors to begin with, but he feels so exposed outside. Not always, but it's getting worse. There has been no new furniture in Diamond Hall, for as long as he can think back. Repairing things takes his mind to places that seem normal – he's read about sanding and priming, filling and fixing. It's what everyone does.

He starts to unpack his purchases: bread, milk, teabags, powdered chocolate for making his sister's favourite drink. He is running low on cash, which will mean a trip to the mainland and his bank. At least over there he can relax a little. No one knows him once he's off the island. He's even had a smile or two in the town centre. But he can never stay there for long; his sister can't be left.

While he heats a pan of milk on the stove, he thinks again about the woman called Laurie Helm. What he remembers about her is the nasty trick she played on him, one that led to consequences for his family she could never have imagined. And now she's turned up again wanting to talk.

What a fool he'd been back then, to believe any of the Chapel Field residents would offer friendship to the Diamonds; he won't ever make that mistake again.

Chapter 6

December 1996

Laurie

The gates of Diamond Hall are chained together with something that reminds Laurie of a bicycle lock. She pushes against them, and they move enough that she could squeeze through if she wanted to. She doesn't. Ed told her to wait by the gates and that's what she's going to do. It's a freezing night with a sky full of stars. The moon is visible as a haze of frosty light. Laurie peers at it and clutches the collar of her new jacket. It's made of felted red wool that's supposed to be warm, but the icy air is sliding up the sleeves and into the neckline so that she already feels numb. In a way, she hopes Ed doesn't turn up. Then she can use that as an excuse when she arrives at Marcus's rendezvous point on her own.

She pulls down her glove and tilts the face of her wristwatch to the light. By half-past nine, she's to be at the bottom of the sea-wood, by the boulders, and she's to have cranked Ed Diamond up to fever-pitch. Those were Marcus's words. As usual, he's gone too far.

47

Just as she's about to head for home, Ed steps from a shadowy patch at the side of the gate.

'Hello,' he mumbles. 'I've been here for a while. Wanted to see if those others were with you.' He eyes the road behind her. 'They're not, are they?'

'No, course not.' Laurie lets herself laugh a little, but her stomach hits the floor. Ed is nothing more than an ordinary guy, standing next to her in his duffle coat, clean-shaven and with his hair brushed into a pony-tail. She wants to weep. What is she doing? Has she no ideas and feelings of her own? Does everything have to revolve around Marcus Butcher? She decides that it doesn't.

'Let's walk along the prom and go to the chippy,' she says, too brightly.

Ed pushes his hands into his pockets and shrugs.

'I've got money. I wasn't sure if you'd been to a chippy before.'

'Why'd you think that? I'm not some kind of weirdo, you know. It's what everyone thinks though, isn't it?'

This isn't what Laurie wants, winding him up before they've even left the village. But if he thinks he's not weird, she'll have to explain.

'It is a bit weird, not going to school.' She casts her glance sideways. 'Weird, but ace.'

They've hit the main road now, their breath hanging about them in freezing white clouds, their pace picking up. Ed doesn't speak for a few moments. Then he laughs. 'Why'd you go to school if you don't like it? That makes you the weird one.'

'You have to go to school, Ed. It's the law.' Laurie realises just how much he might not know. She doesn't want to sound patronising. 'We've all left school now, anyway. College is much better. Don't you get fed up with staying at home all day?'

Ed shrugs again. They make their way through the village

and out onto the promenade. Laurie chats about the things she liked and hated about her old school, about teachers and classes and mass-produced meals, and all the time, Ed seems to be looking at the floor and not taking anything in.

Then he suddenly says, 'I read a lot. I learned that from my dad.'

Laurie feels a wave of sickly regret sweep over her. This guy has a father. He reads. How is it fair, the way Chapel Field has him on the run?

'Is it just you and him in the house? Have you got any other family?'

Ed sighs loudly, and she realises she's said the wrong thing.

'Can we not talk about my family,' he mutters. 'What about yours? Would you want to give stuff away about them?'

'I wouldn't mind. But there's not much to tell.' Laurie shrugs. She feels the point he is trying to make, feels it deep within her stomach. Sharing family information lets others peer beneath your skin. 'I've got a mum I can't stand, no father, and no brothers or sisters. That's it.'

Ed turns away from her and looks across the water, oily and black tonight and scattered with reflected colour from the mainland lights. How must it feel to be on the outside of everything? Laurie has often told herself it's exactly what she wants, but is it? Is being shut out different to being free? She isn't sure, but she needs to get the situation back under her control; being with Ed is not turning out as expected.

'Go home, if you're not comfortable,' she tells him. 'I won't mind. We can meet up another time.' Though what Marcus would say, she can't imagine. She'd probably be dropped from their friendship group. Would that be so bad?

'You mentioned chips.' He shoots a grin over his shoulder. 'Let me have the chips, at least.'

There's something about his smile. It's like the moon

appearing between clouds on a windy night, dazzling and surprising and ice-cold. It makes Laurie's knees tremble. She wants to take his hand and drag him away from the mess she's about to create.

'Okay.' She stretches the word, then touches his elbow lightly to point him in the right direction.

While they walk, Laurie searches her mind for safe topics to talk about. She settles on music, discos and what it's like to try and get served alcohol in pubs when she's not yet eighteen. Ed tells her he's long past eighteen, almost nineteen in fact, and hasn't yet visited a pub. He's not sure he ever will – what would be the need, he says – but he wants to know everything. Within ten minutes, they arrive at the fish-and-chip shop, and he's spellbound once again.

He follows Laurie inside, glances around furtively, then sits down on the window seat, hands thrust deep in his coat pockets and squinting in the harsh white light.

'Two portions of chips,' she says when the woman behind the counter meets her eyes. 'With salt and vinegar, please.' She smiles over at Ed, but he keeps his gaze on the floor. She thinks about how terrifying it would be, the world watching you and hating what they see. There are one or two other people in the shop, and none seem bothered by her presence, or Ed's. She pulls a couple of pound coins from her pocket and hands them over, then waits for the few pence change.

There's a small electronic clock on the wall over the door. It's a quarter past nine. Just time to eat the chips while they walk back to Chapel Field. She's already decided she's not going to fulfil her part in Marcus's plan. She'll deliver Ed back to the gates of Diamond Hall, then face Marcus and the others later. She's starting to like Ed Diamond. He doesn't deserve half the things that are said about him.

She picks up the warm paper parcels. 'Ready?'

He jumps up and suddenly his presence fills the space. She gulps down a strange flutter that starts in her belly and hits the back of her throat. He is eyeing the parcels in her hands.

'Ready.' He inhales deeply. 'I like the smell in here. But it makes me feel hungry.'

'It's meant to,' she tells him. 'That's why they waft it halfway along the street. It brings in the crowds.'

He nods and follows her out into the icy evening. Once they're away from the shop, Laurie passes over his chips, and he takes his lead from her as she unwraps and begins to eat. A smile flickers between them.

When Ed has eaten every scrap, he screws up the greasy papers and tucks them into one of his pockets.

'They were good.' He sighs. 'That was a first for me, Laurie. I'm glad you suggested it.'

She enjoys the sound of her name on his lips. She can't remember sharing it with him. It must have been Marcus who did. Marcus. She looks at her watch. It's gone half-past nine. She imagines him waiting on the beach with Ruth and Pete and Jamie. He'll be kicking at the shingle and calling her fit-to-burn. She doesn't care, only cares that she's brought a tiny slice of happiness into Ed Diamond's life. He is smiling again and asking if she wants to sit on one of the promenade benches for a while. She's about to say yes when she sees a small group of people heading towards them. Before she can think about anything else, she hears Marcus's shout.

'Eduardo Diamond. What you doing keeping our Laurie up? Or is it her keeping you up?' He makes a gesture she doesn't care for, dragging guffaws from Pete and Jamie. Ruth is lagging behind, hunched and shivering in a tiny denim jacket and short skirt. Ed's shoulders sag and he pushes his hands into his pockets.

'Diamond. I'm talking to you.' Marcus is faking annoyance, Laurie can tell, but she's not sure what to say.

'Get lost,' Ed whines as Marcus reaches them.

'Get lost, get lost,' he mimics. 'I think it's you two that've been lost.' He turns to Laurie. 'We've been waiting on the fucking beach for half an hour. Where have you been?'

She doesn't dare look at Ed, knows he will have figured everything out in an instant.

'Lay off, Marcus,' she hisses. 'Just let him get home.'

But Pete and Jamie have got him cornered so that he can't back away and can't move forward. Pete reaches around Ed's waist and puts a hand on his groin.

'Got a hard-on, have you, Diamond? You fucking creep. You make me sick.'

Ed thrusts his elbows backwards and knocks the wind from him. He folds for a moment.

'Ooooh. Narky.' Marcus sniggers. 'Did you really think Loz was interested, you fucking retard. Look at you. Slobbering all over her. She hates you as much as the rest of us do.'

'Marcus—' Laurie wants it all to stop. No matter how she tries, she can't think of a way through. It's too late, anyway. Ed pulls back his arm and smashes his fist full into Marcus's face. There is a collective inhale and time seems to stop for a moment. Then Marcus bends at the waist, clutching his nose. Ed is starting to make the sobbing sound Laurie has heard before. It gets louder and takes on more substance so that it becomes a gravelly howl and then a full-blown wolf-yowl. It doesn't stop Marcus and Pete and Jamie jumping on his back and pulling him to the ground. Then they are kicking and punching and spitting so much that Laurie grabs Ruth's hand and drags her away towards the village as fast as she can.

The first thing she notices when they stop to catch their breath is that Ruth is crying. Her teeth are chattering and loud sobs escape every few seconds. Laurie wonders if they should contact the police. Ruth says no, says Marcus and Pete and Jamie are their friends and anyway, Ed Diamond pulled the first punch; he deserves everything he's getting.

'Why are you crying then?' Laurie spits. 'If you don't care what's happening back there?' She stares into the darkness. There is nothing but a set of car headlights approaching then zipping past.

'I don't want Marcus hurt, that's all. I think I'm in love with him.'

Laurie can suddenly taste grease at the back of her mouth. She remembers Ed's smile, the one that is now likely to be smudged all over Marcus Butcher's knuckles and boots, and she leans forward and vomits up every last chip.

Chapter 7

Summer 2018

Laurie

When Laurie arrives at Pete's house, he is in the front garden, snipping at an untidy hedge with a pair of hand shears. She wants a moment to gather herself after her encounter with Ed Diamond, but Pete spots her straight away.

'Howdy,' he calls as she tries to duck away from the hedge for a moment. 'Not leaving again, are you? Is my house that bad?'

Laurie remembers why she didn't like this guy. 'Don't be daft,' she says. 'I just had a strange encounter with Ed Diamond, of all people. He was in the shop. I tried to speak to him. It's left me stunned, if I'm honest.'

Pete snorts, then throws the shears onto the lawn. 'All encounters with Ed Diamond are strange. Why'd you think yours would be any different?'

'Oh. Sorry. I'm not–' Laurie isn't sure how she's expected to answer, but she's not keen on Pete's tone. She searches quickly for a snappy come-back. 'Still pressing your buttons, is he?'

'The guy's a menace.' Pete gets no further. The front door

swings open and a woman appears. She is small and dainty and has a frizz of hair that seems to defy gravity. In her arms is a small dog.

'Pete, why didn't you call me. I said to call me when your friend got here.'

'Was just about to, love.' He turns back to Laurie. 'This is Gina. The wife. Been married for nigh-on twenty years.'

There's something about the way they grin at each other. Laurie can see that despite her own misgivings about Pete, Gina loves him.

'Twenty years,' Laurie says. 'You must have got married just after I left Chapel Field. Just after Marcus.' She doesn't say any more. This is a present-day visit. The past can stay where it is. She lifts her carrier bag. 'I have gifts. A cuppa would go well with one of them.'

'That's lovely,' croons Gina. She sets the dog down and slips her arm through Laurie's. 'Let's go inside.'

They spend the next half-hour on a tour of the house and family photo archive. Pete has three boys, all in their teens and all with Gina's stature and frizzy hair. She tells Laurie about them – one is a champion swimmer; one can't swim to save his life; the oldest is about to take his driving test – no detail is left out. But it is when Gina mentions her own grandmother that Laurie starts to focus.

'Yeah. She used to work for the Diamonds. Back in the old days. The *very* old days.'

Pete is crashing around in the kitchen, alerting them to the fact that their tea is ready.

'Doing what?' asks Laurie. She's trying to calculate the age Gina's grandmother would be. There's nothing to go on; she's never had a grandma of her own.

'Cleaning, mainly. I think it was when May Diamond became ill. She was Ed's gran. Olivia – that's my nan – wasn't there for long. When Richard Diamond brought his Spanish girlfriend to live in the house, they got rid of poor old Nan. It was in the seventies, from what I can remember.'

'Wow. That's a real Chapel Field story, isn't it.' Laurie can hear Pete calling to them. 'We'd better do what His Majesty says.'

'Better had.' Gina giggles as she leads the way back downstairs. The house is bright and comfortable, nothing like Laurie's mother's. Pete has opened French windows from the kitchen and laid out their mugs and a plate of biscuits on a blue-and-white tiled table on the sunny patio.

'Had a good nosey?' He laughs, giving her a thumbs-up.

'Yes, thanks.' Laurie pulls out a heavy cast-metal chair. 'It's a lovely place. And your kids are adorable.'

'Yeah. From nine at night until eight in the morning.'

Gina sits with them, sliding herself into a chair at Pete's side. 'Laurie tells me she's a teacher of sorts. Disruptive kids and the like.' She picks up her mug. 'That's brave, isn't it? I didn't know you used to mix with brainy people, Pete. I thought they were all like that Jamie character.' She turns to Laurie. 'Did you know Jamie Purcell?'

'I did.' Laurie wonders where this conversation will take them. 'But I haven't heard from him since–'

'I know.' Gina rolls her eyes. 'Since Marcus Butcher. Pete talks in the same way. Everything in his life took place before or after the time of the exalted Marcus Butcher. Can't say I even remember the guy. But I come from the mainland, don't I.'

Pete huffs a little. 'Jamie went overseas, I think. He came to our wedding, but I haven't heard from him since then. It's only me from our gang that stayed the course. Mam left years ago, too. I don't hear from her, either.'

Laurie thinks about Gina's assessment of their past. Was the death of Marcus Butcher, and everything that happened afterwards, a pivotal point in her life? She's not sure it was. Marcus hardly makes it into her thoughts anymore. Ed Diamond has a permanent seat in a shadowy corner, hidden but always present. Now that she's seen him, she wants, more than anything, to put right what she got so wrong.

'Wanting to get away from Chapel Field doesn't make Laurie a bad person, Pete.' Gina is frowning at her husband. 'It's not a badge of honour that you're still here.' She shrugs. 'It's just how things turn out.'

'Whatever,' Pete mutters. 'I never could stand my mother, anyway. I'm glad she *got away*, as you put it.'

Gina slaps his hand playfully. 'Stop that. Parents are people, as I've told you before. They've had a life; it's not for their children to question it.'

Laurie is starting to like this woman. There are no agendas with her and everything she says is tinged with a kind of wish for people to be happy and accepted. Her children are lucky to have that sort of mother. Pete stares across the garden and starts to talk about all the different fruit trees he is cultivating. The conversation is so benign that when he mentions Ed Diamond again, Laurie is hardly listening.

'I mean it though, Loz,' he is saying. 'Don't be trying to talk to Ed Diamond. He's a nutter. We knew it back then, and nothing's changed.'

'Don't call me Loz,' she snaps, making Gina raise her eyebrows. 'That girl is long gone. And if I want to talk to Ed, I will.'

Gina gets up and gathers their mugs. A look passes between her and Pete. His lips press together, and she shakes her head lightly. Neither of them speaks.

'Thanks for the drink,' Laurie says, taking her lead from Gina. 'I must go and get on with sorting Mum's bits and pieces. I'll probably see you around the village at some point. I'm here for a while.' She waves at Pete as she follows Gina into the house. In the hallway, she waits while Gina opens the front door.

'It was nice to meet you,' she says. 'I'd love to talk again, perhaps meet that nan of yours. Olivia, wasn't it? I bet she could tell some tales about Chapel Field.'

'We'll try and arrange something,' Gina says absently. 'See you soon.'

Pete has followed them to the front door. He catches up with Laurie at the garden gate. 'Wait up, Loz,' he says, suddenly breathy. When the front door closes and Laurie is on the pavement, he catches hold of her arm. 'I'm not making it up. About Ed Diamond. You need to steer clear.'

'Will you stop talking in that creepy cryptic way,' she hisses. 'That cruel thing I did to Ed. I'm going to apologise. Marcus paid for what the three of you did afterwards, but I caused it all. I was a horror, back then. My only excuse is youth. If I can tell him none of it was his fault, I might feel this visit was worth something. As it is, I'm hating every minute of it.' She yanks her arm out of his grasp and holds on to her elbow for a moment. Then she storms away from the house and heads for the beach.

Chapter 8

Christmas 1996

Laurie

Laurie lifts the corner of the net curtain so she can see onto the darkening street. Where are her friends? Marcus has a car now, and he's promised to save her from the misery of a Christmas lunch eaten with her mother. The meal itself hadn't been too bad. Janet Helm had roasted a small turkey crown and served it with a selection of vegetables and sauces. Then there'd been Christmas pudding and profiteroles, even a glass of Asti Spumante, but chewing and swallowing food while sitting opposite someone who ate nothing was too difficult for Laurie. She'd begged her mother to eat a few mouthfuls, if only to keep her company. The food remained untouched.

'Stop doing that to the curtains.' Janet is sprawled on the sofa, glass in hand and the almost empty bottle of fizz on the floor beside her. 'Laurie. I said stop.'

Not reacting is the only weapon Laurie has left. Pleading and sympathy and anger have long proved useless against the power of her mother's mind. If it is power. The word implies something positive, proactive even. Janet Helm is neither of those things.

A flash of headlights sets Laurie's stomach fizzing. This will be the first time she's been a passenger in a car that didn't belong to a fully-fledged adult. She's wearing her new fun-fur jacket. It's not as warm as the red wool, but that one reminds her of the night she met up with Ed Diamond. She can hardly bring herself to think about it. From what she's heard, Marcus and the others had given him a good kicking. She won't let herself imagine how that played out.

'I'm going now,' she says as she steps out of the lounge and into the hallway. 'I'll lock the front door and take the key.'

No answer comes. In a dish on the hall table is a handful of change. She picks up some pound coins and a couple of fifty-pence pieces, then pushes them into the pocket of her jeans. Marcus has told her they might take a walk over the fells, so she's wearing her flat lace-up boots for the occasion. She loops a knitted scarf around her neck and steps outside. It's a drizzly evening, bitter with the tang of coal smoke. And so quiet. Laurie pulls the front door closed and locks it, then zips the key into her coat pocket. Her mother will be unconscious soon. If she does need to exit the house, there's always the yard door.

Pete O'Connor is in the front passenger seat. He winds down the window when he sees Laurie. 'Fuck me. It's the Abominable Snowman,' he screeches.

She pulls open the back door. Jamie is already sitting there. 'Where's Ruth?' she asks as she slides herself in. 'I'm not coming with you lot on my own.'

'She's in town. At her nanna's. We're going there now.' Marcus peers over his shoulder at her. There is a glint in his eyes she recognises. 'And you can shut your face, Pete. Laurie looks great. You're the fucking snowman or whatever it is; state of you.'

It feels strange, being in the car with three boys: men, really. They talk around her, about their latest drinking sessions, about cars and about the stash of cannabis Marcus has in the glove compartment. As they leave Chapel Field, she almost asks him to pull over so that she can walk herself home again. But there's nothing at the house for her, so she decides to keep quiet. They drive along the promenade, following the yellow line of streetlights, jostling for position in the conversation. It isn't long before the subject of Ed Diamond comes up.

'Daddy Diamond came round my house, you know. After–' Jamie is gripping Marcus's seat, swinging himself backwards and forwards. With every movement, Laurie catches a faint smell: sweat gone-off and the dirty wax of his coat.

Marcus splutters. 'Funny you saying that. I thought I saw him on our drive the other night. Right by my car. The dogs were barking their heads off.'

Jamie guffaws. 'I hope your old man told him where to go.'

'There was no need. When Mam saw him on the doorstep, she shouted like I've never heard, and he ran away. She was defending me, would you believe. That's a fucking first.'

'He chased me in the street the other day.' Pete has a matching story. 'Said he was going to kill me for laying into Ed. I hardly did anything. It was all you, Butcher.'

Marcus takes a hand off the steering wheel and thumps Pete in the chest. 'Bog off.' He laughs. 'You stuck the boot in as much as I did. Eduardo fucking Diamond won't be chatting up our women for a long, long time.'

Laurie feels the heavy Christmas dinner churning in her stomach. She catches the taste of sage-and-onion in the back of her throat. How dare they talk about her and Ruth like that. *Our women*? Marcus must be getting his education from car and motorcycle magazines; he certainly isn't living in the modern world of the 1990s.

'We're not your women,' she snaps. 'And if I remember it rightly, you're the one who wanted me to throw myself into the path of Ed Diamond. Though why the hell I went through with it, I don't know.'

Marcus lets out a high-pitched laugh. Pete and Jamie accompany him with wolf-howls. Laurie isn't sure what to do. They've bumped across the bridge and are now speeding along the main road through town. She can't exactly throw herself out of the car.

Marcus catches her eye in his mirror. He clears his throat, and the others stop howling. 'Sorry, Loz,' he says. 'We're just being stupid. Ignore us. But something needs to be sorted with regard to the Diamonds. I can't stick them.'

'Why not? What is it they've done?'

Pete turns to look at her. 'They're offcomers. They've no business living in the middle of Chapel Field in that dossy house. My ma can't stand them. She's told me some vile stories about them; sick-making.'

Laurie shudders at his tone. What he's really saying is the Diamonds haven't done anything to deserve the treatment they get, except to be characters in someone else's tale-telling. She dares not voice her opinion. If she lost Marcus's friendship, what would be left for her? Ruth wouldn't jeopardise her own relationship; it is obvious she's head-over-heels in love with him. There is no real attachment for Laurie to Jamie and Pete, which would leave her with a few wishy-washy friends from college, and her mother.

'Guess they don't,' she mutters, then turns her face to the window. They have arrived in an area of the town where tenement flats vie for the skyline with huge industrial buildings. Streetlights tinge the drizzly air with a sickly yellow wash, and no one is about. Standing on the corner of the main street is Ruth, umbrella in hand. Marcus brings the car to a halt in a way that shoots Laurie and Jamie forward so that they must brace against the front seats.

'Fuck's sake,' Jamie spits. 'You're a nut-case, Butcher. Are you sure you passed your test?'

'I aced it, actually. The examiner said I was the best young driver he'd seen in a long time.' Marcus doesn't quite make it to the end of his sentence without laughing, and they all join in. Ruth pulls open the back door and bundles herself in, shoving up against Laurie's legs with her damp jeans, then clambering over her to sit in the middle, where she can have access to Marcus.

'What's so funny?' she says, and they all start laughing again.

Marcus chats with her as he pulls the car away from town and drives out towards the coast. The last houses flash by and the landscape flattens into dark fields reaching up to the line of the sky. The car is moving faster and faster, but no one seems to mind.

In the front seat, Pete is rolling a joint. Jamie is rambling on about a heavy-rock band with a name Laurie has never heard. *Extreme* something or other. He pretends to play guitar and makes high-pitched whiny sounds to match what he's doing with his fingers. It scrapes at Laurie's sense of herself. There is a kind of pressure building behind her eyes; it's the same feeling she had when she thought she was trapped in the lift at college. It's like every atom of her energy is moving into the centre of her body and she can do nothing about it except wait for the inevitable explosion. She tries winding the window down but the drizzle flies in instantly.

'Shut the window,' Ruth screeches. 'Oh, Christ. You're not travel sick, are you?'

Laurie shakes her head but finds she can't say anything. All she wants is to get out of the car, but they are about three miles out of town, on an empty road, on Christmas Day; she's stuck with it.

'How bad was it, dinner with your mother, I mean?' Ruth's question cuts across her thoughts.

'The food was okay, but she didn't eat anything. It's not easy, sitting opposite someone who's starving themselves while you tuck into a large plateful.'

'I bet it's not. My nan tried her best to eat something, even though she's not well. Your mum doesn't know how lucky she is. At least she's got her health.'

Laurie's not sure how to answer this. Does her mother have health? It doesn't seem like it, sometimes. She shrugs.

'Oh, come on, Loz. Perk up a bit.' Ruth takes her hand and rubs the back of it. 'You've got us, now. We'll share a bag of chips with you, anytime.'

The joke is in poor taste, given what happened with Ed Diamond, but Laurie forces herself to laugh and make a comment about curry sauce. It sets off a conversation about favourite foods, and by the time it has run its course, the car is zooming along the wide coastal road, and an earthy, rubbery scent is coming from where Pete is sitting. Suddenly, there is a loud crash and a muffled thud. Marcus has hit something.

'Sod it,' he shouts. 'What the hell was that?' He pulls the car up at the side of the road.

Laurie's stomach flips over. Pete climbs out and walks to the bonnet, then crouches. 'It's a fox,' he calls. 'You've smashed it to pieces, Butcher, you dickhead. Come and have a look.'

Marcus flicks his gaze across to where Laurie is sitting with Ruth and Jamie. 'Stay there, ladies,' he hisses. 'My fucking car better not be damaged.' He shoulders his way outside and disappears into the gloom. Laurie thinks she's going to be sick. A slosh of acid makes its way up from her stomach and burns the back of her throat. Crying isn't an option, but it's what she wants to do. She's never felt more like an immature kid.

Ruth is sitting with her arms folded, drumming her loose fingers on the arm of her denim jacket. Jamie is rolling a cigarette.

Marcus and Pete appear again, at the front of the car. They move into the hedgerow at the side of the road for a moment, then let themselves back in. With them comes the salty-cold smell of the sea.

'It's nowt that I can't sort,' Pete is saying. 'A bit of damage to the plate, is all. I can give the whole car a quick once-over as well, if you like. Just bring it down to the garage after Boxing Day.'

Laurie leans towards Marcus's shoulder. 'Can you take me home?' She is trying to keep her voice calm. Any hysteria will make her the butt of their jokes; she's seen how they operate. 'I'm not feeling very well. Don't want to puke in your car, do I?'

'It's okay, Loz,' he says in a soothing tone she's not heard him use before. 'It was just an accident. The poor critter won't have felt anything. No real damage to the car either. You're just in shock.'

'No, I really need to get home. Please, Marcus. I'll have to walk if you won't take me.' She pulls at the door handle. If she doesn't get to a toilet soon, her guts feel like they might spill themselves.

'Okay, okay.' Marcus doesn't look at her. He slams his hands against the steering wheel. 'Hold on tight, everyone. I'm going to make the return journey in record time.'

Ruth grabs Laurie's hand and squeezes. They are jettisoned back against their seats as Marcus zooms away from the side of the road. Pete squeals in a way that could be fear or delight. Jamie leans forwards, head in hands. The drizzle has built up a pressure now and is more like rain. It splashes under the tyres of the car and pelts against the windscreen.

With no other vehicles about, Marcus acts as if he is king of the road. He crosses into the opposite lane on every bend and does something with the car's revs that cause it to backfire in a way that terrifies Laurie to the point where she recites a prayer in her head. He doesn't let up when they hit the outskirts of the town. It's as though they are in the landscape of one of the new computer simulations Laurie has heard about. There are buildings and streetlamps and roadways but no people and no danger; if you crash, you just start again. Except they wouldn't, would they?

Finally, they bump across the road bridge and onto the island's promenade. Laurie wants to ask Marcus to drop her here, but the rain is hammering, and her jacket won't stand it. A few more minutes will see them back at Chapel Field and then she'll be safe. Facing her mother seems like a better prospect than travelling in the car with Marcus. He's taking long puffs of the joint Pete rolled earlier and rambling about hoping to see Ed Diamond in the road so he can obliterate him. Luckily, there's no sign of Ed. As they hit the slope of the road into the village, Marcus is forced to slow down a little.

'What a ride,' he hollers, grabbing at a handful of his wet hair and rubbing vigorously. 'What a fucking ride.'

'Just drop me at the top of the main road,' Laurie says, leaning towards his ear, but he doesn't respond. His face is turned towards the hunched figure at the side of the road. It looks a lot like Ed's father. He is wearing an old-fashioned oilskin mac and wellington boots. Marcus slows the car as he passes, revving the engine so that the exhaust backfires, then he rolls down the window and laughs in a way that makes Laurie finally spill the contents of her stomach.

Chapter 9

January 1997

Ed

There are no *Happy New Year* celebrations at Diamond Hall. Ed is finally well enough to lie on the sofa and read the latest Phillip Pullman novel. He's been confined to bed for nearly three weeks. Busted ribs, his father said, to match his busted eye and split chin.

When he'd staggered home after taking a beating from those three village boys, Ed had fallen onto the floor of the kitchen and thought he was going to die. He was crying and bleeding and he'd wet himself. There had been no call for a doctor or an ambulance: his father didn't believe in those things. The plight of his sister was testament to that.

What worried Ed more was the state his father had got himself into. By day, he paced the house, crashing around and ranting about pay-back, even though no one was listening. By night, he'd taken to wandering around the village, looking for the culprits and knocking on their doors, seeking parental retribution. None came.

Tonight, he is out again, and Ed is trying not to let himself think about it. His father isn't eating, and his face has taken on a hard edge, as though he's in pain. Not the same kind of pain as Ed is experiencing, but something. The beating was a physical manifestation, it had a beginning and an end. Ed is managing to deal with that. The girl, Laurie, setting him up, is what he's really struggling with. His father hasn't been chasing her though or knocking on her door demanding pay-back. Ed has no idea why not. He hates her more than he hates the others, but for his father, it's all about catching the lads and doing for them. Quite what he thinks he is going to do, Ed can't imagine.

It's a wild night. Rain is pelting against the two skylights over the kitchen, and any heat from the fire is being blown and sucked about by the wind pushing through every bit of faulty joinery. Ed huddles under his blanket and closes his eyes for a moment. Being with Laurie, talking and laughing, had given him a taste of what it must be like to be ordinary, to not be noticed and avoided or worse still, singled out; to be missed when you were not around. He'd really believed she liked him.

At the point where they'd met up with the awful Marcus Butcher, he'd expected her to defend him. Instead, she'd grabbed the other girl by the hand, and they'd disappeared up the slope into the village. He doesn't remember much about what happened after that.

Above the sound of the wind is the wail of a siren. The water has probably flooded over the promenade again, so the fire engines are out. By the size of the moon, it'll be a full tide, though he's no idea when it will reach its peak: he hasn't been outside Diamond Hall since the beating. He's not sure if he will ever go out again.

There's a heaviness at the front of his eyes and he lets them close. What he's taken to doing is filtering out his thoughts and letting sleep come. There are no dreams in his kind of sleep; it's deep and dark and probably something like death.

Is this what Elissa feels? He hasn't been able to help his father with her lately and she's been in bed all over Christmas. They never have conversations; his sister doesn't speak, but he can usually keep her smiling by reading aloud or singing silly songs. Odd times she hums them back to him, but he's no other access to her thoughts.

Now that Ed's feeling less like an invalid himself, he's going to suggest they move Elissa downstairs permanently. Then she'll always have someone around her, instead of being trapped in a bedroom at the back of the house until he and his father can get to her. He'd once suggested there might be agencies out in the world that could help them manage, but his father had exploded with a rage that seemed very close to fear, and Ed chose not to mention it again.

He's not sure how much time has passed when the back door flies open and his father charges into the room. His face and hair are dripping wet, but he's smiling in a way that Ed hasn't seen for a long time. He yanks open the poppers of his waterproof jacket and lets it fall to the floor. Then he's punching the air and dancing around and saying there's been an accident on the promenade. Ed thinks he's dreaming at first and has to blink his way back to reality. But his father is still there, standing in front of him and beaming out news of this accident as though it's the best thing ever.

When Ed has calmed him down enough that he can explain properly, he finds out the accident is actually a fatal car crash, and the victim is Marcus Butcher.

Walney Island, spring 1950
Maisie-Anne Diamond

It was one of those April days, where the sky billowed blue, and the surface of the tide was scattered with sunlight. Maisie-Anne Diamond should have been smiling at the beauty of it, but she felt nothing.

Since Ronnie had been born, there was a heaviness in her body and a blackness in her brain worse than anything she'd felt before. She looked down at him now, asleep in the pushchair and hated herself a little bit more. He'd been a good baby, and Ritchie loved him instantly. Lenny helped where he could but finishing the house had taken most of his time, and now it was complete, he expected her mood to lift. This was what she'd wanted, after all; a place to call home.

She did love Diamond Hall, for all its faults. The windows were in the wrong place and didn't fit properly, and the roof leaked despite Lenny's many attempts to patch it up. He was the problem, always thinking he could tackle any building job successfully and save them a bit more money.

She'd even tried to create a garden on the little bit of outside land left before the sea-wood proper, but the claggy, stomped over soil wouldn't support anything but Lenny's scrap metal.

Maisie-Anne felt she deserved more. When she looked in the bedroom mirror, she saw an attractive girl, little more than a teenager really. Now that her baby-bump was gone, she was slim and lithe enough that men at least should be noticing her. Even when she brushed out her soft yellow hair and wore her best dress, the people of Chapel Field crossed over the road as she passed by.

In the clinic, when she'd taken Ritchie and Ronnie for their weekly dose of rose hip and cod-liver, the mothers she'd often seen walking in the village, would turn to each other, their circle excluding her without a word being said. She understood about the locals being unhappy when Lenny acquired their small piece of land. It had been used for lamping and trapping. Everyone needed the meat from small birds and rabbits to supplement their diet, but there were plenty more fields and scrubby patches of stunted woodland around; more than enough for everyone to use.

Ritchie was swinging his weight against the handle of the pushchair. He hated being left outside the shop to mind Ronnie, so he was acting up in readiness. Some days she felt well enough for trekking across the island to the bigger places, but not today. So he'd have to behave himself and mind his brother and let her buy the things they needed. She'd be as quick as she could: the treatment she received in the shop was no different from anything else she got in Chapel Field; her money was acceptable, but not her face.

'You can pack that in right now,' she said, slapping Ritchie on the back of his hand. 'There'll be no lolly, otherwise.'

As he pulled his hand away, his balance shifted. One of the plimsolls he was wearing came loose, making him stumble, and before Maisie-Anne could catch him, he fell backwards onto the hard slabs of the pavement. She expected screaming, but none came. Instead, his eyes rolled back in his head, and he opened his mouth, just once, then became limp and lolling.

'Ritchie. Richard Diamond, open your eyes.' Maisie-Anne knelt beside him, not knowing whether she should slap his face or his hand or both. She cast her eyes down the street. It was empty.

She thought about leaving her children and pushing her way into the shop for help, but it struck her that none might be offered. Surely people would see this was an emergency. Ritchie was still unresponsive. She tried calling out, but no one came. Just as she reached the limits of her patience and was about to start screaming properly, the front door of one of the terraced houses opened and a woman appeared.

'What's all the commotion?' she hissed, shoving her hands into the pockets of a grubby tabard, and shuffling towards where Maisie-Anne was kneeling. 'What's little 'un doing on the floor?'

'He fell. I don't know what to do.'

The woman looked at Ritchie, then at Ronnie in his pushchair. 'Let me bring the trolley inside. You try and lift t'other one. You can lie him on my couch.'

She dragged at the handle of the pushchair and bumped it over the doorstep. Ronnie lurched forward but his harness kept him sitting safely.

Maisie-Anne slid her arms under Ritchie's legs and around his shoulders, then lifted him from the pavement. He blinked himself awake and began to yell. She carried him into the gloom of the house, wrinkling her nose at the overpowering stench of cat urine.

'In here,' the woman commanded as she disappeared through a door at the end of the passageway. Ronnie was crying now, adding to the stress of the situation. Maisie-Anne felt like joining him. She was a mother, yet she didn't have the first idea what to do. She carried Ritchie into what looked like a kitchen, with a line of pale blue cupboards along one wall and a small sofa next to a fireplace. When she laid him down, the woman was there again, holding out a grubby tea towel.

'Put this under his head,' she grumbled, 'I don't want blood everywhere.'

Maisie-Anne's stomach took a lurch. Blood? She hadn't noticed any blood, but when she looked down at the arm where her son's head rested, there was plenty. The more he cried and thrashed about, the more smeared her arm became.

'Should I telephone for an ambulance?' she stammered.

The woman cackled. 'Don't have a telephone, do I?' She helped Maisie-Anne lay Ritchie on the sofa, then began probing the wound at the crown of his head.

'Scalps bleed a lot. This isn't a deep cut. He'll survive. Just hold the cloth there for now.' She stretched herself upright, pressing her hands to the lower part of her back. 'Would you want a cup of tea?'

Maisie-Anne nodded. 'Thank you. And could you get my other boy out of the pushchair. He'll be panicking.'

Once the kettle was set to boil, the woman stepped into the hallway, and Maisie-Anne could hear her crooning at Ronnie. He stopped crying. Then he was standing in the doorway, reaching towards her, and taking a few tentative steps.

'Tea,' the woman mumbled as she helped Ronnie along. She began crashing about, rummaging through the cupboards, and turning on the taps over an old stone sink.

By the time Maisie-Anne had a mug of tea in her hand, both boys were quiet. Ritchie was lying with his head in her lap and Ronnie sat next to her, clutching a handful of her dress to his face, eyelids drooping.

'Panic over,' said the woman as she settled herself on a kitchen chair. 'I'm Gloria Helm, by the way. I know who you are.'

Maisie-Anne pressed her lips together and braced for what was coming.

'Oh, don't look at me like that.' Gloria ran a hand through her silvery-white hair. 'I'm not one for grudges. If I've something to say, I'll say it.'

'And what would that be?'

'You Diamonds shouldn't have built on that land, up by the woods. How it was ever sold to you, no one can fathom. But I'm not doing what those others want. Can't tell me what to think and feel, can they?' She was muttering and Maisie-Anne

73

struggled to hear. She tried to shift her weight forward, to the edge of the sofa, but Ritchie began to moan. She stroked his forehead and gave him soothing words. Should she have called a doctor? She wasn't quite sure. Something about his eyes looked strange, like they'd lost their focus, but his colour was fine and he was asking for sweets and a drink.

'What is being said about us, Gloria?'

'People want you gone, that's the long and short of it.'

Maisie-Anne wasn't sure how to respond. She took a few gulps of her tea and kept her gaze focused on Ritchie. As far as she was aware, neither she nor Lenny had done anything to merit being got rid of. She wanted to ask why, but what if finding out was worse than not knowing?

The older woman stood up and reached for Maisie-Anne's mug. 'Best get on. Keep a watch on the little lad, but I think he'll be fine. I was a nurse once, you know. Before the war. Only an auxiliary, like, but I know what's what.'

'Thank you for helping me. My husband will be grateful, too, when I tell him.' She freed her dress from Ronnie's clutches and started to manoeuvre Ritchie into an upright position. 'I can squeeze this one into the pushchair, I think. Rather than him walking back to Diamond Hall.'

Gloria let out a spit of laughter. 'What a name for a house. Diamond Hall, indeed. And built over the plague grave, too. You couldn't make it up.' She locked eyes with Maisie-Anne. 'Didn't know that, did you?'

'I've no idea what you mean. What plague grave?' From what Masie-Anne remembered, there was nothing on the land when they first started to build, except heaped tangles of bramble and dried out stumps of ancient elder trees. There was certainly no church or chapel or graveyard. Lenny would never have been allowed to buy that kind of land.

'There's nothing to see, is there; no markers or anything. But everyone from Chapel Field knows how the village was named.'

'And how was that?' Maisie-Anne felt a twist of annoyance in her stomach. This woman said she was plain-speaking, but riddles were dripping from her lips like oily cod-liver running from her son's mouths at the clinic, and she wanted to wipe them away. She pulled both boys towards the hallway, aware of the woman just behind her.

'There was an outbreak of plague on the island,' she was saying. 'Hundreds of years ago now, like. With no one to bury the bodies, they were slung in a deep grave right where your house is. There was going to be a chapel built, as a memorial, but it never happened.' Gloria moved to the front door and pulled it open. 'I wouldn't want to live there, anyroad.' She shivered. 'People don't forget things like that.'

Maisie-Anne gritted her teeth as she strapped both boys into the pushchair. Ritchie had recovered himself enough to be elbowing Ronnie, who was crying softly and half asleep.

'Thanks for helping me,' she said as she navigated the doorstep. 'And I don't care for your story about the grave. I think you've made it up. Silly old bat.' Then she stormed away, head down and shoving the pushchair for all she was worth.

By the time Maisie-Anne reached the narrow driveway of Diamond Hall, both boys were asleep. She bumped the pushchair over what passed as tarmac, and felt her anger rise again at the makeshift nature of the place. Now she'd found out what lay beneath the house, she wondered how she'd ever be able to sleep again. Not that she got much, anyway, and babies weren't the cause of that.

As always, Lenny had a friend who had a friend who could get her some sleeping pills. They didn't work. Not when every wrong thing in her life had a presence and lurked in the hidden recesses of her brain, waiting to show up as soon as the word *sleep* was mentioned. Night after night she lay, listening to their arguments echoing in her head, wishing she could reach inside and throttle the lot of them.

Lenny was standing at the front of the house, dressed in his brown overalls, and hammering a piece of wood onto the door of the porch. It was the name plaque he'd made, and she hated. Like so many things in and around the house, it was recycled when she'd wanted new.

'What do you think?' He stepped away from the porch and swung the hammer over his shoulder. 'No one'll doubt who lives here now, will they?'

Maisie-Anne let her shoulders sag. She leant against the handle of the pushchair and wondered if she had enough energy to carry her through to the end of the day. After what Gloria had said about *Diamond Hall* being a ridiculous name for a house, she wanted to tear the plaque down and break it into tiny pieces. Lenny was doing his best to give her what she wanted; what he thought she wanted. She loved him, she really did. So why did he cause her so much irritation?

'What did you know about the land when you bought it, Len?'

He turned to her in surprise. 'You what?'

'The land. Right here. Where the house is. What did you know about it? You've never even told me how you got it.' She took a deep breath. 'Well, I want to know now.'

Lenny put down the hammer and slid an arm around her shoulders. Then kissed her cheek in a way that made her want to scream. She wriggled from his grasp so that he frowned and pushed out his lower lip.

'Don't start with that,' she hissed. 'I'm not playing games. Tell me. This was council land, you said, and they were happy to make money out of it. You better not have been lying.'

'I never said it was council land.'

'You mentioned the council. I heard you. And don't be telling me I've got it wrong. I'm not stupid.'

Lenny knelt in front of the pushchair and put his index finger to his lips. 'Don't,' he mouthed.

'You're not fobbing me off, Len. I've just been told something horrible, and I want to know the truth of it.' If there was anything Maisie-Anne could use as a hanging-post for her gloom, she wanted it. Perhaps then she could make it go away.

He stood up and clicked the brake on the pushchair with his foot. 'Inside,' he whispered.

With the porch door closed, Lenny began to explain how he'd approached a man he knew on the local council, who assured him the sea-wood was in their possession and a piece could be carved off, for the right price. The deal had almost fallen through when the deeds were checked.

'There had been a petition in, yonks ago, I think, to build a chapel in this clearing. For the village, like. It fell through, in the end.' Lenny shrugged. 'Good for us, though, wasn't it.'

A shivery feeling swept across Maisie-Anne's neck and down her arms. It was just as Gloria had said. A plague pit and a chapel.

'Oh, Christ, Len. An old biddy in the village said exactly that to me today.'

'About what?' He put his hands on her shoulders and pulled her towards him. 'Are you all right?'

She let herself be hugged. This must be why she'd felt so odd. Nothing to do with having Ronnie. There'd always been an air of misery about Diamond Hall. Now she knew why.

'I will be all right, Len. When you move us away from here.' She braced herself for his reaction. None came.

'Did you hear me?' She waited, then looked up at him. 'I don't want to live here anymore.'

Lenny sighed. 'Daft girl. We're going nowhere. And you

need to stop gossiping in the village.' He tutted lightly. 'That bloody lot have had it in for us ever since I started building. Before that, actually. They'll have hundreds of reasons why we shouldn't be here. But, guess what? We're here, and there's not a thing they can do about it.'

Chapter 10

Summer 2018

Laurie

Memories come from the strangest of places. Laurie is driving along the promenade on her way off the island, to visit her mother's bank.

Then Marcus Butcher is there, with his bright hair and wide shoulders, dragging her towards the tide, hands on her waist, pretending to rescue her again. Talking to Pete has dredged up a lot of bad feeling about their shared past, but there were fun times with Marcus, too. He had been a person to follow, all lopsided grin and complete disregard for convention and context. She even thought there might be something more between them once, but her friend Ruth put a stop to that, with her short skirts and her availability.

Then the two-fingered salute he'd been giving to the universe finally bounced back at him. The freak car accident that snapped his neck had shocked Laurie so much, she'd had to take a year out from her studies. There had been no support from her mother.

The traffic lights at the road bridge are on red. While she

waits, Laurie looks across the narrow stretch of water, blue-green now and a reflection of the summer sky, and she thinks about Ed. How must it feel to be stuck on the island with its blinkered community and its suspicion. She isn't being fair: it's a beautiful place, where nature can poke through undisturbed and a constant wind from the sea ensures a clear head and robust complexion. For the Diamonds, she suspects, it's been a prison of sorts.

She is disgusted with the way she acted towards Ed; youth isn't enough of an excuse. She deliberately led him on, made him believe in her offer of friendship.

The rest of the Chapel Field community hated the Diamonds, and without understanding any of their reasons, she'd joined the throng. For most of her adult life she's preached the opposite of this behaviour. Does that make her a liar? She won't know the answer unless she can meet with Ed and talk about what she did and beg his forgiveness. In the meantime, she must pay her mother's last bills then close her bank account. At least some things are straight forward.

The town centre is filled with the buzz of summer-holiday families and groups of teens lounging around the fast-food outlets. Laurie parks her car in a neat side street filled with craft shops and cafés. She is hoping probate has been granted. Her mother left a clear and concise will, all relevant paperwork ordered and available. Nothing like the mess she'd left in the house.

Detachment from the emotional pain of grief has been easy for Laurie; she and her mother hadn't liked each other at all.

Detachment from everything else in Chapel Field is proving a little more problematic. She's even considered not selling the house, throwing in her London life, and starting again. That consideration lasted all of five minutes but being back is unveiling a part of her she didn't know was there, and it's giving her a feeling like homesickness mixed with an unhealthy dose of guilt: perhaps she should have made more of an effort with her mother, whether that effort was returned or not.

Inside the bank, Laurie enjoys a few moments of the air conditioning before she casts about to tell someone she has an appointment. A young woman wearing a crisp white shirt under a navy-blue pinafore leads her through to an office. Its high ceiling and tall windows remind her of the PRU where she works, which is based in a grand Victorian building that used to be railway offices. It's far from purpose-built, but the children seem to like its airy security, and that's more important than anything new and modern and a tight-fit. Most of her pupils would run from a place like that.

The meeting is over in less than fifteen minutes. There are no hitches. Janet Helm had a bit of money, though most of it had been used for her care expenses and her funeral. Selling the house will also give Laurie a small lump-sum, but she's not sure she wants it. There are no relatives and no claims, so she could donate the whole amount if she wanted to. And she might.

As she steps out of the cool spaciousness of the bank, Laurie pauses for a moment and wonders if she might find somewhere to have a coffee and something to eat. She looks along the street.

Standing in front of the bank's cash machine is Ed Diamond, head bent towards the screen and a carrier bag in his hand. Something about him strikes her, as if she's been punched in the stomach and winded.

She hesitates, but only for a moment; this is a second chance.

'Hello, Ed. We keep bumping into each other.' Crass, she knows, but there had to be an ice-breaker sentence.

He doesn't respond, but it's clear he's heard her: he turns his head slightly, then his whole body in the opposite direction.

She moves to stand right next to him. 'Ed. You'll be heading back over to the island eventually. Let me give you a lift, at least.'

He spins towards her. 'I don't want a lift. What part of "get lost" did you not understand?'

'I understood all of it.' She's looking into his eyes now. They are flashing with rage. 'But I'm in such a bad place and you can help me out of it.'

These last words cause a spit of laughter. 'Bad place?' He stretches his brows. 'You're saying that to *me*? You wrote the book on bad places, didn't you? Then circled the worst one and put my name by it.'

'Please, Ed. I'm begging now. Let me at least give you a lift home and we can talk a bit.' Laurie thinks about how this might sound, and changes tack. 'What I mean is, I want to apologise properly. For being a nasty little shit.'

Ed's cash pops out from the machine. He takes it and shoves it into the front pocket of his jeans. Then he swings his body away and strides off down the street. Laurie follows him.

'Oh. Here's the nasty little shit, again,' he mutters, but there is something in his face that makes her carry on with her pleading. His lips are twitching, just slightly.

'Let me buy you a coffee or something. Come on, Ed.' She looks up at him. 'Ten minutes, then you'll never have to hear from me again. Please?'

Laurie is surprised at herself. There's no doubt she'd feel better if she could put things at least halfway right with Ed Diamond. This level of grovelling isn't something she's had much experience of, and she steps away from him for a moment so she can examine her motives – he's standing there with his dark hair and darker eyes, his height and his total vulnerability – and she realises what they are.

Then suddenly he's talking again and saying something

about never having had a coffee in town and she realises he's agreeing.

'Oh. I, er–'

'Changed your mind? There's a surprise. Never done that before, have you.'

'Not at all,' she says lightly. 'I'm just thinking about which café will be best. I haven't been in town for nigh-on twenty years, so I'm not sure where to go. There was a little place near where I parked the car. Will that be okay?'

He nods and holds out his arm. 'Why not. You lead the way.'

Laurie opts for a small upstairs tea-room with a florist's underneath. Ed has to hunch down so that he can access the staircase. They are shown to a tiny table in a bay window, where they slide into old-fashioned pine chairs and try not to elbow each other.

'This is cosy,' she whispers, and when he stretches his eyes wide, she adds, 'Sorry. That was just nervous small-talk. I'm an idiot.'

Ed puts his carrier bag under the table and peers around. 'Do they realise people of my height exist? We're not just in storybooks.'

The comment makes Laurie laugh and they both relax a little. A young woman comes towards them, notebook and pen in hand. She's wearing a white polo-shirt with *Blossom's* embroidered across the front. Ed raises one eyebrow, and Laurie starts giggling again.

They choose mugs of milky coffee and a plate of toast to share.

'This is so weird,' she says when the waitress has gone. 'I never thought you'd talk to me, Ed. I was so vile to you when we were teenagers.' A flush of heat creeps its way across her face. 'Then you took that beating. I'm so sorry. I don't have any excuses. And I shouldn't have left it this long before I apologised.'

Ed runs a hand over the deep scar on his chin. There's no embarrassment, no flash of the anger she's seen before. Instead, he is shaking his head sadly. 'In the story of my life, what you did isn't so important. But thank you for feeling strongly enough about it to apologise. And I'll always have a scar to remind me of it.' He laughs grimly.

Laurie feels a wash of tears well up under her lower eyelids. There are things she wants to say in response, but the words catch in her throat. Ed isn't smiling, but his expression is difficult to read. What must it have been like to live the life of a Diamond in Chapel Field?

'Can I ask you something?' he is saying.

Laurie nods, gulps.

'When the coffee comes, how do we pay?'

Then every bit of trapped angst escapes from her stomach and comes out of her mouth as a burst of hysterical laughter. 'I'm paying,' she says when her breath comes back. 'But you can watch and learn.'

It isn't long before the waitress is carrying a tray towards them. Ed sits with his hands between his knees as she unloads their drinks and toast and asks if they need anything else. Laurie shakes her head and offers thanks, while Ed picks up some packets of sugar and stares at them.

'This is all new to me,' he mutters. 'I just dig my spoon into the bag, at home. Smells good, though. What kind of coffee is it?'

'I'm not sure. They'll have a machine out back, or something. I usually have instant coffee. I'm not a connoisseur.'

Ed looks at her quizzically, then shakes sugar into his drink. 'Why are you in a bad place, anyhow?' he asks as they pass the plate of toast between them. 'You said you were. In a bad place, I mean.'

Laurie doesn't want to use her mother's death as an excuse. He knew about Janet Helm so he must have realised Laurie has hardly been the dutiful daughter. She's already decided she will never lie to Ed again. Not after what happened before.

'I think I probably said it to get your attention, if I'm honest. I've lived a different life for the past twenty years, and never allowed myself to think about Chapel Field. Now I'm back and seeing the place through a slightly more grown-up lens, I feel sick at what I did.'

'Wasn't just you though, was it?' Ed has stopped looking at her and is staring at the surface of his coffee. 'It's the whole place. Everyone hated my dad, so they also hate me.'

Laurie wants to throw her arms around him. She remembers only too well how local people shunned Richard Diamond. They'd stood on the corner of every village street and shared stories of his terrible deeds. Not that she could remember anything specific, apart from that one last act.

'I wish I could make things different for you, Ed. I really do.'

He shrugs.

'Well,' she says. 'There is something I can do. I can talk to you and be seen with you while I'm living back in the village. Let them all make of it what they will. I don't care.'

'Don't get yourself into trouble on my account,' he mutters. 'I'm used to being shunned. You're not.'

'I have plenty of *shunned* in my job, make no mistake about it. I can do *shunned*.'

Ed laughs quietly. 'This has all been about me, hasn't it? I'd like to hear about your job, if you want to tell me. I don't know much about anything outside the village.' He reaches for his carrier bag, then tries to ease his legs from under the table. The bag slips sideways and spills its contents. Laurie leans down to help him. The bag is white, with a *Boots* logo on the front. Protruding from the top is a large pack of sanitary pads.

Ed

Ed has lived his life with no intention of ever interacting with anyone on a level deeper than the polite disregard he has for shopkeepers, bank clerks and taxi drivers. Then Laurie Helm turned up and he's being sucked in all over again. There is something about her; he feels connected. Now, she's seen the contents of his shopping bag. This is what happens when he lets people in.

When they leave the café, he gets her talking about her job and keeps the questions coming. She works in a type of school, she says, where the children can throw abuse one minute and love the next, such is the unpredictability of their lives. Her words make him wonder if this is the kind of place he would have ended up, had he ever attended school. During his teenage years, he can remember being full of rage one day and weeping with complete despair the next.

His father hadn't known quite how to deal with him, other than to provide food and clothing and books. What pushed Ed into a heated rage more than anything else was when he saw people his own age hanging around together, talking, laughing, touching even. He'd been drawn to those groups even though contact with them invariably ended with torment.

As they walk the length of the high street, Ed thinks about how they must look to others: Laurie, with her soft hair and wiry frame, laughing upwards as she talks, and him with his well-washed jeans and carrier bag, nodding down at her, listening intently but also not. They could be any couple, enjoying a shopping trip on a day in summer. What would happen if he was recognised. Would the spell be broken? Would there be jeering or quiet ignorance? The poignancy of the situation is bringing tears to his eyes, and he can't allow that. He changes the subject, asks her about the other friends she hung around with and what they're doing now. They stay off the subject of Marcus Butcher.

When Ed buckles himself into the passenger seat of Laurie's car, he asks her how she went about learning to drive and the trials of travel in a big city like London. That she loves the place is clear. From her perspective, there is no downside to city living, and he wonders what it would be like to move away from the island and reinvent himself. He could never do that, because of his sister.

They trundle across the road bridge with the other traffic and when the tide comes into view, Ed wants to jump from the car and get back over to the mainland as quickly as possible. Though the water is beautiful, with its glittering flex-and-flow and its patchwork of blue and greens, to him it represents the worst kind of trap.

Then Laurie is apologising again, reminding him of that awful fake-date and the bags of chips, and of Marcus Butcher.

Ed smiles and says he's faced far worse but what he really wants to do is tell her he'd probably still have his father had it not been for that cruel and twisted friend of hers.

Chapter 11

January 1997

Ed

In the early mornings, before anyone else in the house is out of bed, Ed has taken to leaving Diamond Hall and walking along the beach. It gives him physical therapy as much as an escape from his father's ranting. The bruised ribs have almost healed, and there will be a permanent scar on his chin, but he's lost a lot of his muscle bulk from all the lying around. Not that he had much, but now his arms and legs are skinny to the point of showing the outline of every bone.

It's been quiet in the village since Marcus Butcher's car crash. There have been no more back-firing cars at the gates of Diamond Hall and on the odd time Ed has had to walk to the shop, there's been a hush in the streets that couldn't be blamed solely on the days and days of rain.

When he reaches the shingle path today, the first orange light of dawn is appearing above the mainland skyline. Most other mornings have been thick and dark with drizzle. Inhaling the freezing sea air sends a buzz through his body; he's wide awake in an instant. The tide is incoming, dragging boats against their moorings and groups of wading birds skyward and screeching. He starts to run. Fast breathing hurts his ribs, but he feels free.

It is possible to get from where Ed is now, right to the tip of the island. He'd need an hour or so, then another to get back; he doesn't usually go all the way. Today, he wants to breathe in the feeling he's getting and never let it go. Diamond Hall will have to manage without him for a while. It won't be for long; it never is.

When he reaches the dunes at the end of the path, the sun has lifted and is casting the sea and sand with deep orange light. Ed climbs to the highest vantage point and scans around. To the west is the Irish Sea. In front of him is the eastern silhouette of a town just starting to wake. Grey stripes of cloudy condensation from chimneys and vehicles cut into the morning sky. If he could feel like this for ever, he'd not want anything else. He'll never leave Chapel Field. How can he? The responsibility of that shrivels his freedom.

By the time he makes it back to Diamond Hall, the sun is high, and a clear yellow. He'd passed a group of people on the road up to the house. Something about their clothing made him look twice rather than hide his gaze and move away. Was this what people wore to church or some other smart occasion? Heavy dark coats over neat trousers and skirts, clean shoes, and cleaner expressions? His father would know what was going on. Prowling the village looking for information had become his new obsession. One that Ed would rather he didn't have.

No sound comes from inside the house, no clanging of saucepans or whir of the washing machine. It is silent. Ed is about to go and check the bedrooms and see who is sleeping late, when he spies a piece of paper on the kitchen table. Not a piece of paper, a flyer. He lifts it up to read and his stomach lurches. It is a photograph of Marcus Butcher, surrounded by ornately printed words, spaced down the page and continuing on the back. This is the order of service for his funeral, and it's happening today. Ed glances at the wall clock. Not just today, but within the next hour. Without waiting or thinking too much, he heads out of the house again. That his father will be at the island's church is not in any doubt; whether Ed can get there before he does any damage is another matter.

From Diamond Hall, he runs onto a small side street then to the main road. It is clear to him now, that this is the day of Marcus Butcher's funeral. There isn't a house without some kind of decoration or memorial: photographs, flowers, banners adorn every gatepost and windowsill. By the time he gets to the start of the promenade, he has to pick his way through the gathering crowds who stand aside for him with a kind of disapproving glee. He keeps his eyes fixed somewhere above their heads and hopes his father hasn't made it to the church.

Laurie

After days of rain, the morning is bright and clear, and dry enough for Laurie to walk through the village to Ruth's house. She's managed to find a black anorak in the cupboard under the stairs and she's dressed it up with a black-and-white silk scarf of her mothers, and black gloves. It's Marcus's funeral and she wants to look respectable.

Every house she passes has something to mark the occasion: a banner in the front window or a bouquet of flowers taped to the gate. People are already gathering in small groups, their cold breath hanging in clouds, their feet shuffling to try and get some warmth. There are children and adults, youngsters and elderly folk, arms latched and supporting. This is Chapel Field at its best.

Ruth's house has a photograph of Marcus pinned to the front door. It is surrounded by hand-made pom-poms in a pattern of pale blue and white. He'd been an ardent fan of the town's football team and played for one of the island's amateur clubs. He has become everyone's property now that he's died, yet when he was alive, many had complained about his antics. Not Ruth, though. She'd been in love with him, she said.

Laurie knocks at the door then turns to take some deep gulps of the icy morning air. No one has asked her how she feels or offered support. Whenever she tries to rationalise what's happened, she ends up seeing Marcus smashed up in his car or lying in a hospital freezer or in a coffin, and she starts to feel dizzy.

Being strong for Ruth is how she's to be today, but is that possible? Before she has the chance to worry further, the door opens and Ruth's mother is there, smart in a black suit but wearing her carpet slippers.

'Come in, my love,' she says and reaches for Laurie's hand. 'Our Ruth is in bits, as you can imagine. Go on up and see if you can fix her face.' She gestures towards the staircase leading straight up from the tiny hallway. 'She's done her mascara five times already.'

Laurie finds her friend sitting on the edge of her bed, hands on her thighs, eyes closed.

'I'm not going,' she stammers. 'I can't go, Loz.' The stammering turns into full-blown sobs.

Laurie kneels in front of her. 'You don't have to. But you'll feel sadder if you don't. I guarantee it.'

Ruth stays sitting, slumped and quiet, while Laurie bustles around the bedroom, picking up a pallet of powder and make-up brushes, a comb and a couple of hair slides. She's soon managed to fix her friend enough that she looks less raw.

'I hope you've got something warm to go over that,' she says, eyeing the flimsy black dress Ruth is wearing. 'And you'll need gloves and a scarf. It's freezing out there.'

They make their way downstairs. When she sees her mother, Ruth begins to cry again, and stands for a few minutes in her embrace. She allows herself to be slid into a dark-coloured pea-coat a few sizes too big. Laurie wraps a wool scarf around her neck, then pushes a wad of tissues into her hand.

'We'll set off now,' she tells Ruth's mother. 'Any more waiting around and she'll be fit for nothing. We're meeting Pete and Jamie at the pub. We'll see you in the church.'

She takes Ruth's arm and leads her outside. They walk together, footsteps falling in time, saying nothing. It reminds Laurie of walking to their high-school assemblies: there had to be perfect behaviour, and the only reward was the moral droning of teachers and grumbling stomachs of kids who had hours to wait until lunch. When they arrive at the pub, Ruth has a little colour in her cheeks and is starting to take notice of what's going on around her.

'There's the guys,' she says. 'They look smart, don't they, Loz?' Her bottom lip trembles a little. Pete is dressed in a black suit with skinny-legged trousers. His hands are pushed into the pockets and his complexion is lilac with cold. The overcoat Jamie is wearing must belong to someone taller and larger. He is clean-shaven, and his hair is neatly combed.

'Hello, both,' he says. 'You okay?' His expression is hard-set; he looks tired.

'We're getting there,' Laurie replies, 'but you don't look so good. Should you be here?'

'Got to give Butcher a good send off. No more than he deserves.'

Pete stares at his feet, and Ruth holds her arms open for him. He stoops into her embrace, whispering close to her ear. Then Laurie loops her arm through Jamie's and begins to walk with him along the main road towards the promenade. Ruth follows, clutching Pete's hand.

The tide is high and full, a sombre and glassy blue. Along the edge of the road, people huddle together, dressed warmly against the weather but smart enough for this to look like no ordinary gathering. Ruth begins to sob again. Pete slips an arm around her shoulder.

'Let's walk on for a bit,' he suggests. 'Get ourselves nearer to the church, or we'll never get a seat.'

Laurie doesn't feel like arguing. What she really wants to do is go home and pretend none of this is happening. Since the incident with Ed Diamond, she hasn't been able to shake the feeling that there's a darkness in the world she has no knowledge or experience of. It sits in her stomach like a stone and stops her from enjoying any of the things she used to love. If it's called growing up, she wants none of it. Jamie leads her along the promenade, but they stop when a shout goes up. Someone has spotted the funeral cortège emerging from the lower slopes of the village.

It is a shock to hear the clip-clopping of hooves as the mourners fall silent. Laurie isn't sure what she expected, but when she cranes to see, the promenade is empty of vehicles apart from a glass-fronted hearse being pulled by four black horses. An open-topped carriage is drawn by two more. She clings to Jamie's arm as the procession approaches. People begin to throw flowers onto the road; it's winter so they are mostly tulips and red roses and fake paper sunflowers. She wishes they'd thought of bringing something.

Ruth is crying even harder, if it's possible, and Laurie wants to yell that she should stop making everything about herself. She lets go of Jamie's arm and takes her friend into a full embrace, keeping her own gaze firmly fixed on the approaching horses. Each has a blue-and-white feather headdress, and her first glimpse of Marcus's coffin shows her the same colours, woven through a beautiful display of roses formed into one word. *Son.* In the carriage are four people. Marcus's family. She hardly knows them.

'He's here if you want to look,' she whispers to Ruth. No answer comes. Instead she is held tighter and harder. Pete has covered his eyes with one hand and Jamie looks above the cortège, to the sky.

Suddenly, a commotion comes from their left, just along the road. Someone is shouting, raging. It's Richard Diamond. He is wearing a checked shirt and dirty jeans, and he's standing in the middle of the road, trying to wave down the horses.

Ed

He crosses the road, thinking that the crowds are slightly less on the other side, though what they're waiting for, he can't fathom. Then a kind of hush falls and he hears hoof-beats. Nobody moves and Ed wonders what he should do. Across the road he is sure he sees the girl at the centre of his misery: Laurie. She is clinging on to another girl and they are both crying.

Emerging from a bend in the road are four horses pulling a glass-sided carriage with a coffin inside. Ed has never seen anything like it. Before he has time to think about what is going on, his father is there, in the middle of the road, ranting at the top of his voice and smashing his fists against the glass. Ed must get him away; some of the men in the crowd look as though they want to kill him. He pushes through to the front of the crowd and plunges into the road.

Laurie

'I'm so fucking glad you're dead, Butcher,' Richard Diamond is shrieking. 'So fucking glad. I hope you didn't die quick. I hope you suffered like you made my kid suffer.' The words seem to come from somewhere else, so high-pitched and desperate they sound. The coachmen pull up all four horses and they paw the ground nervously while Richard continues his rant. It's when he moves past them and towards the hearse that the crowd gasps, though no one stops him.

'Did you hear that, Butcher. You're dead, and that makes me so happy.' He smashes his fist against the glass sides. The woman in the carriage behind starts to scream.

'And you can shut the fuck up,' he continues. 'You should be glad a son like him is no longer in the world. What he did to my Ed is a disgrace. And I doubt you even care. Well, your vile son finally got what he was owed, didn't he. Alle-fucking-luia.'

It's at this point Laurie thinks she might faint. One of the coachmen climbs down from his seat at the front of the hearse. Then Ed Diamond appears from the other side of the road and grabs his father by the back of his shirt collar. Laurie hears him shouting *idiot* and can do nothing but stare as he is dragged away.

Ed

Ed grabs at his father's collar and gets a tight grip so that he can drag him away without giving him the chance to twist free.

Someone in the crowd is shouting about police, and Ed wants to ask them where the police were when Marcus Butcher and his friends were trying to kick the life out of him.

He fixes on the end of the promenade and keeps dragging his father until he's sure both of them will collapse from lack of breathing. All the time they are moving, his father is shouting something that sounds like *I done him*.

At Diamond Hall, Ed shoulders open the back door and pushes his father in. The ranting stopped halfway along the promenade. There is no explanation for the claim that he was responsible for Marcus Butcher's death. Richard Diamond looks no more dangerous than a tired old man, body deflated and quietly sobbing. Ed throws him onto the sofa and exhales everything he has been holding in. He bites his teeth together and runs a hand over his sweat-covered face.

How could his father be so insensitive? There'll be no reconciling the Diamonds with the rest of the world, he knows that, but any chance to have at least a quiet life will be gone now, smashed against the altar of Marcus Butcher.

No sound comes from his father. It would be pointless trying to have a conversation with him about anything. This is what he does; opts out of the world by sleeping. Ed hears sirens, distant at first, then louder. He leaves his father and goes back outside. Within a few seconds a police car has drawn up at the front gates and two uniformed officers are rattling to gain access. He watches as they slide through a gap in the fence, then he runs back to the house as they start calling his surname, over and over.

Ed offers no resistance when they push open the front door

and make their way to the kitchen, where his father is sprawled, eyes closed. They shout his name, then the taller of the two touches the arm of the other. All is quiet for a moment.

Ed is more worried about Elissa, but he says nothing; she will sleep through the loudest, messiest happenings and never respond to them.

One of the officers has knelt by the sofa. He's lifting Ed's father's wrist and putting his ear over the gaping mouth, then he is shaking his head and whispering to his colleague: *he's gone.*

Chapter 12

Summer 2018

Laurie

There's someone knocking. Laurie can see the outline of a figure behind the stained-glass panel in the front door. Visitors are the last thing she expects. This morning has been about emptying her mother's wardrobes and bagging up her clothes.

'Hiya.' Gina is standing on the doorstep, smiling out a greeting. She's dressed for the day in a blue summer frock patterned with daisies.

Laurie wipes her greasy hands on her leggings. 'Hello. Nice to see you,' she says, somewhat confused.

'You did say you'd like to meet with Nana Olivia? I'm heading up there today, if you wanted to come.'

If she'd thought about it properly, Laurie would have declined the offer. She needed to be rid of her mother's clothing by the end of the day; a local charity shop was expecting her donation and she liked to keep her word. But her conversation with Ed and the glimpse of his chemist purchases has ignited something in her imagination. She has questions, and she can hardly ask him, though he hadn't completely declined her invitation to meet up for another chat.

'That'd be great,' she says to Gina. 'Can you give me a few minutes to get washed and changed?'

'Sure. Visiting time starts after lunch and extends into the evening, so we vary it. Olivia likes to be surprised.'

'Where is this, exactly?' Laurie beckons Gina inside.

'Oh, yes. It's a residential home on the outskirts of town. Abbot's View, it's called. Not far away. I've got the car.'

'That's good. Mine's full of tat at the moment. I'm gradually managing to off-load it. Make yourself at home. I'll just be upstairs.'

Laurie leaves Gina to find somewhere to sit and makes her way to the bathroom. She washes her face and hands and brushes her hair back into a pony-tail, then shakes out a clean T-shirt from her suitcase. It's slightly creased but fairly new. She tucks it into a pair of jeans and slips her feet into sandals.

The thought of talking to someone who has seen the inside of Diamond Hall is making her stomach fizz. Whether it's with excitement or something a little more suspect, she doesn't want to think about. She'll take whatever information she can get.

'Okay,' she says as she strides back into her mother's lounge. 'It's a mess, isn't it? The house, I mean.'

Gina turns from where she's peering at the framed photographs on the mantel above the fireplace. 'Oh, it's not that bad.' She hesitates. 'Was she an elderly lady, your mother?'

Laurie shakes her head. 'Not really. She was in her late sixties. That's not old. She let things go at the end, I think. I wasn't here, as you know.'

'Pete's told me you didn't get on. That's a shame.'

'There's not much I can do about it now.' Laurie shrugs. 'Shall we go?'

She leads Gina out onto the street, pulling the door closed

behind them. There is not going to be further conversation about Janet Helm. Not yet, anyway.

On the drive away from the island, Laurie keeps Gina busy with questions about her children. She doesn't need much encouragement to explain every aspect of their lives and loves. She glows with pride when she tells of their sporting victories, exam successes and quirky personalities. Laurie can't help thinking that if every child had a parent like Gina, special schools and PRUs wouldn't have half as many attendees.

The residential home is on the main route out of town. As Gina pulls the car onto the forecourt, Laurie peers upwards at the Victorian gothic splendour of the place and thinks about how much her mother would have hated it. There will be regular mealtimes and walks around the immaculate gardens, socialising and people checking up. Everything that Janet Helm held in contempt.

Gina locks the car behind them and leads Laurie in through huge double doors, studded with panels of tinted glass. Behind a pass-coded barrier is a reception area that's cool and airy and smells of burnt toast.

'Mrs O'Connor. Nice to see you.' A man holds out his hand in greeting. He looks young, with his neatly clipped beard and tattooed forearms. His aqua-coloured tabard is immaculately clean and pressed. Gina smiles a hello then introduces Laurie as a friend of the family. They are taken through to a bright drawing room where a mixture of employees and elderly people are engaged in conversation or activities such as reading newspapers and magazines. A few are listening to a radio. Gina moves towards a tiny lady with soft silver hair. She is looking out through a pair of French windows, and she is drawing.

'Hi, Nana,' Gina says, kneeling beside her. 'Oh my word, that's beautiful.' She beckons Laurie over and points to Olivia's drawing. It is of the tree just outside the window, its texture caught on the page in a way that makes her want to reach out and touch. 'This is Laurie, Nan. She's Janet Helm's girl. You remember Janet, don't you? She's come to say hello.'

'I love your drawing,' Laurie says, unsure about whether she should shake the lady's hand or hug her shoulders softly as Gina has done. Olivia is peering at her with an unsettling intensity.

'Hello, both.' Her voice is sharp and clear. 'Janet Helm? Course I remember her. Who wouldn't. I'm sorry for your loss, my dear.'

'Thank you,' Laurie says, then pulls up a chair beside her. 'You're not going to say I look like my mother, are you? I know it's not true.'

Olivia reaches out and touches her cheek. 'No, that's not what I was going to say. It's just–'

Laurie smiles.

'It's just that you're so pretty. I wish I was young all over again, but knowing what I do now. Us old crowd always say that, don't we. Someone might actually listen to our advice, one day.'

Gina goes across the room to the tea trolley, while Olivia changes the subject, chatting about the weather and the lunch she's just had and the state of the latest prime minister, explaining how she'd do things differently. When there's a lull in the conversation, Laurie brings up Diamond Hall.

'That place, yes. Used to work there, didn't I,' Olivia tells her. 'May needed me. She wasn't a well woman.'

'Who's May, if you don't mind me asking?' Laurie hasn't heard that name before.

Olivia takes time to think about this, so Laurie is sure she's going to get a perfectly accurate answer.

'Maisie-Anne Diamond was Lenny's wife. He built the place for her, but she was never happy. People hated the

Diamonds, even then. She was Ritchie and Ronnie's mother; lovely boys they were. Gone now too, I suppose.'

'I'm not sure about Ronnie. Was *Ritchie* Richard Diamond? Ed's father?'

Olivia tuts. 'That's him. Had a funny eye, didn't he, from an accident in his past. The eyelid drooped, like he was winking all the time. Not at me though; he didn't like me, that's for sure.'

'Did you stay on at the house? Helping out Richard's wife, I mean.'

'For a short while.' Olivia looks away as Gina returns with three drinks in regulation sage-green cups.

'I'll bring us some biscuits, shall I, Nan?'

'Can't have tea without biscuits,' they say together, then laugh. It makes Laurie feel a longing for the family she's never had.

'What happened to Maisie-Anne?' she can't resist asking. If the Diamond saga were a book, she'd be completely hooked and turning the pages as fast as she could. Olivia puts down her drawing and accepts a cup and saucer.

'Well,' she says, lowering her voice to a whisper. 'She did away with herself. With pills from the doctor, of all things. Ritchie came home then and bought his pregnant Spanish girlfriend with him. They stopped needing me, so I was let go. My face didn't fit, anyway. I was a bit older than that crowd.'

'Oh, that's so sad.' Laurie takes a sip from her cup. It tastes of dust.

Olivia grins. 'I can make a better cuppa in my room, thank God,' she says. 'But I never complain. They really look after me here.'

'Only the best for you, Nana.' Gina has returned. 'They've got your favourites.' She holds out a plate of Bourbons. 'Mine, too.'

Olivia dunks her biscuit then enjoys it for a moment before

she puts down her cup and peers at Laurie. 'You do have a look of her, I can see it now. Janet, I mean. But she was far too skinny. You're lovely.'

Being compared to a mother Laurie has no feelings for, is difficult. As is the fact that the mother must have had a relationship with people in Chapel Field, when she seemed not to care one jot about her own daughter.

'Thank you,' she says. 'Were you friends with her?'

'She was at Diamond Hall a lot after Ritchie came back. I knew her from there. She was more a friend of Alina's, in a funny kind of way. And they didn't need me, as I said.'

Laurie is stunned. Her mother at Diamond Hall? In the seventeen years they'd lived together, there had been no mention of this, or anything else much, if she's honest. Some of the blame for that must lie with her. She'd stopped talking to her mother when she'd hit her teens. It was a protective mechanism against all the digs about her looks and her weight. She realises now they'd never had a proper conversation about anything.

Gina kneels in front of Olivia and starts fussing with the blanket she has over her legs. Laurie moves away and stares out through the French windows at the garden. It is laid out with rose beds and perfectly flat paths and lawns. It's the kind of garden that tempts you to take a walk, and it looks like that's exactly what Gina has planned.

'She's supposed to have a stroll every day,' she calls. 'We'll take her, shall we. Her mobility isn't good, so it'll need both of us.'

'I'm still here, you know,' huffs Olivia. 'No need to talk about me in third-person.'

Between them, they help her to her feet, Gina holding one elbow and Laurie the other, and then take small steps out through the French windows and into the warmth of the day. Olivia is very frail. Laurie could pick her up and carry her around the gardens without working up a sweat. Every few steps, they stop and admire the roses that form part of each display in the borders.

'Nana went to art college, you know,' Gina is saying. 'She's got a wonderful talent.'

'I did. In the very early sixties. And what great fun it was, too.' Olivia giggles to herself. 'I could have been a famous artist, but I fell pregnant with our Alison instead, and the art went down the pan.'

'That's not true.' Gina laughs. 'Nan used to exhibit in local shows and exhibitions. Her work's quite well known.'

Olivia snorts loudly.

'It is,' Gina continues, but Olivia stops her.

'I was an amateur. Now, Ritchie Diamond and his art; that was the real thing. I learned a lot by watching him, but Alina didn't like it. I was older, you see. Janet was a much better friend for her. Shame, what happened.'

Laurie has been sucked in all over again. There's something about asking direct questions. She doesn't want to show just how nosy she's being, but she has to know what Olivia means. 'Shame about what?'

They have reached a wooden seat and pergola, threaded through with climbing roses and honeysuckle. Olivia frees herself from their support and perches as daintily as a bird.

'Well,' she says, 'Alina had an accident, right at the end of her pregnancy, didn't she. It was twins and she was enormous. Both the babies were delivered safely, but she never made it, poor woman.

'The baby girl had some brain damage, too. I don't think she made it to adulthood. The boy, Eduardo they called him, still lives at The Hall, doesn't he? I get all the gossip from our Gina.' She pats her granddaughter's hand, but Laurie has stopped listening.

What Pete told her was true; there is no sister living at Diamond Hall. Richard Diamond has been dead for many years, as far as she can remember, which means Ed is living there on his own. She hasn't forgotten the woman she'd seen in the woods to the side of the house. Perhaps Ed is in a relationship and is keeping it to himself. She can't think any further while Gina and Olivia are trying to engage her in more conversation.

'I don't call it gossip, Olivia,' she says. 'I call it history.'

They all laugh at that.

It takes more than an hour to complete a full tour of the gardens. Olivia keeps them entertained with stories of Abbot's View's bingo nights and Christmas parties, but all the while, Laurie is thinking about how she can engineer another meeting with Ed Diamond.

Chapter 13

Summer 2018

Laurie

The morning is thick with heat, the sky so low Laurie feels she could touch its heavy lilac clouds. She's grateful for the early arrival of the house clearance people who have just collected the last of her mother's belongings. Another hour and they would have been working in the rain. She's been thinking a lot about Ed Diamond. Is he as dangerous as Pete O'Connor makes out? Everything she knows about the Diamonds has been based on hearsay. When she tots up what's true, using the evidence of her own eyes, there is very little. That fact embarrasses her. Leaving aside everything from before Ed was born, her own reactions to him have been focused on the things Marcus Butcher told her and on village gossip.

Though she's taken a walk every day since she'd met with Ed in the town centre, she hasn't seen him again. She can hardly ask the locals about his well-being or whereabouts.

Now that her mother's house is empty, she can see the bones of it and start to get it into shape for selling. When the summer is over, she'll leave the final threads to the estate agent and return to her London life. If she never encounters Ed again, will it matter?

She looks through the lounge window and up at the sky and decides that it will. Without thinking too much about what she's doing, she lifts her raincoat from a peg by the back door then steps into the yard. It is little more than a square of concrete, cracked, and pitted with weeds. At the far end is an outhouse with a broken door. It is here that her mother kept items necessary for supporting domestic life: a watering can, brush and dust-pan, various buckets. There is also a small step-ladder. It's made from aluminium and very light. Laurie slips her arm through the top rung and carries it into the back street.

The quickest way to the fence around Diamond Hall is through the sea-wood at the edge of the beach. The streets are quiet, and she's soon made it to the outskirts of the village and onto the shingle path.

The mudflats are fully exposed and popping with life. When the tide is this far out, it's hard to imagine the place as an island. Laurie looks across to the mainland. The uneven, dark cloud could burst open at any minute and wash away every trace of summer. She's going to have to move fast. She hitches the ladder high up over her shoulder and begins to clamber up the banking and into the first tangle of trees and scrub. Any daylight is held back by the dense overgrowth.

Laurie almost changes her mind. She could have gone to the gates of Diamond Hall and rattled them until Ed answered. People would have seen and heard, though. She's not ready to bring that kind of attention to either of them. Cowardly, really.

When she reaches the fence, she realises she's underestimated how high it is. It's not the climb she's worried about, it's the scaling it from the other side if Ed's not there to let her out through the gate. She opens the ladders and sets them down. From the highest step she can only just reach the top of the fence. It's going to take a lot of upper-body strength to pull herself over, but if she doesn't do it straight away, she might not get another chance: rain is plopping down from the foliage, which means it must have already started falling heavily above the wood.

Her pupils would have told her a rope attached to the ladder allowed it to be dragged up and over when she needed to escape. They spent much of their lives talking about how to break out of the PRU. It had never happened, as far as Laurie was aware, but the conversations gave them the chance to taste rebellion, despite the confines of the place.

With a few heaves and some shin-bashing, Laurie has cleared the fence and landed lightly on her feet on the other side. Her stomach lurches when she realises she is trapped on Diamond land without having thought about the risk. What if there are dogs? Or worse? She doubts anyone from the village has been this near to Diamond Hall for a long time. In her youth, they would dare each other to push through the old wooden fence and run at the place. Pete had even thrown eggs, once. The worst that ever happened was getting caught on an arc of bramble and taking a tumble. They were never chased by Richard Diamond. If they passed him in the street, he would wave a fist or call out, but there was no pursuit. Would it be different if Ed saw her? She has no way of knowing.

When the house comes into view, Laurie stops for a moment. It is a huge concrete monstrosity, with gables sticking out at odd angles and tiny windows that seem too small for the vastness of the walls. There is a small garden at the back, giving way to a flat expanse of mud covered with paving slabs in the formation of a pathway. Against the side of the house is an array of dustbins and boxes. Everything is neat and tidy and blank.

A porch sticks forward onto the mud. Laurie makes her way towards it. There is an outer door, with an oval of carved wood announcing the place as *Diamond Hall*, and an inner door with a panel made from diamond-shaped panes of green glass. She knocks hard against the wood and waits. No answer comes. From here, it is possible to look right along the driveway to the gates that open out onto a quiet street in Chapel Field.

She remembers waiting by them to meet Ed, on that horrible night. Along with all the folk in Chapel Field, she never humanised the Diamonds, never thought that behind those gates was a family, trying to get by. Part of the problem had been the hidden nature of their lives, the way they didn't interact. It wasn't enough of a reason for them to be treated as they were. And still are.

She knocks again and Ed appears on the other side of the panelled door. He yanks it open and glares at her. 'How have you got in here?'

Laurie isn't quite sure what she should say. The truth of it is she's trespassing. Rain is splattering onto her hair and shoulders, and she flips up her hood. 'I climbed the fence.' She tries to make a joke of it. 'I wanted to see you, didn't I? See if you were okay.'

Ed makes a sound, something like thunder, in the back of his throat, and Laurie realises she really shouldn't be here.

'People don't want to know if the Diamonds are *okay*,' Ed says in a low voice.

'I'm not people.' Laurie shakes the peak of her hood before it collapses under the weight of water. 'I'm getting soaked.' She is surprised when Ed steps back from the outer door and beckons her into the porch.

'I can't believe you climbed the fence,' he says. 'It's supposed to be good enough to keep the world out. I'm going to have to get it shot through with electricity.' He runs a hand over his face and there is the tiniest twitch of a smile. 'I can't let you come right in though, Laurie. I'm sorry. We– I don't do visitors.'

She glances over his shoulder and catches a glimpse, through the diamond panes, of a pine-panelled ceiling and floral-shaped pendant light.

'I'm here, now. What would it matter if I came in for a bit?'

'No.'

'Well, come and have a coffee at my mother's house, then. I don't care if anyone sees us.'

'I can't just– No. Another time, perhaps.' Ed is shivering slightly, in his T-shirt and jeans and bare feet. The rain is dragging down the stifling heat of earlier. A line of cold water seeps through at the place where Laurie's hood joins the rest of her jacket.

'It's number twenty-one. On Beaconsfield. If you did fancy coming,' she says.

He nods. 'I know it.'

'There're things I wanted to ask you, as well. If you could find time for a chat. I go back to London in a couple of weeks.'

That she's being this pushy is coming as a surprise. She'd scaled the fence without thinking about it too much, but now she's here and almost begging Ed to interact, she's embarrassed. The thought that her mother has been inside the house has captured her imagination in a way the person never could. Then there's the woman she'd seen. Was she lurking somewhere inside? A secret girlfriend, perhaps? According to Pete, Ed lives here on his own. His other suggestion is too horrible to contemplate. Nothing about Ed makes Laurie feel uneasy; there's no way he would be impersonating a dead sister – that's another one of Pete's weird grudges.

'You'd better get going,' Ed is saying. 'The rain's getting heavier.'

'Please come for a visit, Ed.' Laurie brushes a hand against his bare arm. It is ice-cold.

'I'll try to,' he mutters. 'But I'm not sure. You'll need a key.'

He rummages around in a small wooden crate on the window ledge of the porch.

'To the gate, I mean.' He holds up a tiny key. 'Unless you want to take your chances with the fence again. You can give me it back another time. Just click the padlock shut again after you're through.'

The strangeness of the situation is not lost on Laurie. She's been given a key to the gates of Diamond Hall. By the current owner of the house. A guy she once duped into a situation that got him a beating. A guy who, when she looks at him now, makes her thighs tremble and a red flush spread across her face. She has the sudden urge to escape.

'Thanks,' she says, taking the key and backing out of the porch. 'See you soon.' Then she turns her back on him and runs towards the gates as if she were being chased by the dogs she'd imagined earlier.

Ed

As she runs towards the gates of Diamond Hall, Ed thinks Laurie might be crying. He's not sure why, it's just a feeling. She doesn't look back, doesn't seem to be wiping her eyes or anything, but the way she'd looked at him when she took the key, it meant something. He's not sure what.

He closes the door of the porch and lets himself into the house. Luckily, Elissa is still in bed, or her interest would have been pricked. There are days when she's fully alert to everything, and today is one of those. She'll be wanting her raincoat and a walk later, he is sure. She'll have some colour in her cheeks once she's been outside, though it never lasts. If Laurie had seen her, what would have been the reaction? He shudders at the thought. One of the last conversations Ed had with his father was about keeping his sister out of harm's way. Would people really try to take her away if they knew she was here? As always, his lack of knowledge about how the world works is letting him down.

Would there be any harm in paying a visit to Laurie's house? He's sure he can trust her, despite what happened when they were younger, and he'd so like to gain an insight into what it's like to be part of the normal world. She has some questions for him. He has many for her, too. If he gives his sister full attention today, she'll be so tired tomorrow, he'll get a couple of extra hours to himself. Then he'll call on Laurie.

Elissa is sitting on the edge of the bed when he goes into her room. Normally, he has to get her up. While he helps her wash and dress, she directs her smiles towards the sound of the rain. He brushes the long dark hair, so like his own, and braids it tightly. She refuses his offer of breakfast, though it is nearly noon. When he takes her to the back door, she points to her orange raincoat and almost claps her hands together. It's been a long time since Ed has seen any gesture like that. It makes him smile. Underneath her seemingly endless problems is a woman not much different from him. He loves rain, too.

Outside, Ed can smell the sea, which means Elissa will also be able to. Not that she's ever seen it. Even living this close to the tide, he would never take her beyond the confines of Diamond Hall, though he knows she would love it, would love the glitter of light on the water's surface and the mesmerising waves.

He pulls her hood up, but she shakes her head so hard, he lowers it again, laughing as she turns her face up towards the huge raindrops plunging down between the side of the house and the undergrowth of the sea-wood. Slowly, they walk together on the paved path his father laid, then out into the wood proper. He never takes her as far as the fence. There's always the possibility that someone is peering through. Laurie's been there twice now, so he's sure others must have done the same.

They spend most of the afternoon walking in wide circles around the Diamond land. Ed talks to his sister about the things they see: the standing water, the mud, early leaf fall and a nosy blackbird that calls an alarm whenever they pass by. There's never a response, but he knows Elissa enjoys listening by her smile. When they are thoroughly wet, he leads her back to the house. Her eyes sparkle and there is the faintest tinge of pink above each cheekbone. If his father were here, he'd praise Ed for his attentiveness, for his care of the daughter who looked so much like his wife.

In the kitchen, Ed strips away his sister's wet coat and boots, and brings her fresh night-clothes. When she is dry and settled on the sofa, he covers her with a blanket and heats up a pan of milk for her favourite drink.

There's never any conversation and he's usually happy with that. Today, he would like to share his burden with someone else, someone who could make him feel like he was important for no other reason than he was Ed Diamond.

Tomorrow, he will go and meet with Laurie.

Chapter 14

February 1997

Laurie

Laurie sits in her bedroom and peers at the pile of work she has to get through. Studying is difficult at the best of times, but the thought of Marcus Butcher lying in a coffin, is clouding her vision and churning her stomach. A friend of hers, dead. How is it possible? She needs human contact, and in the absence of anyone else, she will seek out her mother.

When she lets herself into the living room, Laurie is surprised to see a man perched on the edge of the sofa. There's something about his slicked-over blond fringe and shiny slacks showing a glimpse of white socks, that makes her stomach lurch. This can't be one of her mother's friends; he looks no older than twenty. But by the clouds of musky perfume and singing coming from the landing, it's exactly what he is.

'Oh, sorry,' she mutters then backs away.

'No need to be sorry, love. It's your house.' He runs his hands along his thighs and peers over her shoulder. 'Your mam's here now, anyway.'

Laurie's mother totters in between them. Her pencil skirt is so tight it shows the bones of her hips, and she lays her hands there as if emphasising the fact.

'I thought you were going to your friend's tonight.' She glares at Laurie. 'We'll want some privacy later, won't we, Jace.'

The man licks his lips in a gesture that makes Laurie's stomach tighten.

'I was going to do my homework tonight. I'll stay in my room.' She turns to go. What her mother doesn't know is that completing a few bits of homework isn't going to be enough to pull Laurie out of the mire. Her mock A-level results had all been fails. Mainly because she couldn't focus on anything but the thought of Marcus, under the ground, rotting away. Gone. Just like that.

'How did I get such a swotty daughter,' her mother is saying to this Jace. 'She'll be boring you with tales of going to university in a minute.'

'I am going to university. It's not a tale.'

'I haven't said you can or signed anything.' Janet Helm is standing in front of the mantle-mirror, fluffing her hair and turning up the collar of her hand-made satin blouse. She lets out a long sigh. 'Why can't you put as much effort into your appearance as you do into stupid homework? You might get somewhere then.'

Laurie spits out her response before she can close her mouth and contain the words. 'Like you have, you mean.'

'Girls, girls.' Jace stands up and walks over to where Janet is preening. He puts his meaty hands on the waistband of her skirt. 'Play nicely.'

'Listen to you.' Janet giggles. 'Anyone would think you were a policeman or something.' She turns to Laurie and adds, 'He is, you know.'

'What?'

'A policeman. Of sorts.'

Laurie looks at Jace again. No policeman she can think of would have hair long enough to style. And he wouldn't wear a shiny, skinny suit. She huffs.

'I'm a special,' says Jace. 'Do all the good stuff, without having the paperwork.'

Laurie stares at him. 'I don't believe you,' she snaps. 'What's a special, anyway?'

'Don't be so bloody rude.' Janet links her arm through Jace's. 'I love a man in uniform. Show some respect.'

Jace licks his lips again, and Laurie wants to slap first him and then her mother. But where would that leave her? She'd probably be arrested or something.

'I can tell you a bit of police gossip if you like,' Jace is saying. 'You'll have to believe me then.' He slides his gaze sideways. Janet is watching him, open-mouthed. 'Old Man Diamond died a couple of weeks ago. After the funeral incident. You didn't know that, did you?' He punches his chest. 'Boom. Just like that, had a heart attack, didn't he.'

Laurie tries to swallow down her alarm. The last thing she'd heard was that Richard Diamond had been taken away by the police after his outburst at Marcus's funeral. Now, this man is saying he's dead. How would that be for Ed? Surely he hasn't been by himself in the house all this time. She looks at her mother. Jace's story has captured her interest. She is shaking her head and clutching at the lapels of her blouse.

'No,' she breathes, and for a moment none of them speak. Then Janet gathers herself and says something like *serves him right*. Laurie gasps. She has to get herself out of this situation: it's making her feel as though she's being poisoned.

'How can you talk like that?' she hisses. 'Do you ever think about anybody but yourself? Do you *care* about anybody?'

For a moment, Laurie thinks her mother might stride across the room and thump her.

Janet's face has narrowed into the meanest of expressions. 'Caring about someone is a two-way street,' she mutters. Then Jace is all over her again and kissing the top of her head and Laurie makes her escape.

'I'm going to Ruth's,' she says as she slams out of the room. 'At least her mum is nice.'

Ruth's house is the last place she wants to go. Her time will be taken up with soothing and encouraging her friend, letting her cry over Marcus, then listening to tales of how wonderful he was, when all she wants to do is beg for some support of her own. In the days since Marcus's funeral, Laurie has felt herself sinking. It's a physical feeling, like there are weights on her shoulders and the backs of her eyes are being slowly painted black. There's a rawness, too, so that she wants to cry at the slightest thing. Getting away to university has been a tiny light in the creeping darkness, but there's not much chance of that now. If she doesn't get the grades she needs, she's going to re-sit the exams and apply next year, and every year until she succeeds.

As she grabs her coat from the end of the banister, she hears the rise of her mother's voice. Time to escape. She's not allowed a front door key of her own, so she'll end up cadging a sleep-over with Ruth. Not that she minds. They all benefit, but it doesn't get her studying done.

The air outside is damp and briny-smelling. Around each streetlight is a halo of yellow mist. The pavements are slippery and wet. Laurie turns up her collar and shuffles along carefully; she's only wearing her slippers. She laughs at this. It's so typically Chapel Field. People visit the village shop wearing pyjamas or a housecoat and carpet slippers, and no one bothers about it.

On the walk to Ruth's house, Laurie thinks about Ed Diamond again. Would he really be allowed to stay in Diamond

Hall on his own? Has he had to organise his father's funeral without any help? If she hadn't agreed to Marcus's stupid prank in the first place, none of the horrible events that followed would have happened. That's her thinking, but she dares not speak it to anyone. The Diamonds have no support in Chapel Field and whatever happens to them, they deserve, or that's what people think.

Only, she doesn't believe it. Which means there is no way she could continue to live in the village. If she doesn't get to university this year, she will get there eventually. It will be her only escape.

She peers down at her feet. The tips of her slippers are stained dark, and her toes feel wet. Every window she passes has a glow of light behind closed curtains. There will be families she knows, watching television, talking, laughing, enjoying their time together, safe and warm on this murky evening. It's never been like that for her. Not for Ed, now, either. A couple more minutes' walk will bring her to the gates of Diamond Hall. She could try and attract his attention and see if he needed help. She could apologise. She could do something, anything that might make her feel better about the whole rotten situation.

By the time she reaches the gates, the tears Laurie has been holding back have overflowed and are stinging their way down her cold cheeks. It's just possible to see the house from here, and as always, the gates are padlocked shut. She pushes her fingers through the chicken-wire covering and tries to rattle the wood against itself. The gates move slightly, but not enough to make much sound.

A picture of Ed comes into her mind; how his face changed from stormy to summer when he smiled over the bag of chips; the dark hair and darker eyes. If what Jace said was true, Ed would be sitting in the house, alone, trying to come to terms with the loss of his father.

'Ed,' she calls, softly at first, then, 'Ed. Ed, it's Laurie. Ed. If you can hear me, come to the gate.'

She's mindful of attracting any attention, then hates herself for that feeling so that she wants to slap her own face. She could squeeze herself through any of the gaps in the fence, but it would mean actually having to face Ed. The truth is, she's as much of a coward as any of the other residents of Chapel Field. She rattles the gates a few more times, then wipes her face with the cuff of her coat and heads back along the road towards Ruth's house.

Ed

In the dark shadows of the kitchen, Ed waits for the inevitable to happen; someone is trying to get onto the Diamond Hall land; he can hear the gate being rattled. In the weeks after his father died, he'd been expecting this day to come. Now it has, he's ready to fight. He looks at the fine rain clinging to the window. Inside each droplet is a tiny glint of moon; beyond this, just night. He knew they'd come when they couldn't be seen. Who would have the gall to break open the gate and walk up the drive, in full view of Chapel Field's rubberneckers. That's what his father called them, those who hated but couldn't tear their eyes away.

There had been a letter, in the days after, those terrible days when Ed couldn't think what to do. It had come from the borough council and was addressed to *The Occupier*. When he'd finally got the nerve up to accept this was him, he'd torn it open and found a curt explanation about a private corporation burial for Richard Diamond, and an enclosed death certificate. Nothing more. Was he supposed to act on the letter? How? As an eighteen-year-old, he was legally responsible for himself so perhaps no one cared what he did. They certainly didn't know about his sister. If the truth of that situation was ever discovered, he would lose her. He shakes his head; he can't allow himself to think about it; his life would be over then, too.

Whoever is trying to get into Diamond Hall would have no reason to challenge him. The box of money his father kept, the bills and papers, Ed has access to everything, and as far as he can make out, the Diamonds have broken no rules. Though his whole body is trembling, his stomach knotted so tight he thinks he'll never be able to eat again, he is ready. But no one comes. He's not sure if this is worse, being left alone and ignored and invisible.

He lets an hour pass, then decides it will be safe enough to open the front door and look outside. Whoever was trying to break open the gate must be gone by now. He steps out through the porch and walks halfway down the drive. It is so quiet. Not even the gentle fall of rain creates any sound.

Disorientation accompanies his realisation that there will be no one in the world thinking of him, wondering how he is. There are two choices: he can give in to the desperately sad feeling that has been inhabiting his body for the past few weeks, or he can put it to one side and create a life for his sister and himself at Diamond Hall. He wants to cave in, but who would care? He looks up at the sky. The moon becomes visible for a moment, between slabs of heavy raincloud, then it is covered again. He won't give up. No matter how much he is hurting, there will be a time when it passes. He will live for that time, and for Elissa.

Chapter 15

Summer 2018

Laurie

I t's still raining when the estate agent's sign goes up outside the house. Laurie stares at the bright yellow panel with its navy script telling the world they could buy the place if they wanted. Though it's never felt like her home, tears well up and she has to choke them back. They're for the loss of Ed Diamond as much as anything. His promised visit hasn't happened, and in another week, she'll be gone from Chapel Field for good.

She ducks back inside and closes the front door. She's spent the last few days setting up the house for brochure photographs. Every room is clean and minimally dressed. There's a bed, a sofa, some kitchen basics, and net curtains at every window. The back room hasn't been included in the photos: it contains two boxes of things Laurie can't bear to throw away, and the painting that has fascinated her since she first saw it. These items are going with her back to London.

In the kitchen, she fills the kettle and sets it to boil. Seeing Gina again might settle her mind about Ed. There are things she wants to know, though she'd hate to give the impression she is only interested in visiting Olivia to glean information. The lady seemed lovely, and interested in Laurie as a person in a way her own mother had not been.

She and Ed are very much alike in that respect, with no place in a supportive extended family, nowhere much to belong. She'd quit lying to herself years ago, though, and the truth is she feels something for Ed she'd like to explore further, Diamond or not. Which annoys her all over again because what kind of person does that make her? Just as bad as the Laurie Helm of her youth.

She doesn't have time to think further because she hears a light tapping on the front door. The estate agent guy must have forgotten something. It's not the estate agent guy standing on the step, though: it's Ed.

'Hello,' she manages, though her stomach has hit the floor. 'You must have heard me put the kettle on.'

Ed tucks a hank of dark hair behind his ear and smiles slightly. Laurie beckons him inside and can't resist casting a glance over his shoulder and into the street.

'It's taken me a long time to get the nerve up to come,' he says grimly as he follows her down the hallway and into the kitchen. 'I wasn't sure–'

'About what?' She pulls out one of the two stools tucked neatly away and gestures for him to sit.

'I wasn't sure you meant to invite me, that's all. I'm a Diamond. The hated Diamonds.' He lowers himself onto the stool, which is far too small. 'I've never been inside a single house in Chapel Field. Never thought I would, either.'

Laurie holds up two mugs. 'I'm glad you decided to come.' She smiles. 'What will you have to drink?'

'Anything,' he says. 'I don't mind.'

While she makes them each a mug of coffee, Laurie chats about her house-clearing endeavours and how much junk her mother had accumulated over the years. Every one of her words is measured before she utters it. Natural conversation isn't possible with a guy who's been through so much. He must know she's faking. When she turns to hand him his drink, he is casting around the room in a way she finds surprising.

'You've seen inside other buildings, Ed. The bank, at the very least, and shops. This house isn't modern, I know, but there's nothing interesting to see here.' She slips the last three words into index-finger quotation marks, then wishes she hadn't.

'It's not that.'

'What then?'

Ed takes a sip of his coffee. Laurie waits.

'I've no idea how other people live.' He shrugs. 'I feel embarrassed by that. And sad. I've never understood why my family are so excluded. Oh, I know my dad did a bad thing. But people hated him long before that. I wanted to ask you why, Laurie.'

There is an honesty about his expression, like he's been cracked open exposing the raw. This is Ed without his shell; she must be careful.

'I don't think it was personal so much as doing it to fit in. Hating the Diamonds, I mean. No one ever said why, they just followed the crowd.' She shakes her head. 'Horrible, really. And I'm not excusing myself, but I did the same.'

He considers this for a moment, then lets out a long sigh. 'As far as that Marcus guy was concerned, it was personal. He was gunning for me. You can't deny it.'

'He was, and I'm sorry. It was a long time ago. And Marcus Butcher didn't exactly get off scot-free, did he?' Whatever Laurie expected they would talk about, it wasn't this, but Ed is determined.

'Why do you want to know me now, Laurie? You've been

away from here for years and I doubt you've even given me a thought. Why now?'

She could lie, could make up some story about trying to find closure now that her mother is dead, but there's something so open and naïve about Ed. She can't bring herself to trick him.

'You're right. I haven't thought about you, or this place, for years. But not for the reasons you're probably thinking. That night, when we had our date–'

Ed lets out a fake splutter of laughter.

'Well, whatever you want to call it. I started off doing it because Marcus wanted me to, but after we met and talked, I thought you seemed okay. I liked you. So I wasn't going to go through with the rest of the plan. That's not how it worked out, in the end.'

'Damn right it wasn't.' Ed slams his mug down on the table and some of the coffee slops out. He stands up, towering over Laurie. A flash of fear shoots through her body, but she is certain he'd never hurt her. When she looks into his face, there is nothing but sadness.

'Give me a chance to put things right, Ed. Not for me, for you.'

'All the goodwill in the world isn't going to make that happen,' he says. 'And you've already done the apology bit.'

'Let's start from here, then. We could be friends. I know that sounds twee, probably insincere too, but I mean it. I don't give a shit what people around here think of the Diamonds.'

Ed is shaking his head and moving towards the kitchen door. 'Friendship? You've got no idea what my world's like, have you.' He thumps a hand against his chest.

'Why did you come here, Ed?' Laurie spits. 'To laugh at me? Is that it?' She faces him, bracing herself for some truths that may well cause injury.

Instead, he takes three strides towards her, grips her

shoulders, and drops a rough kiss on her lips. 'That's what I came for,' he growls. 'Full of surprises, aren't I.'

Laurie jumps away but takes both his hands in hers. 'Weirdly,' she murmurs, 'I'm not surprised. I've felt something brewing between us, too. Though I hardly know you.'

Ed pulls his hands away and charges towards the front door. If she does nothing else, Laurie knows she must keep him here.

'My mum used to hang out at Diamond Hall,' she calls. 'I wanted to ask you about it.' His hand is on the front door. 'Please don't go, Ed. I promise I won't be anything less than honest with you.'

He pauses just long enough for her to realise she's captured his interest.

'Mum was friends with your mother, apparently,' she continues. 'Can we at least talk about that?' She waits. There is a tension across Ed's shoulders. She can see it through his T-shirt, in his muscles and bones.

He leans his forehead against the door for a moment, muttering under his breath. Then he turns to face her again. 'I'm useless at dealing with people, as you can imagine.' His eyes are shining. 'Don't muck around with me, Laurie. I'm begging you. I'd rather just go home and forget about us meeting.'

She holds out her hand. 'If you can trust me, I'd like to help you, be friends, whatever. I've no reason to be lying, have I?'

He takes her hand, and she leads him back into the kitchen.

'Let's start all over again,' she says as he folds himself onto the stool for a second time. 'I'll make you another coffee.'

Ed

As he watches Laurie move around the kitchen, rinsing mugs and clipping their sides with a spoon, Ed feels his heart thumping against his ribcage. He can hear it in his ears, and he wonders if the sound is escaping his body. If she's heard it, Laurie isn't responding. She's just continuing to make his coffee like she said she would. Then she's suggesting they go on a tour of the house so he can see *how the other half live*, whatever that means. He's not good with innuendo, though he does recognise it. There's been so much time in his life for television and reading, but it's the real world that eludes him.

He is starting to find Laurie's company quite entertaining, the way she seems so serious, then peppers her thoughts with bad language; the way she doesn't try to hide the terrible relationship she had with her mother; the way she smiles. She takes him through the house, pointing out ancient wallpaper and carpets with raised-up textures. He doesn't tell her those same things are available to see in Diamond Hall. She wants to know if he's got any photographs of his mother and hers together. He can only say he hardly knew his own mother and his father kept very few photos of her, and spoke her name rarely. He can talk about his father's brother, Ronnie Diamond.

That makes her stop in her tracks and focus on what he's saying. That Ronnie is long gone from Chapel Field and any life with the Diamonds makes him a safe topic. But Ed has seen a photograph of him on the deck of a huge grey battleship, grinning and wearing the uniform of the Royal Navy. Laurie wants to know more than this, but it's all he has.

She tells him about her mother's family then. Or lack of it. Janet Helm had been brought up by her grandmother, another resident of Chapel Field. There had been no aunts or uncles, or siblings, only Laurie. There was no sign of a father. It makes him realise how wrong he's been to assume every family's story, apart from his own, is about happiness and normality and contentment. Laurie is as disconnected as him, it seems.

Laurie

Ed seems to be relaxing into her company. He laughs when she tells him about some of the strange items her mother collected over the years. He's never heard of crocheted blankets or onyx cigarette lighters, though he knows all about smoking and the way it affects health. He's well-read and she wonders again about how it must have been to miss out on schooling and all its intricacies.

When they come out of the front bedroom and onto the landing, he looks towards the closed door of what Laurie has started to call the junk room.

'That's where I've stashed everything I can't bear to chuck out.' She laughs. 'Do you want to have a look? It's mostly boxes.'

'Yeah, I'll have a look.' Ed is running his hand along the dark-wood banister. 'This is beautiful. There's a lot of good solid wood in this house. I know you don't like it, but I do.'

Laurie pushes open the door and they step into the room. In one of the boxes is a photograph of Laurie's mother, one of the few she has. When she pulls it out to show Ed, he takes the frame from her hands and peers closely. It's a coloured photo, grainy and muted, and shows a group of women, skirts short and hair bunched, with the sea behind them.

'That's my mother, in the yellow sweater. Skinny, isn't she?' Laurie moves to stand next to him. 'I've no idea who the others are.'

'When was this taken?' Ed is frowning.

'I'm not sure. I don't think I'd been born, though, so it's probably late seventies. My mother always said she hated what having a baby did to her body. That didn't make me feel great, I can tell you.'

Ed passes the photo back to her, but he isn't listening to her rant about Janet Helm. He is staring at the half-covered painting propped against the wall behind the boxes. Laurie follows his gaze.

'Oh, that.' She pulls the old sheet away and rolls back the plastic. 'Strange, isn't it? I've no idea how it came to be in this house. My mother was no artist, so I guess someone gave it to her. Or she bought it. What do you think?' She lifts the painting clear of the boxes. 'I like it, in a weird kind of way, so I thought I'd take it home with me.'

The colour has drained from Ed's face. He is blinking and holding a hand to his throat. Laurie lets the painting slide to the floor so that its edge rests against her toes.

'Ed. Are you feeling all right?' she asks.

'It's one of my dad's paintings,' he stammers. 'I mean, it's one he painted. I can tell. There were lots like it at Diamond Hall.' He reaches out and touches what Laurie thinks is part of the texture, a raised area in the bottom left-hand corner.

'That's his signature. It's how he did it.'

Laurie covers her eyes with her free hand and shakes her head. 'Are you saying my mother had one of your dad's paintings? What the hell–'

'Can I look at that photo again?' Ed is asking. She has no idea what is going on. Gina's nan had been right, obviously. Janet Helm was a visitor to Diamond Hall, and somehow she'd gained one of Richard Diamond's paintings. Laurie lifts the photo from where she'd laid it, just under the flaps of the box. She hands it to Ed. He scans it again, then nods.

'It's what I thought, when you first showed me. My mother's

128

here, too.' He runs a thumb over the image of a darker haired woman. She is wearing an orange dress with white flowers along the hemline and around the neck. 'I've seen another photo of her wearing this dress.' He continues to stare, and Laurie isn't sure what to do. But the connection between their parents is intriguing and she wants to find out more; this is the most interesting she's ever found Janet Helm.

'I wasn't making it up when I told you our mothers knew each other,' she says.

Ed passes the photo back to her. 'I didn't think you were.' He looks at the painting again. 'Dad told me everyone hated our family, so I was to avoid people at all costs. But there must have been a time when that wasn't completely true. Though it doesn't explain why your mum would have one of his paintings, does it?'

'Perhaps she saw it and liked it, so he gave it to her as a gift.' Laurie lifts her shoulders. It hardly matters now, though Ed seems worried. 'I'm more interested in the photo. What was your mother like?'

'I don't know,' Ed snaps. 'I wish I did. Dad never spoke about her and once he'd set his mind in a certain way, there was no changing it.'

'What about your sister? What's the story there?' As soon as she's uttered those words, Laurie realises she's gone too far. Ed is shaking his head and moving towards the door.

'I don't want to talk about my family,' he is saying, 'and I have to go now, anyway.'

For a second time, Laurie finds herself chasing Ed along her mother's hallway. When he reaches for the door, she places her hand on his. His chest is heaving, and he won't meet her eye.

'Don't go,' she pleads. 'I won't press you on things you don't want to talk about, but honesty is a two-way street, as they say. There's no reason for you to hide your backstory, is there?'

He dips his head. 'Other than being a Diamond. And we all know how that goes.'

'Do you know what,' Laurie says suddenly. 'Diamond or not, I'm going to walk with you back to your house. Oh, don't worry, I didn't mean I'd want to come in. Sod the *haters*, I'm taking you the long way round.'

She slips her feet into a pair of trainers and glances at his face. He is frowning but she can see the slightest hint of a smile on his lips. He pulls open the front door and they step together into the damp morning air.

The street is quiet, and as they walk, Ed tells Laurie about his own love of painting and about how he's sold every piece of his father's art, over the years, to keep the money flowing.

'I sell my own pieces, now,' he says. 'They're not really what I want to work on, but there's a market for seascapes, so that's what I paint.'

'I did wonder about the paint stains.' Laurie laughs.

'It is what it is.'

As they reach the main road, a bus is pulling up. The stop is the final one on a long route from the town centre, and a few people are making their way from their seats and out onto the street. Laurie senses Ed's unease, and she slips her arm through his.

'It'll give them something to gossip about,' she whispers.

A young woman wrestles a baby-buggy down the steps of the bus. She doesn't take much notice of them. Behind her comes an older couple, clutching shopping bags and each other. Laurie hears them huff as they move to avoid Ed. One or two other people notice him and avert their eyes, but Laurie makes a point of talking loudly about the weather and laughing and leaning into him.

They make it past the bus and push on towards the pub.

Suddenly, there is Pete O'Connor, in collar-and-tie, wearing an identification lanyard and carrying a laptop in a case.

'Lozzer.' His top lip twists upwards. 'What the fuck?'

She can feel the tension flooding through Ed. He lifts his elbow slightly, like he wants her to set him free. She doesn't.

'Hello, Pete,' she says smoothly, though her heart is hammering against her ribs in a way she can't explain. 'You're looking very smart. Break-time, is it?'

'You having a laugh, or what?' He glances at Ed. 'Keep your grubby paws off her, Diamond, you loser.'

Laurie clings on tighter.

'Pleasant as ever,' she says to Pete. 'Good to see you. Catch up soon.' Her knees are trembling as she pulls Ed away and strides with him along the street. The many tense encounters she has with her pupils have never left her feeling like this. It's an adrenaline rush, but magnified hundreds of times; she's a teenager all over again.

'God, Laurie. That was awful,' Ed says as they make it past the pub and head towards another crowd outside the shop. 'What are we doing?'

They pass a pair of giggling teenage girls, all crop-tops and skinny jeans, and eyes on one mobile phone screen. Neither of them appears to notice Ed, or they simply aren't interested.

'Don't over-think it,' she says. 'Most people's heads are so far up their own arses; they wouldn't notice if you were the Queen.'

Ed throws back his head and laughs in a way that cheers Laurie on. She squeezes his arm tighter, and they make their way to the edge of the village, and on towards the beach.

Ed

He leads Laurie off the road and onto the shingle path at the edge of the beach. He's never walked through the village with such fear or with such a feeling of exhilaration. Invisibility has always been something to strive for.

Today he's been noticed without it leading to anything. Apart from with the guy he's sometimes seen around, the one who he's sure was part of Marcus Butcher's gang. Though he's heavier and his face has taken on a smudgy shapelessness, Ed is sure the man Laurie named as Pete is the same one who'd kicked him once he was on the floor. He'd split his chin with a hefty rubber-soled boot.

It's Pete's wife, Laurie tells him, whose family has some sort of connection with Diamond Hall. A grandmother who worked for Lenny Diamond, or something. Ed has very little idea about life before he was born; his father hadn't been one for dwelling on the past. It does make him wonder if there was a time when to be a Diamond, in the village of Chapel Field, wasn't such a bad thing. If his mother had friends and they visited the house, perhaps her life hadn't been as harshly isolated as his. He'd be glad if that were true. Though she has never felt like a presence in his life, Alina Diamond must have meant something to his father. He married her, after all: she'd given him children. Ed wonders if the way he feels when he's with Laurie is something like what his father felt with his mother. That thought makes him smile. Then Laurie asks him what he's chuckling about, and he can't tell her, but it makes him smile harder.

On the beach, they discuss the best places to walk and enjoy nature, and Laurie tells him how she gets her fix in London, about running somewhere called Hampstead Heath, and about Kew Gardens and Richmond Park. Listening to her is fascinating. It shows him aspects of the world he hardly knew existed. When she adds that she's heading back to London at the end of next week, his spirits plummet again. He so wants to confide in her about his sister and the life they've carved out for themselves, a life Laurie could add to, he's sure, now that he's had a taste of her company. But it's not possible. Not when she's leaving.

She must sense his sadness because she points out that she will keep visiting Chapel Field until her mother's house is sold, and she can come back anytime he wants to see her.

When they arrive at the other end of the beach and the road that leads to the gates of Diamond Hall, Laurie asks again if she can come in and have a quick peek at the place. He can't allow that. Something pushes up in between them then. It's a tangible thing with a brittle edge and he wishes he could smash it down. There is a moment when he almost agrees, then he sees his life through the eyes of someone else and shuts that thought down.

Laurie asks him to visit her again, and soon. She wants him to bring any photographs he has of his mother and any other relatives. He tells her he will, but as she walks away, he doesn't know if he can bear to see her again. It hurts his heart too much.

Summer 1978
Richard Diamond

Ritchie Diamond pulled the cigarette from between his lips and threw it onto the stone steps. A few glowing tobacco embers bounced, before he ground the whole thing to death with the heel of his new shoes. Alina had found a toilet and was relieving the burgeoning pressure on her bladder. The giggling posse of so-called friends had gone with her.

The doors of the registry office creaked open, and Ronnie

came out, squinting against the punishing sunshine. 'You've gone and done it, bro.' He laughed but Ritchie sensed the sarcasm in it.

'I want my little ones to be Diamonds, don't I, not kids with some random Spanish name.'

Ronnie pushed his hands into the pockets of his tight-fitting suit trousers and kicked at the cigarette stump his brother left.

'Really?' He snorted. 'Any other name but that, surely? Look at what it's done for us.'

Ritchie would rather not think about any truths hidden in his brother's words. Coming back to Chapel Field wasn't exactly a choice, but he had to make it work. The same thing mustn't happen to Alina as happened to his mother. May Diamond had lived a life of pure misery. He has no memory of her smiling or showing the slightest bit of joy. She'd died like that, too. He shook away those thoughts.

'You're looking at a new generation of Diamonds,' he said buoyantly, just as his new wife pushed her way outside to join him. Her waist-length dark hair was topped with a wide-brimmed hat, and her long white dress had been made especially for her by a new-found friend, Janet something or other. This woman was walking behind, holding the excess dress material and Alina's small posy. She was slim and blonde, with a cheeky gleam in her eye which she flashed at Ritchie whenever she got the chance.

'Hello, husband,' Alina crooned in her heavily accented English. 'Have you missed me?' She draped an arm around his shoulder and leaned into him.

'I didn't need to miss you; we've got years together now.' The rest of the wedding party filtered out through the doors. His father was being helped along by a woman who had been cleaning at the house, and her sister. They were Olivia and Emily, as far as he could remember, though the surname escaped him. He was useless with names. Working as a potter and painter in Spain required him only to use his artistic talents, not his memory. Alina helped with that; it was how they'd met in the first place. He was glad she'd made some friends already. Diamond Hall needed visitors more than ever.

Ronnie had brought a young man with him to the wedding. He had a camera and tripod and was setting them up on the pavement at the bottom of the registry office steps. Though it was a hot summer's day, he was wearing a beautifully cut velvet jacket and matching slacks. His face was shiny, his cheeks flushed. 'Gather around the bride and groom everyone,' he was calling. 'I'll just be a minute.'

Another young woman blinked her way into the sunlight. She pulled the doors closed behind her.

'That's everyone,' she shouted, with a flick of her blonde pony-tail. Like the other women, she was wearing a full-length dress, but hers was sleeveless. It showed off her large bosom and lightly-muscled arms.

'You need to be in the photo, Jen,' Alina said to her. 'Come, stand by me.' She seemed more interested in the other women than she did in capturing a romantic moment with Ritchie, but he didn't mind.

Ronnie's photographer friend was being very hands-on, arranging them in artful poses and slapping his temples when they didn't instantly comply. The sooner they could get out of this heat and back to Diamond Hall, the better. At least he could have a cold beer and a sit down. His shoes were pinching enough to have drawn blood.

When the photographs were taken and everyone had kissed everyone else, Ritchie led them away to where their cars were parked. He offered to drive the ladies and left Ronnie to follow behind with his photographer friend, and Lenny. His father hardly knew what day it was, let alone that he'd just been to a wedding. Richard had finally found him a nursing home place, where he could be cared for properly. Lenny's deterioration had happened since May died, according to this Olivia woman. And now, she was sliding herself into the passenger seat as though she was more important than the others. Ritchie didn't like her much. On the days when she'd come to Diamond Hall with the pretext of cleaning, she'd spent too much time talking about her own teenaged daughter, then grilling him for information about his own life and his art. He'd been left feeling wrung out, like anything personal had been taken from inside his body and laid out for all to observe. Alina didn't seem keen on her, either.

As they crossed the bridge to the island, Ritchie got his usual feelings of claustrophobia. It was the only way to describe the panic that caught in his throat so that he could hardly breathe, and the gripe of his stomach when he crossed the water. It looked beautiful today, a mix of sky-blue and jade green, its surface scattered with gold. Beautiful but terrifying.

Alina and the younger women, packed tightly into the back seat of his Capri, were singing. It was a welcome distraction. He joined in, making them splutter with laughter. Olivia huffed, turning her attention to whatever was outside.

'Your new hubby is quite a catch,' said the woman named Janet. She was sitting directly behind him, and he felt her fingers in his hair, just where it met the collar of his shirt. 'Artistic and a wonderful singer. Lucky you.'

Alina snorted with laughter. 'Hands off.' There was more laughing and some words he couldn't quite make out. His anxiety was receding now. As they reached the lower slopes of the village, he thought about the times he and Ronnie had made their way home from school along this very route. Though they hadn't had friends as such, they'd had each other, to share jokes and be a human defence against the way they were excluded by the other kids. He never quite understood why the name

Diamond caused such extreme reactions. Alina Diamond laughing along with other women made his heart sing.

The gates of Diamond Hall were open, and Ritchie swerved the car through from the road in a way that made the young women screech and pretend to fall against each other. He laughed off more of his anxiety. As long as he didn't think too hard about being trapped on the island, he could cope with living here again. Soon, there would be children to keep him occupied. When Alina fell pregnant, he had visions of her barefoot in the Spanish sunshine, showing off a dark-haired baby to his customers, with him smiling along indulgently but leaving her to it. The reality couldn't have been more different: there were two babies, the hospital had told them. Then his mother had died, leaving his father barely able to cope. Ronnie could never live back at Chapel Field, not with his life-choices, which meant Ritchie had all of his taken away.

Alina and the other women held up the hems of their dresses and tottered across the hardened mud of the yard. One after the other, they disappeared through the porch of the house. His brother and the photographer walked up the drive towards him; they must have ditched their car on the other side of the gates. He waved, then entered Diamond Hall for the first time as a married man.

The kitchen area was decorated with white balloons and garlands of plastic flowers. Their big trestle table had been covered with some white glossy fabric and laid with platters of sandwiches. Alina was already breaking open a dark-green bottle of the champagne he'd purchased for the occasion. The other women were fussing with plates and glasses and dragging chairs together.

'Everyone get a glass,' Janet was calling. 'Here's the dishy bridegroom, right on cue. Come on, Ritchie. Here's one for you.' She handed him an overflowing glass. They jumped away and giggled as the golden liquid spilled between them. He held out his arm for Alina. When she tucked herself under it, Janet somehow managed to snuggle under his other one. He felt her slide an arm around his waist, under the jacket of his suit. From across the room, Olivia glared at him. He wasn't sure what the problem was; he'd never been good at reading body language or responding to it. If she was cross about something, he wished she would just say.

'Help yourself to the grub, everyone. There's plenty.' Janet seemed to have taken over the running of what Alina wanted to call their wedding breakfast, but which seemed more like a late lunch. The woman was lifting a platter of egg sandwiches and holding it at arm's length. 'These are a bit whiffy, but I'm sure they'll taste okay.' She moved towards Ronnie, who was standing over his father and helping him take sips of the champagne. 'You gorgeous fellas will have one, won't you?'

Ritchie wished she would tone it down a bit. It was like she was the bride, the centre of everything. The other women had moved to stand with Olivia, their smiles fading as quickly as the drink was going down. The woman named Jen glowered at him, and when he met her eye, a jolt of something hit him in the stomach. She was attractive in an obvious kind of way, with all her assets on show.

'Don't call my sandwiches whiffy, Janet Helm,' Olivia was shouting across the room. 'I don't remember you being here last night to help me make them.' She muttered something to her sister, whose sunny expression had soured. 'And you can stop showing yourself up as well.'

Alina cocked her head at the change of tone and put a hand protectively over the tiny mound of her stomach. 'Ladies, the sandwiches are perfect. I'm grateful to you all for everything you've done to help me.' She pointed at the decorated walls. 'It is all lovely.' She tried to take the sandwich platter from Janet's hands, but Janet resisted.

'There's only one person showing themselves up, Olivia Johnson, and that's you,' she muttered. 'It's a wedding. You're allowed to smile.'

Ritchie laughed, hoping the others would follow his lead, but there was a tension in the room that felt so heavy he needed to sit down. He took Alina by the hand and pulled her onto his knee as he sat.

He tucked her hair behind her ear.

'That Olivia woman has been griping since she got into my car,' he whispered. 'She's a bloody nuisance.'

'But she's been looking after your mama, my love, and Lenny. She must be a good person, deep down.'

'I don't like her.' He shrugged. 'Sorry, but there it is.'

Janet put the platter of sandwiches back in its place on the table. 'I think I'll pass,' she said, looking directly at Olivia. 'Got to watch my figure, haven't I.' She twirled around with her hands on her hip bones. Ritchie couldn't help staring. So he didn't see Olivia grab her sister's arm and drag her out of the kitchen. And he didn't see Jen following close behind. It was only when he heard the slam of the front door that he realised all of Alina's friends, bar Janet, had gone.

Chapter 16

Summer 2018

Laurie

It's a beautifully faded summer's evening. Laurie decides she should go and retrieve her mother's step-ladders from the Diamond Hall fence. She's not heard from Ed again, and she's leaving for London in a few days.

The forecourt gardens along the street have fuchsia and buddleia bushes dripping with dying blooms, and some spill out over walls and through gates. One seagull chick is still whistling from a nearby roof; late, Laurie thinks, and no parents in sight. The air tastes of smoke and earth.

It is only when she's on the shingle path to the beach that a sound puts her on high alert, a shout, coming from somewhere inside the wood. More than one voice and drifting from a direction she can't quite work out. She clambers up the bank to where the ladders should be. They're still there and none the worse for being out in the rain for a few days. She hears another shout. It judders across the stillness of the evening, and she cocks her head to try and clarify where it is coming from; something is happening at the gates of Diamond Hall.

She leaves the ladders and follows the line of the fence, pressing down nettles and brambles carefully with her trainers so none reach up and catch at her bare ankles. There's no sign of anyone on the other side, but the shouting is getting louder, and rhythmic. Then she realises it's not shouting at all, it's chanting. The smallest frisson of fear starts to make its way from her stomach to her throat; whatever is happening doesn't feel good.

At the gates, she finds a group of people, Pete O'Connor included. They are facing in the direction of the house and calling *Diamond out* at the tops of their voices. Some have grabbed the bars of the gate and are yanking them backwards and forwards. Laurie dashes towards Pete.

'What the hell are you doing,' she cries, pulling at his arm. 'This is private property. Ed's property.' She turns to the small crowd. 'Whoever's in charge of this shit-storm, you'd better call off your posse. I've got my phone here and I'm about to get in touch with the police.' She waves the device in front of her, hoping none of them will realise she's quite scared.

'I'm in charge.' Pete takes her to one side. 'And since when did that imbecile Diamond become *Ed*. Oh, yeah, that's right. He's your boyfriend now, isn't he.' The words fire out of his mouth, then he sticks out his tongue in a fake gag.

'Don't be so pathetic. Oh, wait. You're jealous.' Laurie isn't quite sure what she's saying, but anger is digging into her mind and finding words she wasn't expecting. 'I knew it then, and I know it now. If anyone's got a screw loose, it's you.' She thumps two fingers against her temple. Adrenaline is zipping around her body and putting her on the highest alert.

Pete stares and puffs out more snide laughter. 'Diamond is a nutter, Loz. We've had enough of him prowling around dressed as a woman. We've got our children to think of.'

'Oh, my God.' Laurie wants to slap his smirking face. 'He's

not prowling around dressed as a woman. You lot will say anything.'

'What *lot* is that?'

'Diamond haters. And I've got news for you, Pete O'Connor. You're not juveniles anymore, causing a bit of anti-social behaviour. You're adults. For Christ's sake, move on.' She walks away from him very slowly, making a show of using her phone. 'I mean it,' she calls over her shoulder. 'Get them away or you'll all be facing a police caution.'

Pete hesitates. He looks towards the gates, where his cronies are still chanting and rattling, then back at her. 'I don't understand you,' he spits. 'In Chapel Field for five minutes and you're trying to run the place. Why don't you just fuck off back to London. That's what you did before, isn't it? Do it again.'

Then he moves towards the other people and begins slipping his arm around shoulders and whispering in ears. Within a few minutes, they are breaking away in small groups and heading along the road towards the village proper. Pete shouts something that she can't quite hear but she doesn't need to; his intentions are clear; she's now as damned as Ed Diamond.

And then she remembers him, stuck inside the house. Did he hear the chanting and threats? What happened to set them off? She must know. Instead of heading for home and calming her jangling nerves, she decides to do something that probably isn't sensible. She's still got the key to the Diamond Hall gates on her own bunch. She's going to try again to get inside the house and talk to Ed.

Once she's sure everyone has gone, she checks both ways along the road. It's empty. There are a couple of houses further down, and if they see what she's doing, she can hardly make it any worse for herself. The padlock comes away easily in her hand, and she squeezes herself through a small gap and locks the chain behind her.

It's getting dark now, and swarms of midges are hanging about in the green twilight. As the house comes into view, she can't see any sign of life, no lights or twitching curtains. It's quite overgrown along the driveway, so perhaps Ed hasn't seen what's been going on. She hopes that is the case, though she cannot fathom why Pete was accusing him of prowling about dressed as a woman. Ed's never denied there's a sister living at the house. He's never confirmed it, either.

She knocks as hard as she can on the porch door, but no answer comes. When she tries the handle, she finds the door is locked. It's impossible to look through the diamond-paned inner door from here, so she moves to a window and taps lightly against the glass. Not a sound or sign of movement come from inside. It's possible that Ed has gone out. Which means the sister is in the house on her own. If there is a sister. Laurie tries to drown out the stream of confused thoughts flowing across her good sense. In her experience, if you dig down far enough into the seemingly bizarre, there is a logical explanation waiting to be discovered: she fully intends to dig.

A path made from broken paving slabs lies along the side of the house. Laurie follows it, ducking to avoid the overgrowth of elder and hawthorn and trying not to step in the mush of red and black fruits littering the ground. When she reaches the back corner of the house, the ground opens out into a garden of sorts. There are some raised beds, formed from planks of thick wood nailed at the corners. A few late flowers, dahlias she thinks, stretch upwards from the beds, desperate for light. Flat against the back of the house, is another door.

'Ed. Ed, it's Laurie,' she calls as she slams her hand against the flaking green wood. When he doesn't answer, she turns the handle and pushes. The door opens straight into what looks like a kitchen, and sitting on a tatty sofa, staring at her, is Ed. His face is drained of colour. He jumps to his feet as she steps inside. Before she can think much further, he takes three strides across the room and throws his arms around her.

'I need some help, Laurie,' he chokes. 'Help me.' He feels so tense in her arms, and he's freezing.

'Course I'll help you,' she murmurs. 'I take it you heard that rabble at the end of the drive. They need a rocket up their arses.'

Ed steps away from her and smiles slightly. Whether he's shaking with fear or the cold she can't tell. The room is chilly and smells damp, but it looks clean and it's very tidy.

'I'm sorry,' Ed says. 'I'm just so glad to see you. Even though I've got used to coping with all the rubbishy things thrown at the Diamonds, this has got me worried.' He takes Laurie's hand and pulls her towards the sofa. 'Sit down, and I'll return the favour and make you a cup of tea.'

'Tell me what's happened, first.'

'I will,' he says. 'But I'll have to start at the beginning. It might take some time.'

While Ed boils water on a gas ring and makes tea in a pot using real tea leaves, he tells Laurie about Elissa. She's his twin, she's disabled and frail. His father had been terrified she'd be taken away by people with power and Ed followed the lead he was given to keep her hidden. She'll never have an independent life, but she's his sister and he loves her above everything. He hates that he has to go out and leave her, but she sleeps for big chunks of time and there's never been a problem.

He walks her around the Diamond Hall land every day, which is all she seems to want. He reads to her and talks to her and feeds her. There's never any conversation because she doesn't speak, but she smiles, and it melts his heart.

By this point, Laurie isn't sure what to believe. Either Ed is exactly what Pete said he was; or an adult woman has been locked away in Diamond Hall for many, many years, sometimes completely alone, and has had no advocate other than her brother. Neither option is anything but dreadful.

'Someone was prowling along the edge of the fence while my sister was out in the garden. She doesn't usually bother going anywhere I don't take her, but on this particular day, when I looked away for a moment, she wandered off. I caught up with her pretty quickly, but she'd reached the fence, and someone was there.' Ed brings two mugs of tea over to the sofa. His hand shakes as he passes one to Laurie. 'I thought it was you at first; you were there that other time. But whoever it was shouted something.'

'What?'

Ed shrugs. 'I'm not completely sure, but it sounded like *Diamond, you paedo.* If it means what I think it does, why are they shouting it at me? What's going on, Laurie?'

She needs to be careful. There's been no sign of this *Elissa* yet. 'It's based on a real word, which I guess you know. Some people throw it out when they really want to cause hurt, regardless of the truth. Pretty awful, I know. But don't worry about it at the moment; I think I need to meet Elissa. Where is she now?'

'She's asleep. There's a room back there; it's where she lives, mainly.' He thumbs towards a set of double doors with frosted glass panels. 'It used to be another sitting room, when Dad was alive. I thought it would be easier to have her down here.' He gets up from the sofa and holds out his hand. Laurie takes it and lets herself be led into Elissa's room.

It's sparsely furnished. There is a television on a small table in one corner and a wall of shelves, stuffed with magazines and ornaments and books. An armchair is pulled up against French windows and behind the door, pushed up to the wall, is a single bed. It is layered up with blankets and a beautifully embroidered quilt, and here, with her head on the pillows and sleeping peacefully, is Ed's sister. Laurie knows this immediately, because the resemblance is striking. Though Elissa's face is thinner, the cheeks smoother, it could be him, lying there.

'Oh my goodness, Ed,' Laurie gasps. 'She's lovely.'

Ed

There's terror in his heart as he leads Laurie into Elissa's room, but Ed has realised something; he can't continue managing on his own. Chapel Field residents seem bolder, nosier somehow. Perhaps it is people generally who have changed. It's only a matter of time before one of them pushes their way into his life and shines a light on how he's been living and turns it into a challenge.

Not like Laurie. She's treated him with nothing but respect, and now she's slipping an arm around his waist and staring at his sister and saying how well she looks, but he can tell Laurie is shocked. She is focused on the fact that when he goes shopping or over into town, Elissa is left alone in the house. His reassurance about security doesn't seem to mean anything to her. She mentions potential fire risks and burglars. Of course he's thought about these things, but he and Elissa have to function on a basic level. They have to eat.

Laurie tells him that there's a system in place to help people like his sister, that she should have specialist care. This is what he'd thought she was getting. No one would care more for her than him.

There's a different kind of care, Laurie is busy explaining, where nurses would come to Diamond Hall and work with

Elissa and attend to all her needs. He is listening, but all he can think of is his sister being driven away from the house in an ambulance and never coming back. It happened to his father; it could happen again.

There's money available to help him support Elissa at home, Laurie seems to think. As helpful as that would be, Ed can't fathom how he could claim money without anyone interfering in his life. He understands such things as tax and other payments, but he's never put into those pots, so he'd surely not be entitled to anything. Laurie's explanations and insinuations are making his head spin. She's asking to see birth certificates and photographs and wanting him to wake Elissa up so that she can meet her properly. He doesn't know if he can.

Laurie

'She'll wake up when she's ready,' Ed says, closing the door gently behind them. 'Stay for a while.' He glances at the wall clock. 'I guarantee she'll be awake in about an hour.'

Laurie looks across the kitchen to where Ed left the teapot. She needs something to settle her stomach. While she's relieved that there is a sister, now that she knows, her presence can't be ignored. She'll need to treat Ed kindly, though. The poor guy is clearly terrified she's going to phone the authorities at any moment.

'I could do with another cup of tea,' she says. 'Any left in the pot?'

His shoulders lower a little as he picks up their mugs from the floor beside the sofa and rinses them. Ed is a couple of years older than her, as far as she remembers. Richard Diamond died in the same year as Marcus, which means Ed has been looking after his sister in this house for almost twenty years. How is that possible? What she can't get her head around is that the people of Chapel Field have no idea what he's been through.

Ed brings her tea, and they sit together on the sofa. It is made from a soft green fabric, like velvet, and is worn to almost threadbare on the arms. There is a tiny television and a radio on the one long kitchen countertop, and a microwave that looks like it has been hanging around since the nineties. When Laurie thinks about every one of her experiences in the last twenty years – university, travel, her first job – and about the people she's met, it's difficult to imagine Ed's story playing out in Diamond Hall, hardly changing since the death of his father.

'Tell me what would help you the most,' she says to Ed. 'I won't do anything you don't want me to.'

He doesn't speak for a moment. Then he sighs. 'Can I tell you the things I don't want? I think that would be easier.'

'Sure.' She pats the sofa. 'Sit. And spill.'

When he sits down beside her, Laurie experiences a sadness so profound it almost has a taste, yet he is smiling.

'You can always make me laugh,' he says. 'The thing I don't want, above all else, is to lose Elissa. I'm happy to build the rest of my life around caring for her. I don't think I could cope if she was taken away.'

Laurie takes his hand. He feels cold. 'You've got some strange ideas. You're an unpaid carer, in essence. Putting your sister into a situation that costs money isn't something that would happen unless you wanted it to.'

His gestures say he's agreeing with what she says, but Laurie can still see fear in his eyes.

'Honestly,' she whispers. 'You won't lose your sister.'

He nods. 'I know it's not going to change, but another thing I don't want is the constant heckling from people like that Pete O'Connor guy. I hardly know him, Laurie. Or any of the

Chapel Field residents. Yet they make me feel so low, when I see them. I just want to shout and bawl at them about what they think I've done.' His eyes fill with tears. 'What have I done?'

This is something Laurie can't explain to him. She can hardly explain it to herself. There was a time when she'd been tangled in the consensus of the village that the Diamonds were the bad guys. It didn't need explaining; it simply was. That the Diamond family have always kept themselves hidden away from a village that thrives on sociability, isn't enough of an explanation. It feels weak, but there is nothing else she can offer.

There must have been a time, when Richard Diamond was younger, when the family were more accepted. Her mother and Olivia had both been inside Diamond Hall and had lived to tell the tale. Marcus Butcher's funeral hadn't been the pivotal point for all the hatred, she's sure, but it certainly wouldn't have helped. There's nothing Ed can do about that, anyway. Perhaps just seeing him around the village, accompanied by Laurie, might help to change people's mindsets, but she's not convinced. There's not a hearts-and-flowers ending to this story, she suspects.

'You haven't done anything,' she tells Ed. 'From my memories of being young and living in the village, there was an understanding that the Diamonds were not nice people and you kept away from them. So we did. Once or twice I asked my friends about it and that was all we could come up with.'

He shrugs and takes a gulp of tea. 'My dad didn't exactly help though, did he. All the trouble he caused. He hated that I took a beating, you know. He could cope with all the ignorance, he said, but not that. Those evenings before he died, before that lad's funeral, he'd taken to wandering the village, looking for those he thought were to blame. And God knows what else.'

Laurie taps a finger to her lips. 'I have a vague memory of it.

He went knocking on doors and moaning at parents. Pete O'Connor was one of them, you know.'

'I thought so. I've seen him in the village, but I never get a proper look.' He shakes his head. 'It's done now, anyway. I just want to live my life out in peace, without people shouting abuse.' His voice cracks a little and Laurie puts her hand on his shoulder. She needs to focus on what can improve for him.

'Have you got paperwork and stuff?' she asks. 'Bills? Those kinds of things? I can have a look through if you like. It might give me some ideas for what you can change to help you and your sister.'

Ed puts down his mug and gets up from the sofa. Laurie watches him as he walks across the room. Aspects of him make her feel like she's with a stranger: he's so thin that she can see the bones of his shoulders beneath the faded T-shirt. His elbow joints remind her of those she's seen on skinny six-year-olds. Yet he's familiar, too. When they fall into conversation, it's like the background gaps don't need filling. And now he's coming back to her and he's carrying a cardboard box that's almost lost its shape. He puts it on the floor, and Laurie has to lean away from the smell of damp and mildew.

'This is everything I've got,' he says as he carefully pulls open the flaps of the box. 'There's birth certificates and suchlike, and the letter I got when Dad died.'

'Did you find out what he died from?' Laurie takes each piece of paper he passes her and tries to create an order. 'Was he having treatment for anything?'

Ed shakes his head.

'We don't have a doctor. Or a dentist. Is that wrong?'

'That's the first thing you need to do, then.' Laurie is trying hard to keep her reactions to herself, though she's struggling with the thought of Elissa not having access to medical help. It's the twenty-first century, for goodness' sake. How can people remain this hidden? There's not an aspect of her pupils she doesn't know about. The more off-grid their lives, the bigger the file.

'I can't just walk into a doctor's surgery and ask to be registered, can I? Would I not get into trouble?' Ed is frowning and Laurie wishes she could take away his confusion.

'The whole world isn't against you,' she says. 'You and Elissa have rights. It's your mindset that needs to change, as much as anything.'

'I get that. It's difficult, though, when there's people like that Pete guy glaring at you wherever you go.'

'Pete was, and will always be, a bit of an arse.' Laurie waits while Ed has a small fit of giggles. 'But his wife is nice, and I'm sure she'd be willing to meet us halfway. She's a health worker, by all accounts. I could talk to her about your situation, if you like.'

Ed goes quiet then, and Laurie isn't sure whether she's moving too fast for him. She can't guarantee there won't be repercussions when Elissa's situation is revealed to the world, but she can't afford to lose any ground either.

The box contains every utility bill that has ever been sent to Diamond Hall. Ed has kept everything, including receipts for art materials he has bought, and bills of sale for some of Richard Diamond's paintings. She stretches her eyes as she scans down. One of them fetched more than £10,000.

'Jeez, Ed,' she gasps. 'I didn't realise your dad's work was this collectable.' She waves the tatty piece of paper at him. 'You'd better have that one back, the one my mother has. It'd give you another heap of cash if you sold it.'

'No. I don't want it back. There must be a reason why your mother had it, and it's yours now.' Ed rocks back on his heels. 'I've found some photos, if you want to look.' He fans them out in front of her. There's nothing recent. When she looks more closely, Laurie is drawn to a photograph of a wedding. She spots her mother straight away, in a floor-length green dress, her blonde hair loose around her shoulders.

'Is this your mum and dad?' she asks, though she knows the answer.

Ed has moved onto the sofa next to her and is watching Elissa's door. 'Yes,' he says absently.

'Do you know who the others are?'

'Uncle Ronnie's there. And my grandfather, Lenny. Your mum, of course. And I think the woman who cleaned for them is there, too, with her sister. I don't know the other woman.' He pushes the photographs into her hand. 'Have a proper look,' he says.

There's another shot of his father and mother. Alina is wearing a dress Laurie has seen before, orange, with daisies at the hem and neckline. There's one of an older woman sitting on a dining chair, outside the porch of Diamond Hall; this is Olivia, she's sure. She has on an old-fashioned tabard-style apron and there's a cat at her feet. There's also a black-and-white photograph of a patch of woodland.

'That's what it looked like before the house was built,' Ed tells her. 'Lenny took it, apparently, as a souvenir.'

Laurie is intrigued. She wants to ask Ed if she can borrow the photographs and show them to Olivia, but before she can say anything else, he shoots up from the sofa and heads towards the doors of Elissa's room.

'She's awake,' he calls.

Ed

Elissa is sitting up in bed when Ed enters the room. It is shadowy at the back of the house, and if he's not careful, she'll fall asleep again without having anything to eat or drink. He flicks the switch on the small bedside lamp and the flash of pinkish-orange light makes his sister gasp. As he pulls back her sheets and blankets, he talks to her about their visitor, though she'll hardly grasp what that means. Her lack of understanding has never stopped his conversation.

He helps her to stand, then wraps her in a soft purple dressing-gown. She smiles when he jokes with her about what they call the *disappearing* slippers, then he pulls them from under the bed, with a mock-bow. Her hair is mussy at the back, and he smooths it down and tucks it into her collar, then he takes her hand and leads her into the kitchen.

Laurie stands and takes a few steps towards them. From her face, he can tell she's not sure how to act. He introduces Elissa as though she's an ordinary woman, not one the world hasn't seen for more than thirty years, standing here in her night-time clothing and smiling though she has no idea what is happening. Laurie holds out her hand.

Ed realises she hasn't yet understood; there will be no response from his sister apart from her smile. This is the first time he's seen Laurie's cloak of confidence slide away. It's on the floor; she's crying.

To hide his embarrassment, he sits Elissa on the sofa and covers her legs with a crocheted blanket.

While he's doing this, Laurie is asking if she can help, as though something abnormal is happening. It's not. This is his normal routine. In a moment, he will make toast and a milky drink for his sister, and they will watch the television, or he will read to her. Sometimes he will help her to have a bath and by the time the afternoon wears on, she will be ready for bed again. The art of living seems to tire her so much, but her health hasn't changed for many years, so he's not worried. Laurie clearly is.

While he does his work in the kitchen area, he tells her to sit with his sister and talk to her. As he fills a pan with milk, he hears Laurie mentioning the items in the room, the books, the television, even the colour of the lampshade. She's not yet realised everything said must be rhetorical; his sister will never answer.

When he cuts two thick slices of white bread and lights the grill of the cooker, Laurie moves to talking about the outside, about birds and gardens and the sea. She must be used to having one-way conversations with young minds. He can recall her telling him about her work in London, and he's sure he remembers a comment about her going back there at the end of the summer. Well, it's almost at an end. Perhaps when she leaves tonight, he'll not see her again. If she doesn't tell anyone what she's found out about Diamond Hall, none of them will be any worse off.

He thinks about that moment when he'd kissed her. It meant something, he's sure it did.

He calls across the soft hum of Laurie's voice, to ask if she'd like more tea. She jumps up and says she'd better go home as there are things to do, and when he turns to look at her, there's something strange about her expression, like it's a different person behind her eyes.

She's polite and says she will see them both very soon, but he doesn't believe her, believes instead that it's the last time he'll set eyes on Laurie Helm. The thought catches at the back of his throat and he thinks he's just done the worst possible thing.

Chapter 17

Summer 2018

Laurie

When she presses the red screen-button to end the call, Laurie sits in the semi-darkness of her mother's living room and wonders what the hell she's just done. Asking for time away from work on compassionate grounds doesn't sit well with her.

When her mother died, earlier in the year, she hadn't taken even one day's leave. On the phone, her boss had sounded confused but relieved; there had been a consensus in her workplace that the grief would hit home eventually. This is what she's let him believe.

The truth is very different. Ed Diamond has hooked his way under her skin, like a thorn from the stem of a rose. She's tried and tried to dislodge him, but there he is, still trapped. Seeing Elissa had been the defining moment. There's no way Laurie can go back to London, knowing what she knows about the situation in Diamond Hall.

She lets the atmosphere of the house settle around her. When she'd first arrived here, echoes of her mother and their unpleasant relationship bounced from the walls of every room. Now, stripped of clutter and clunk, the place feels like it has a new story to tell. Ed has been in this room. His energy has deflected that of Janet Helm.

What Laurie wants to do is pay another visit to the O'Connor household and talk to Gina again. Though it's a Saturday evening and the residents of Chapel Field like to kick back, close their curtains on the world and crack open their drinks bottles, she's sure Gina wouldn't mind. Then there's Pete.

Before she can talk herself out of it, Laurie lifts her jacket from the banister in the hall and slips her feet into trainers. She picks up the front door keys and steps outside. The evening air is soaked with the tangy scent of bladderwrack. The tide must be high. Laurie has already fallen back into island mode, judging every day against tide-times and sea-wind. She zips up her jacket and steps briskly along the street in the direction of the O'Connor household.

Her judgement had been correct. All the curtains in the windows of Pete and Gina's house are closed. When she taps on the front door, no answer comes. As she waits on the step, she looks back at the street. Is she doing the right thing here? Blasting open the privacy of the Diamond family in a place where she knows it could be used in the worst possible way. Perhaps she should go home and have a rethink.

Then the front door opens, and Gina is standing there and calling her name, and she is smiling. 'Laurie. I was only thinking about you this morning. Are you a mind-reader, or what?'

'Oh. Hi. I was just about to go.' Laurie glances up at the house. 'I thought you might be away.'

Gina shakes her head. 'The others are. I'm here on my lonesome.'

'Holiday?'

'Not exactly. Reece has just passed his driving test. Pete's managed to get him a car, would you believe, though the insurance premium is phenomenal. The car's a right old banger of a thing, with spoilers and a customised exhaust. Bright blue, as well. He'll be a magnet for police to pull him over, that's for sure. The lad has driven the family up The Lakes for an overnighter in a caravan, of all things. I didn't fancy it.'

'I'm with you on that one,' Laurie says. 'I had one caravan holiday when I was a student. Even that young, I said *never again*.'

Gina pulls back the front door. 'Come on in.' She laughs. 'And I won't mention the word caravan.'

The television in the lounge is switched on and flashing out a detective drama. There is an open novel on the sofa. A family-sized bag of crisps sits next to a coffee mug on a small table in front of the fireplace. Everything is in silhouette. Gina comes into the room behind her and taps on a floor-lamp with her foot.

'That's better,' she says, gesturing for Laurie to sit down. 'I'm glad of a bit of company. For all the moaning I do about how over-packed this house is, when my lot are not here, I miss them. I'll be one of those mothers who cry when their children leave home. Actually, I think Pete will be the same.' She clutches at the collar of her furry dressing-gown. 'Hope you don't mind the nightwear. Can I make you a coffee or something?'

Laurie nods and Gina pads into the kitchen, continuing to chatter above the sound of the kettle being filled and cups chinking together. It's impossible to hear what she's saying, but that doesn't seem to matter. Laurie sits back on the sofa and enjoys the cosy lamplight and homely smell of drying washing.

'Do you think that's too much to ask,' Gina says as she comes back into the lounge carrying two mugs on a tray.

'Sorry, what?'

157

'Expecting our Josh's headteacher to email back straight away. I know it was a Friday, but I would never have got in touch if I didn't think it was urgent.'

Laurie has only picked up half the story, though from what she's gathered, all three children have been schooled at the huge local academy. Which means the headteacher will have a personal assistant who should be straight on to urgent emails, even in the holidays. When she points this out, Gina frowns.

'Exactly my thoughts. So I'll be on the doorstep of that school, come Monday, training day or not.'

'Tiger-mom.' Laurie laughs. It's not the first time she's had this thought; having Gina on-side would be a great strength. 'And on that subject, would you have time to help me with something?'

Gina cocks her head in a way that says she doesn't believe Laurie would ever need help.

'Well, not me exactly. More, erm, Ed Diamond.'

Silence stretches between them. Laurie picks up her coffee and takes a sip. She dares not look up; she's clearly said the wrong thing. Eventually, Gina gives a small huff and clears her throat.

'Pete said you'd got involved with Ed. He's livid about it, you know. It's a bit of a sore subject between us. Live and let live, I say, but Pete, he can't.'

'It's more for Ed's sister, that I'm asking for help.' Laurie has to drop Elissa into the conversation; it's the detonating factor.

Gina's expression twists into a confused frown. 'There is no sister.'

'Oh, but there is. And I've met her.'

'Christ Almighty, Laurie. Are you sure?' Gina has moved to the edge of the sofa. Her hands are on her thighs, and she looks like she's about to jump out of her own skin.

'I've met her, Gina. She's disabled and Ed's been looking

after her in that house, forever.' Laurie stretches this last word with her hands. Her emotions are on show, and she can't help it. Which serves to convince Gina that she's telling the truth. Then the woman does jump up from her seat and scans the room as though someone might be lurking in the corner and listening.

'Tell me everything,' she demands, her hand on her chest. 'Oh, my God, I can't believe it.'

———

When Laurie has explained the situation, she pleads with Gina to visit Diamond Hall. If she sees Elissa with her own eyes, perhaps she'll believe there is nothing sinister going on. As it is, Gina is shaking her head and saying *poor lass* over and over, until Laurie wants to take her there and then.

'If I do come with you,' Gina says, 'and I'm at all worried, I'll have to call it in. You realise that, don't you?'

Laurie nods with a confidence she's not feeling. The whole situation with Ed and Elissa is worrying. How could it not be? But Gina's husband has to take some credit for that, and she knows it, though there's no denying Laurie herself has been part of the terrible outcomes for the Diamonds. Which is why she's going to do everything she can to improve them. Or, that's what she's telling herself. She's no fool. Her authentic self has flagged up an attraction to Ed Diamond, and there's no point lying about it.

'We'll go in the morning. First thing.' Gina picks up their coffee mugs. 'Pete and the kids won't be back until the afternoon. But, Laurie–'

'Yes?'

'I'll have to tell him. You do realise that.' She shrugs. 'Who knows. It might make him go a bit easier on poor Ed.'

People going easier on Ed is the least of Laurie's worries.

She can't get the picture out of her mind of Elissa, coloured blanket over her legs and staring off into the distance. She wouldn't look out of place in the residential home with Gina's nan. Yet the poor girl can't be forty years old. What quality of life has there been for her in Diamond Hall? It would break Ed to let her go, but does that give him the right to dictate the next forty years of his sister's life.

'Let's leave Ed out of the equation, Gina, when we visit tomorrow. Base your thinking on the evidence of your own eyes. Listen to your heart.'

Gina walks with her down the hallway. 'My God, Laurie,' she gasps. 'You're in deep with this family, aren't you.' She pulls open the front door and lets in a burst of briny night-air. 'Call for me in the morning and we'll take it from there.'

Chapter 18

Summer 2018

Laurie

It's a bright Sunday morning when Laurie walks to Diamond Hall with Gina. The streets of the village are empty and there's a layer of chill in the salty wind. Gina is wearing a navy-blue uniform and carrying her nurse's bag. She's chatting about how she wants to give Ed confidence that she is a genuine health professional, without terrifying him.

Above them, a dart of geese flap their way towards the open horizon. Laurie shields her eyes and watches them go. It's what she should be doing, leaving the convoluted life of Chapel Field behind as she did once before. Last time, there was nothing of consequence to hold her back; now there's Ed and Elissa.

They reach the gates of the house. Gina hesitates. She's not a born-and-bred local but the tales must have had an effect. When Laurie opens the padlock and loosens the chains, she tilts her head and raises her eyebrows.

'God Almighty! You've got your own key. Imagine what Pete would say.'

Laurie winks as she pulls back one of the gates. 'Imagine.'

They walk together through the shadowy gloom that obscures the house. Gina slips her arm through Laurie's. The woman is genuinely nervous about this visit. She must have seen most things, in her job, but as Laurie often points out to her London colleagues, truth is much, much stranger than fiction. Laurie has worked with children who are seething with anger at the life they've been handed; whose parents would rather spend money on tanning salons and nail extensions than feed them, and parents who allow their offspring access to their own deviant world so that they can become an emotional support.

Yet the gut-punch she'd felt on meeting Elissa was way outside her experience. It will be the same for Gina, she's sure.

'It'll be fine,' she says, patting Gina's hand. 'The Diamonds are not the way people have painted them.'

Gina huffs. 'Nana wouldn't agree with you.'

Laurie gestures towards the house, which has now come into view. 'She said Richard Diamond didn't like her, but she must have been okay with them at some point, because she worked here, didn't she?'

Gina inhales sharply. 'I never actually believed this place existed; how stupid is that? Pete goes on and on about it, to the point where I've stopped listening.'

Laurie is surprised to see Ed standing in the porch. He is wearing a faded blue-and-white shirt and a pair of jeans. He waves a hand in greeting.

'How did he know we were coming?' Gina hisses.

'He must have heard the gates,' Laurie whispers, painting on a smile, then louder, 'Hello, Ed.' The strangeness of the situation is playing out across Ed's face and down into his body. He's biting his bottom lip and standing in a lopsided way, with one hand in his pocket and the other reaching around to the pony-tail he's made with his hair. That he's terrified is obvious.

Laurie runs hundreds of scenarios through her mind, and

comes up with the fact that joviality as a way of coping would be the most patronising thing ever.

'If you're not happy with us being here,' she tells him, 'we'll go and no more will be said.'

'This is the right thing to do.' Ed beckons them forward. 'Come in. Please.'

Laurie introduces him to Gina as they move awkwardly together into the main room of Diamond Hall. She can just about stop herself from opening her arms to Ed and hugging him.

'My sister is in bed, but she's awake and sitting up, having her breakfast.' He thumbs towards the double doors. 'Go in, if you like. I'll make a pot of tea.'

Gina holds a hand up to Laurie and mouths *you stay*, then shoulders her way through the doors and closes them behind her.

'Is that okay?' Ed turns to Laurie. 'Have I done the right thing, letting your nurse friend go in there on her own?'

Laurie can't stop herself then. She slides her arms around his waist and rests her head against his chest for a moment. He relaxes into her.

'You go in, too, if it makes you feel better. I can rustle up a pot of tea. I think.' She peers up at him.

He is grim-faced. 'I feel better when you're here,' he murmurs. 'Safer.'

Laurie's stomach flips over. She's not sure, but fear might be the cause: does she want to be someone's safety-net? 'You're not in any danger, not anymore. Neither Elissa.'

'You've no idea what real danger is, though, have you, Laurie.' He steps out of her embrace. 'I don't mean to cause offence or anything, but being a Diamond, in this village, has meant a low-level fear of hatred every single day of my life. It mounts up and does the same damage as if you were being chased by a pack of starving lions.'

His analogy makes her smile.

'You've been watching too many nature programmes,' she says. 'Sorry. I'm not being flippant.' When he tilts his head, confused, she adds, 'What I mean is, there's been nowhere for your worries and fears to go, has there. Apart from back inside your own head. Time to voice them.'

Ed considers this for a moment, then says, 'Well, here's one. What will happen when you go back to London? It's soon, isn't it?'

'I've some news about that.' Laurie takes his hand and moves him towards the sink. 'Fill the kettle and I'll tell you what I've done.'

While Ed moves around the kitchen, setting out mugs on a tray and measuring out tea into a chipped brown pot, Laurie explains how she's put herself on compassionate leave for a few weeks. She peppers the explanation with hints that there are personal reasons for her decision, and watches for his reaction.

'Why would you want to be with me?' he asks when she pauses for breath.

'I like you, that's all. I mean, it's not all, but–' Laurie finds herself struggling for words; every one of her choices tastes of the crass way it will sound.

Ed interrupts. 'No, that came out wrong. It sounded like I was asking for compliments. What I meant was, there's too much baggage that comes with the Diamonds. It'd be a relationship killer.'

'Ah, so we're definitely talking relationships,' Laurie says, with a tilt of her head. She is rewarded with a beaming smile that feels like coming home. Then Gina is back in the room, carrying a tray with the remains of Elissa's breakfast, and his attention is diverted.

'I'll need to talk to you now, Mr Diamond, if that's all right?' she says. Laurie looks at her face, and catches the tiniest trace of a smile.

'Of course. And please call me Ed. My dad was Mr Diamond, not me.' They laugh at that, and some of the dread that's lodged itself between Laurie's stomach and her throat, creeps away.

Gina explains to Ed about registering himself and his sister with a doctor so that he can access care services and equipment which could help him. When she explains about him being entitled to monetary allowances for Elissa, he stretches his eyes in disbelief. Her suggestion that trained health professionals could come to the house and help him, is met with even more incredulity. Laurie wonders if fear is behind his reaction, but he doesn't hesitate when Gina asks to see their birth certificates to collect certain details.

Ed carries the cardboard box to the kitchen table. As he unpacks it in a hunt for the certificates, Laurie picks up the pile of photographs from before. Gina recognises her nan straight away.

'Oh my God.' She peers at the shot of Richard and Alina's wedding. 'That's Nana. Doesn't she look young. She's with Auntie Emily. That's her sister. I don't know the others.' She hands the photo to Laurie. 'Who are they?'

'My mum's there. Can you pick her out?'

Gina looks closer but shakes her head. 'She's not the bride, obviously. So she must be one of the other two women. They're both very pretty.' She shakes her head. 'I don't know.'

'The bride and groom are Ed's mum and dad. That's my mum, there.' Laurie points to the slightly taller of the two blonde women. 'I've no idea who the other one is. That guy is Ronnie Diamond, Ed's uncle.' She runs her hand over the photo. 'They've all got thick, dark hair, haven't they, the Diamonds?'

Gina is flicking through the other photographs.

'This is Nana, too,' she says, handing Laurie the one that shows a woman sitting outside the porch of Diamond Hall. 'It must have been when she worked here. Bless. She'd love to see these. Would that be okay, Ed?'

Ed looks puzzled. 'Pardon? Oh, yes, sure, take them.' He has almost reached the bottom of the box. Piles of papers have spilled across the table and the mouldy smell is catching at the back of Laurie's throat.

'Finally,' he suddenly gasps. 'I thought I'd lost them.' He hands a plastic wallet to Gina. 'Just check it's what you need.'

While Gina flaps open the wallet, Laurie cranes to see. The information on each certificate is printed over pale green watermarked paper and signed in ink at the bottom. The parents are named as Richard Leonard Diamond and Alina Diamond, neé Casstella, and the date of birth is the same on both, showing Laurie she was right about their ages. Ed is named as Eduardo Richard Diamond, and his twin sister as Elissa Janet Diamond.

Ed

Though he's vaguely aware of Laurie's sharp inhale, Ed is focused on his own thoughts. When she asks him why his sister would have Janet as a middle name, he can't think of the answer she might want. He has looked at the birth certificates once before, and he'd rather not remember the occasion.

Getting himself and Elissa away from Diamond Hall had been his motive; that, and a search for any thread of Spanish family that might offer some comfort or solace or just a respite from the despair he was feeling. The idea had come and gone. The despair hadn't. He'd discovered things about the Casstellas that were best forgotten. When the family realised the man who'd married their daughter might have money, land, a house even, their interest had been piqued. Ed shut down all correspondence, after that. He'd wanted human contact; they wanted what they were owed.

All he can offer as an explanation for Laurie about the birth certificate, is that her mother may have helped his father after Alina died, and perhaps they'd become close. When he puts words to his thinking, it makes him so uneasy he has to focus on something else. He can tell Laurie isn't happy with his answer, but he has nothing more to offer.

His thoughts are snarled up with what she's revealed: she feels something. For him. How is that possible? And how does it play out? He's never had a relationship with someone on his own level. He's been a dutiful son and brother; he's had success there. What would a relationship with Laurie make him? A boyfriend? Lover? He shakes away these thoughts because Gina is trying to pin him to a time and date for someone to come and assess his sister properly.

The pace and structure of his life are changing much faster than he'd anticipated, and it's scaring him. There's no way of telling if he's made the right judgement. All he is certain of is that from the moment he met up with Laurie again, the life he'd been leading felt wrong. He had made his peace with never being accepted in the village and never being free of his sister's care. Now, he's no longer at peace and it's hard to know why, but Laurie is at the bottom of it, he's sure.

She wants to have her mother's painting valued and sold so that he can use the money to make some alterations to Diamond Hall. She's asked for details of the collector so she can use a computer to look him up and get in touch. Ed's only ever dealt with him through postal correspondence, but Laurie seems intent on having her way, and he doesn't have the energy to argue. The truth is, he wants her and Gina to go, and give him some time to process everything.

He walks with them to the front porch, and finds himself agreeing not to leave Elissa on her own anymore, even if she's asleep. Laurie tells him she will sit with his sister if Ed has errands to run, and Gina chimes in with some details about respite care. This will mean leaving his sister in the hands of strangers and he's not sure if it's something he will ever be able to live with. There's also the offer of taking her for an outing; Laurie has a car and she's happy to accompany them to the shops, she says.

He can't answer any of their questions or comment on their thoughts because he has no idea how Elissa would react to any of it, and she is his priority.

The outcome he sees is that he won't be able to comply with anything being asked of him, and that will lead to more hatred of the Diamonds, and he'll be back where he started.

As he makes his way inside the house, Ed thinks about the things he has let Gina and Laurie take away already. The photographs falling into other hands could hardly cause him any problems, but what if the birth certificates were used against him? How this could be, he isn't quite sure, but he's well aware the world has moved a long way forward of what he thinks he understands about it. He knows Laurie would want to stop anything bad happening, but he's not sure if that's in her power. He lets himself into his sister's bedroom. Caring for her will be a welcome distraction this morning, and she'll want to be outside as soon as she's ready.

The routines of walking and talking, bathing and dressing keep Ed completely absorbed for more than an hour. By the time he lifts Elissa's coat from a peg by the back door, he feels calmer. He's learnt to live just for the moment he's in; but meeting Laurie and listening to Gina have given him a glimpse of the future, and one that might hold something more than he thought. While he walks around the fading gardens with his sister, Ed can't help but smile. The tiniest seed of excitement has planted itself in his stomach and in his mind.

December 1978
Richard Diamond

Standing in front of the open fire, Richard Diamond huffed to himself as he took a sip from his glass. It contained a good amount of the punch his wife had made. The taste was a mix of cherry liqueur, cloves, and the sliced oranges she'd floated on top. He spat his mouthful back into the glass and slammed it onto the mantelpiece. Once again, he was feeling out-numbered.

He'd asked Alina to try and organise some male company for him at this party, but he was on his own. Unless he counted the brother Olivia had brought along with her – Rob or Bob or something – who couldn't have been more than twenty. What would they have in common? Olivia was hardly his number-one fan, either. They'd let her go as a cleaner, but she often came to the house on the pretext of checking how Alina was. Janet Helm was here again, too, with her flirty looks and wriggling hips. If Alina continued to keep him at arm's length, something was going to happen between him and Janet, he was sure.

The double doors of the other lounge had been wedged back with two dining chairs, and he could see Emily, Janet and Jen moving in time to a pulsing beat from the record-player speakers. The sight of long hair skimming slim waists set his stomach fluttering. If he couldn't share a drink with male company, he might as well enjoy what he'd got.

'Room for another,' he shouted as he stepped between furniture and the Christmas tree. 'What do you think, ladies?'

The women opened their circle to let him in.

Janet beamed. 'Rikki Diamond, you old snake-hips.'

'Less of the *old*, woman.' Richard danced towards her as she held out her hands. He took them and they swung together for a moment. When he let her go, Jen pushed herself in between them.

'My turn now,' she said coyly, and Richard obliged. She pressed herself against him, and he felt that familiar jolt. His free hand slid around her waist. If he was being denied the male company he wanted, he might as well enjoy himself. He wasn't sure why his efforts to bond with the men of the village came to nothing. He'd tried being friendly, tried drinking in the Chapel Field pub, even tried standing at the gates of Diamond Hall and people-watching, hoping to catch some interest, but nothing worked. He felt as shunned as he and Ronnie had been, when they were kids.

The woman named Emily was peeling Jen away from him and slipping herself in as a replacement. Something about her reminded him of Olivia, the way she had of smiling out disapproval; Emily had it, too.

He put his hand to his chest and faked a cough. 'Sorry. I think I need a drink. Catch you in a minute.' He put her to one side, though she continued to dance, and made his way into the main room. The dining table was covered with bottles and cans, and tubs of crisps and peanuts. In the centre of it all was Alina's glass punch-bowl, still full of the dark orange concoction. He grabbed a can of beer and popped the ring. His wife was leaning against the sink, filling a large glass with water.

'Hi, darling,' he said as he moved to stand next to her. 'How's things?'

She took three swallows of water, then turned her body away from him.

'Okay.' Richard gulped down some of the beer. 'What have I done this time?'

'I don't want you running your hands all over my friends. It's not nice.'

'They weren't complaining,' he spluttered, before he could stop himself. Alina turned to face him. She laid her hands against the huge mound of her belly.

'I'm complaining,' she spat. 'Me. Your wife. You should do what I say.'

'Some wife.' Richard swigged from the beer can again, then wiped his mouth.

Alina huffed out a laugh. 'What does that mean? As if I didn't know. I've got news for you, Richard Diamond. I'm pregnant.' She pointed to her belly. 'Very pregnant. I can't do those things you want.'

'You make me sound like some kind of pervert,' Richard snapped at her. 'I'm not the one in the wrong here. I'm not even allowed to cuddle you. What wife refuses that, pregnant or not?'

'This wife.' She slammed her glass onto the countertop and clumped away. Richard stormed across to the drinks table and picked up two more cans. If he wasn't allowed to mix with Alina's women-friends, he'd find this Bob guy and see what he had to say for himself.

Bob was sitting in an armchair by the French windows of the back lounge. They were open slightly and he blew cigarette smoke out through the gap. Richard held up the cans.

'I'll join you,' he said, passing one to Bob. 'Got a spare fag?'

A deep red flush spread across Bob's face. 'It's Ritchie Diamond, isn't it? Thanks for asking me to your party. It's cool.'

He glanced around the room. 'I reckon there's one guy for at least every two girls. Great odds.'

'Yes, I'm Ritchie. And yeah, great odds.' Richard held up his can. 'Cheers.' He settled himself on the floor with his back resting against the wall and angled his head towards the icy air drifting in from the open windows. 'What do you normally get up to at New Year?'

Bob passed him an open packet of cigarettes and his half-smoked one, then watched while he lit up. 'I mainly go into town,' he said, 'at New Year, like. But I'm not gonna lie: who wouldn't want a look inside Diamond Hall?'

'It's nothing special.' Richard swung an arm above his head. 'As you can see.'

'That's not what I mean, mate.' Bob took a swig from his can. 'It's more what the place stands for.'

'Oh, and what's that?'

Bob shrugged. 'Dunno exactly.'

Richard reached around the open French windows and flicked at his cigarette. He didn't want to press this guy for information. The poor lad looked hardly old enough to be drinking, with his baby-blond hair curling over his shirt collar and his neatly-pressed jeans.

They sat together in silence for a while, watching the women swaying to the beat of the music. When Emily and Jen wandered away, Janet danced towards them, barefoot and breathy.

'Hi, fellas. I need a rest, after that. Shove up.' She pushed against Bob's thighs and slid herself into the space she'd made. 'I don't even know your name, Olivia's baby brother.'

'It's Bob,' he muttered, flushing deeply again.

Janet looked down at Richard.

'Isn't he cute.' She laughed softly and leaned her head against his arm. 'Wish I had a brother like him.'

When she began stroking his hair, Richard couldn't bear to look. He wanted this, someone fawning over him, stroking *his* hair, making him feel important. If he couldn't have Alina, he'd have someone else. He threw his cigarette outside and made his way back to the drinks table. The punch still hadn't been touched. He picked up a pint glass and scooped out enough of the orange liquid to give him a good drink. It went down in one. Then he refilled the glass and took a handful of peanuts. With his mouth full and his blood beginning to fizz, he sauntered across to where Jen was perched, unfastening the buckles of her shoes.

'I don't know how you girls do it,' he said, wiping away traces of salt from his lips.

Jen looked up at him. 'Do what?'

'Wear those ridiculous heels.'

He licked his lips as she removed the shoes and pointed her stockinged feet at him. 'Make your legs look longer, don't they.'

'Yours look just fine to me.' Richard met her gaze. 'Stand up a minute, and we can test them out.'

Jen kept her eyes locked on his, then got up and pushed herself against him. 'See how small I am without them. I barely reach your chest.'

The alcohol and heat flooded his body. No one would care if he kissed this woman, no one would even notice. It was a party, after all; Alina couldn't expect him to behave himself at a party. Jen stretched her arms upwards so that she could hold the back of his head. Before he could think any further, she pressed her lips to his and he couldn't stop himself responding.

Suddenly, he felt a hand on his arm. He pulled away from Jen and she slid down to floor level again.

'Ritchie. Stop.' It was Janet. 'Alina's seen you. She's upset.'

Richard wasn't sure if he cared or not. He'd lost focus, his body taking him places where his mind hadn't allowed him to go for a long time. If he could take Jen to his bedroom right now, he'd be happy.

'Sod Alina,' he hissed. 'She doesn't want me anyway.'

'So you're doing this to make her jealous.' Janet shook her head. 'Nice work.' She flicked her gaze towards Jen. 'You're a one, you are. Get upstairs and apologise. Now.'

Jen had slumped against the sofa cushions, her round face smudgy with drink. 'Got nothing to be sorry for, have I?' she muttered. 'Me and Ritch fancy each other. It's a party.'

When Janet grabbed at her arm, Richard thought he'd better intervene, but Jen allowed herself to be dragged off the sofa and across the room. He watched them go, thinking this was exactly the reason why he didn't trust himself to mix with women. The drama they created around the simplest thing was more than he could deal with.

'You all right, mate?' Bob had made his way to the drinks table and was eyeing up the punch. 'Is it drinkable? Looks a bit orange for my liking.'

They had a bit of a giggle while Bob made a show of serving himself the punch, using the silver ladle to fill one of the tiny glass cups. He pinched his nose and gulped down the drink in one mouthful.

'Your turn,' he said, handing the ladle to Richard. 'Down in one. Let's see if we can't empty the bloody bowl.'

The game continued. Bob seemed to have an endless stomach capacity. Richard could feel a prickle of sweat forming across his forehead. The sickly liquid was choking him. He wasn't himself, trying to keep up with younger men, chasing after women when he was married and about to become a father. What was he doing?

'I'm going to have to concede defeat,' he said as Bob filled his mouth with a handful of peanuts. 'I'd better go and find my wife.' He rolled his eyes, then hated himself even more for the gesture of apology. He loved Alina, he was sure of that. Once the babies were born, he'd find a way to win her back. Her huge belly had been coming between them for far too long.

'She's upstairs.' Olivia appeared at his elbow and was treating him to one of her best frowns.

'Right, thanks.'

'Pregnant women should be cosseted if you want my opinion,' she huffed. 'And there's you, chatting up everything in a skirt, and right in front of her.'

'I don't want your opinion, thanks. I have enough of my own.'

'Funny.' She tugged at the hem of her dress as though reminding him she was a woman, too.

'Wasn't meant to be.' He cleared his throat. 'Look, if you want the truth, I'm getting quite fed up with you turning up at my house and sticking your nose into my business. I'm grateful for your help with my mother, but really, you're not needed anymore. Spend a bit more time with your little one. She might appreciate the input.'

Olivia glowered at him. 'You're not a nice man, Richard Diamond. Leaving Lenny and May to cope on their own was bad enough. Now you're back here and eyeing up any woman that comes within smelling distance, though you've got the loveliest wife going. You've got a screw loose.' She tapped one finger against her temple so that he wanted to slap it away. Another clever quip was forming on his tongue when a shockingly loud screech came from the direction of the stairs. He stared at Olivia.

'What the hell–'

'Go and see.' Olivia thumbed over her shoulder. 'Quickly.'

Richard stormed from the living room. His wife was lying on the hallway floor. Her sunshine-yellow dress had ridden up over her bare legs. She looked as if she were asleep.

'Shit. Shit, shit, shit.' He knelt beside her, trying to contain the stomach full of punch that was threatening to make its way up and out through his mouth. 'Get an ambulance. Someone, get an ambulance.' Suddenly, Janet was by his side and taking charge, and all he could do was hold tightly to his wife's hand and pray.

Chapter 19

September 2018

Laurie

Ed stretches his eyes in disbelief when Laurie shows him the photograph she's taken of Richard Diamond's painting.

'The quality's perfect,' he says, peering at the screen. 'As good as I've seen in books. How does a mobile telephone do that?'

'I'll show you again.' Laurie looks around the lounge for something to take a snap of. While Diamond Hall might be clean and organised, there are no luxury items, no ornaments or plants. 'Let me take a photo of you.' She holds up the phone. 'Smile.'

'Don't, Laurie.' He shakes his head. 'I hate seeing myself. The only time I look in a mirror is when I shave.'

As she lowers the phone again, there is a knock on the door.

'I bet that's a first,' she says. 'A proper visitor. I noticed you had the gates pinned back. It'll be Gina bringing her social care people, I expect.'

It hasn't taken more than a couple of days for a team to be

put in place to help Ed manage his sister. Gina has been true to her word. She's used every bit of her power and influence to get things moving. Highly irregular, Laurie suspects, but absolutely what tiger-mom Gina would do.

'Are you going to answer the door?' Laurie smiles as Ed gets to his feet and begins plumping the sofa cushions. 'No need to do that. Go on.' He's put on a fresh shirt for the visit and combed his hair into a low pony-tail, but there are lilac shadows under his eyes and he's jittery beyond belief. No matter how many times she's tried to reassure him, he still believes the world will treat him harshly, as it has for more than thirty years.

Ed has helped his sister wash and dress and she is sitting in her armchair by the French windows, smiling and oblivious to what's happening. The plan is that he and Laurie will use the time to walk into the village and pick up some groceries. Not a necessity, but it will give Ed the chance to practise leaving Elissa with people he classes as strangers.

He brings Gina and two other women into the room and Laurie stands up to greet them. One is older, with blonde hair going to grey and wearing a dark red overall that shows off her wiry frame. The other is much younger, sweet-faced and soft. But when she grips Laurie's hand, there's a strength that's reassuring. The key to getting Ed through this situation is to keep talking to a minimum, and mobilisation to the max.

'Get your coat and shopping bag,' she tells him, 'and don't be going back in there to see her.' She shakes her head and matches it with a wagging finger. Ed pushes his hands into the pockets of his jeans and stares at the floor. Gina talks him through some basic details, then he does what Laurie asks, racing towards the front door in a way that makes her want to hug him and soothe him as though he was a child. Which in many respects, he is.

As Gina leads the other women into Elissa's room, she

mouths to Laurie that she hasn't told Pete anything about what she knows. *It's not my story to tell*, she seems to be saying.

Laurie gives a thumbs-up and rushes away to catch up with Ed.

Outside, there's a fresh chill overlaying the fading summer air. September has a particular smell: a mixture of powdery mildew on wet leaves and grass that's been cut too wet. It reminds Laurie of returning to school, of new shoes that pinch and the beautiful cage of classroom life; she's missing it this year.

Instead, there's Ed, with his shadowy eyes and taut body language, and his desperate need of her. It's a new phase in her life and she's heading into it without the slightest notion of how it will end. That thought sends a rush of adrenaline around her body and for a moment, she feels invincible.

Then Ed slips his arm through hers and she's back down to Earth and wondering how the people of Chapel Field will greet them this morning.

'We've got a half-hour,' she says to him as they stride out together. 'What do you want to do first?' No answer comes. 'Well, you must need bread and milk and stuff. Do you? Or we could leave the shopping until last. You decide.'

Ed lowers his head and says nothing.

'Ed? This is excruciating for you, I know. But it's the right thing, isn't it.'

'You keep saying that.' He lets go of her arm.

'Because it's true.'

He turns back towards the gates of Diamond Hall. 'I can't do it, whatever you say. Anything could be happening to Elissa, and I've just abandoned her.'

Laurie jumps in front of him and takes his hands. 'Stop,' she says. 'Stop right there. In your more lucid moments, you said you'd get like this, and I was to talk you round. The way you think of the world isn't exactly right. I can understand it, I really can. But many people are better than you give them credit for.' She locks her gaze onto his. 'Like me, for example.' Laurie has prepared herself for this moment. It had been easy to convince Ed that he could make the huge leaps of faith that freedom required. They'd batted opinions back and forth for many hours, always in the safety of his home. He was stepping out today as a different person, and she very much understood how that felt.

'Ed. Do you trust me?'

He nodded.

'Well, trust the process then. I guarantee there will be good outcomes for you and your sister. Even if it doesn't feel like it, at first.'

Ed's shoulders slide downwards, and he lets out a long sigh. 'I understand what you're saying but it's hard. Too hard.'

Laurie can feel his pain, but she can't allow him to quit. If she'd been asked to explain her reasoning, she couldn't. There are no words. Instead, she slips her arms around Ed's waist and waits until he relaxes into her embrace. This has been her method of dealing with his anxiety, and it always works. Ed puts his hands on her shoulders and lifts her away.

'You're too good,' he murmurs. 'Keep me talking while we head to the beach. Then talk some more. Don't let me fail, Laurie. Please don't let me fail.'

Tears catch at the back of Laurie's throat. She hates drama but has found herself immersed in it. There's something about this guy. His presence digs down to the very heart of her, and she's not used to it. There have been children in her care that she's bonded with, and some adults, too, but she's been more than happy with her own company, over the years; she's never subscribed to *a part of me was missing* brigade. But it's exactly how Ed makes her feel.

'Let's go,' she says, affecting a breezy air, and she leads him away from Diamond Hall again, following the scent of the sea.

The tide is ebbing away as they arrive on the beach, leaving a line of tangled black seaweed, large shells and bleached driftwood. Ed lets go of her hand and starts to kick at the debris, hunching forwards and peering closely. 'I used to think I'd find treasure, when I was a child.' He laughs.

Laurie joins him, toeing between the clotted seaweed. 'Like bits of sea-glass?'

He shakes his head. 'Actual treasure. Gold coins and stuff. I think I read too many stories about pirates and their hoarding. I loved those stories. I used to imagine I could get on one of the boats moored out there–' He gestures towards the white painted yachts dragging at their chains. '–and escape from everything, go where no one knew me. That was before Dad died.'

'What exactly happened to him in the end?' Ed has told her enough times that he doesn't want to talk about past history, and she remembers hearing Richard had a heart attack. 'Sorry. You can tell me to butt out, if you like.'

This makes him laugh. 'Butt out? I love your phrases. I guess it means *mind your own business.* I think I told you Dad died on the same day as he made a complete fool of himself at the Butcher funeral. I didn't hear much after the ambulance took him away. There was just a letter and some forms to fill in. I didn't take much notice, if I'm honest. I was too panic-stricken. I don't even know if there's a grave or anything. Is that very bad?'

'It's not bad, just really sad. I can't believe social services left you to your own devices. It wouldn't happen now.'

'I was eighteen. They wrote me off.' He lifts one shoulder in a half-shrug.

Laurie seizes the opportunity, though she knows she should leave it well alone. 'What about your mum? What happened there?'

Ed has collected a few stones. He pulls his arm back and launches one across the jade green surface of the tide. It bounces twice then disappears. 'I only know she died having me and Elissa. There was an accident of some kind; she never got to meet us.' He turns to look at Laurie. 'I don't feel much of a connection with her. You've seen the couple of photos; you know as much as I do.'

'Our mothers must have been friends,' she says. 'Which is strange, when mine never mentioned yours. It was a long time ago, I guess.' She's about to ask him what kind of accident, when they are distracted by the crunch of feet on shingle.

A dog-walker is approaching, a woman. The dog is bounding towards them in a flurry of sandy fur and lolling tongue. 'He's friendly,' she calls, 'don't worry.'

Ed and Laurie stand together as the dog gives them a quick sniff then continues its quest. The woman hurries past with a simple smile and cheerful greeting. They return the favour.

'Okay?' whispers Laurie.

Ed gives her a half-smile. 'I'm not visible when I'm with you.'

'That's the point. We probably look like a couple of nondescript people out on a walk. When you're on your own in the village, everyone notices you.'

Ed rounds on her. 'So you're saying I bring the negative reactions on myself, by just being me?'

'No. That's not what I'm saying. It's more–'

'What?'

'You have to break the cycle of being the old Ed who expects to be ignored, or worse. Be the new guy, the one who smiles and is more open.'

'So it's my fault.'

Laurie sighs. Trying to find words for something way beyond them, is causing anxiety. There has to be a different way. She stomps towards him and reaches her arms around his neck. When she kisses him, he pulls back at first, then lets himself be coaxed.

'A few weeks ago you were telling me to get lost,' she says when she pulls away. 'Where's all that hatred gone now?'

'You made me give you a chance.'

Laurie watches his face. Suddenly, he breaks into a smile. It's beautiful.

'Now pass it on,' she says. 'Make people act differently. Be the new Ed.'

He slides an arm around her shoulder and laughs to himself. 'Okay, let's go to the shop and I'll give it a try.'

Ed

Laurie kissed him.

He's a grown man with years of turbulence and strife behind him, yet he's grinning like the teenager he can hardly remember being. Not that he'd grinned much, back then. He's hoping the energy he's getting from being with Laurie will carry him through an interaction with the horrible man who serves in the shop. Though he has no reason to treat Ed with contempt, it's what always happens. In his more childish moments, Ed thinks it must be because he smells or something, though the real reason is infinitely more ridiculous: a grudge going way back.

Laurie has linked her arm through his and is chattering about the art dealer who has bought all the other paintings by his father. She is going to connect with the guy electronically and send photos of what must be the final Richard Diamond piece not in a collection. Ed has never met the guy or any of the people who work for him. Not that it matters. The money raised kept him and Elissa afloat in the early days. Ed's own agent is an anonymous person, too. Ed has told Laurie about his little studio in an upstairs room of Diamond Hall, but he's not showed her any of his work yet. Time enough for that.

When she asked him about paying tax on his earnings, he'd switched off. He needs to tackle the world in manageable chunks, not huge swathes that might knock him off his feet. It's hard enough letting people into the house and allowing them access to his sister. He asks Laurie about the time, and she assures him there are still ten minutes left of their half-hour. Enough to get to the shop, then escape as quickly as they can manage.

Outside the shop, a couple of people are gathered and talking. When they catch sight of Ed, silence descends. Laurie keeps a tight hold on his arm and pushes her way between them, offering a smile and a greeting. Nothing is returned.

Ed follows her inside as she lifts a shopping basket from a pile by the door. She scans across to the counter. He's there. The guy with the dark red hair and thick beard. And he's glaring with those hooded eyes and that sneer. Laurie calls a snappy hello.

Whenever he's in the shop, Ed's mind goes blank, which is why he always makes a list of things he needs and tries to keep focused on it. There's no list today. Instead, Laurie is asking him questions and acting like there's no palpable hostility zipping around the place, like it's an ordinary late summer's day with everyone going about their business as usual. He tries to remember what she'd told him about making eye contact and smiling. The problem is, people are doing what they always do, they're turning away from him and hiding in the aisles.

At the counter, he stands with Laurie as she lifts her basket and slides it towards the man. He coughs, just once. She asks him if everything is okay, and he cocks his head in reply but won't meet her gaze. When she requests a carrier bag, he yanks one very deliberately from a hook just behind him and slams it down next to their provisions. Ed wants to escape. He often feels like this, and has come away empty-handed on more than one occasion, then had to walk the length of the promenade to find another shop.

His wallet is in the pocket of his jeans. His hand is shaking as he fishes out a twenty-pound note and is about to pass it to Laurie. She nods towards the man, who is now picking at a tooth to the side of his large front ones and staring at the ceiling. He snatches the note from Ed's hand and in a few seconds is dropping some coins on the countertop. Laurie is packing the carrier bag and muttering something about manners. Ed doesn't stay to see how the tableau ends; he's outside before he responds in a way that would embarrass them both.

He can feel Laurie's anger. She's shoved her arm through his and is almost dragging him along the road back to Diamond Hall. When he suggests this visit to the shop wasn't as bad as some he's had, she snarls and spits like an angry cat. He tells her this and she starts to laugh.

While she rants, he pretends to listen, but what he's really doing is thinking about his sister. More than anything, he wants to see her. Until he does, he won't believe he's done the right thing in leaving her alone and trying to create a new persona for himself in the village.

When they arrive back at the house, Ed rushes through the porch and into the kitchen. There's no sign of anyone and the glass doors to his sister's room are shut. He pushes them open.

Elissa is sitting on a stool having her hair braided by the wiry woman, while Gina and the other woman are standing just outside the French windows, talking and pointing and adding

185

writing to a clipboard of paper. They all turn and look at him, nodding their hellos.

His sister is exactly as she was, smiling and looking so young now that her hair has been given a childish style. He hears Laurie asking if any of them would like a cup of tea, but the women say they are nearly at lunch-time and they have certain things they must do before then.

Gina asks him to walk with her to the gates of Diamond Hall so that she can explain everything that's been said and organised. He wants Laurie there too. The other women say goodbye to Elissa as though she really counts as someone. He appreciates this and tells them so. They take their leave in a giddy way. Ed feels a flush of heat across his cheeks.

As they walk away from the house, Gina explains about regular respite care for both him and his sister. There will be the opportunity for her to attend a facility away from Diamond Hall, where specialist services exist. He tells her he will think about it, but Laurie wants to know more. She and Gina discuss a lot of things.

Ed's attention drifts. He can't help noticing the fading beauty of the trees in the sea-wood and the way the sky billows blue and cheerful above them. There's a feeling of lightness in his body. Like the weight he's carried around for so many years is finally starting to shrink. He's passed the initial test: he's left his sister in the care of someone else for the first time since his father died. Laurie's kissed him, and she's on his side. There's a confusing aliveness sweeping through him and the only way to handle it is to let it come.

When they reach the gates, Gina holds out her hand and thanks him for the support he's given his sister and how welcoming he's been to her and the other health care workers. He's about to tell her there's no need to thank him when he catches the look on Laurie's face. She's staring over his shoulder, at the street beyond. When he turns, there is the man named Pete O'Connor. He's stomping towards them, giving Ed a look that he remembers seeing, once before.

Laurie

'Oh, Christ.' Gina holds up her hands. She turns to Laurie. 'What's he doing here? He should be at work.'

Pete is acting as if he hasn't seen either of them. He stomps right up to Ed, so that their chests are almost touching. 'What are you doing near my wife, Diamond? If you've caused her any problems, you're dead.'

They are similar in height, and Ed isn't backing away. Laurie's not sure how to handle the situation. There have been many instances in her life when she's dealt with warring teens in the wrong way, and it's caused a bigger issue. Human behaviour doesn't follow rules or patterns, that's one thing she does know for sure. She makes a snap decision: she's going to use distraction.

'Pete, Gina's been helping with Ed's sister,' she says.

'What fucking sister?'

That he has heard her is enough. The brittle moment has softened.

Gina tugs at Pete's arm. 'The sister you didn't think Ed had. Turns out she does exist. She's been living at Diamond Hall all this time.'

'Bollocks.'

'No, sweet, it's not.' Gina manages to move him away from Ed, who's not giving any ground. 'And what're you doing here, anyway? What's happened at work?'

'Nothing's happened at work. Someone said they'd seen you

going into the Diamond place this morning. I laughed at first, but they insisted. I told my boss there was a personal emergency and he let me pop out.' He glares at Ed. 'Look at the state of you, Diamond. I don't want our Gina anywhere near you.'

Laurie looks at Ed's face. His gaze has dropped, and his shoulders are following. She wants to tell him to fight back, to knock the hot air and bluster out of Pete O'Connor once and for all. Then she's transported to that day on the promenade, Pete kicking and Ed on the floor. She steps towards him and slides her arms around his waist.

'Ignore that idiot,' she whispers. 'Let's go back to the house.' She turns to Gina. 'Thanks for everything you're doing. It's really appreciated. I'll be in touch.'

'Over my dead body,' she hears Pete shouting as they walk away. 'I haven't forgotten what you lot did to Marcus Butcher. None of us will forget. I'm getting social services on to you, so watch out.'

Ed says nothing as Laurie leads him back up the drive of Diamond Hall. She wonders whether she should have locked the gates. Though she's been trying to wean him off locking himself away, Pete's outburst must have shaken him. She's feeling a bit unsettled herself. To have that amount of hatred levelled against you is unnerving. No wonder Ed spends his time looking over his shoulder and worrying.

'What a wimp Pete O'Connor is,' she says, thinking she might try and make light of a situation that feels anything but. Ed doesn't respond. 'His face when he realised there absolutely was a sister. Hilarious.'

Ed pulls himself out of her grasp. 'This is my life we're talking about. Not some pageant. You don't understand any more than the others, do you? There isn't *a* sister. It's *my* sister, my only family. This is all too much for me, sorry.' He storms off, heading towards the house. Laurie wants to give him space in which to be angry with her and the rest of the world, but he's had so much of that in his life already. If she takes even one step away, she can see him shutting down for ever. He hasn't got far. If she runs, she can catch him before he goes back into the house and locks her out of his world.

'Ed. Ed Diamond,' she calls as she hurries towards him again. 'Don't be such a sulky little shit. You're a grown man. Stand still and listen to me.'

He's arrived at the porch and has his hand on the door. Then he stops and turns to face her; he is smiling. 'Don't be too free with your compliments, will you. I wouldn't want to get above myself. Anyhow, are you coming in or not?' He holds open the door and Laurie steps inside, matching his grin as she passes.

'This is a real improvement,' she says.

He tilts his head towards her. 'What is?'

'You, standing up for yourself.'

'I'm not sure I did that.'

Laurie follows him into the kitchen. He holds up the kettle.

'Yes, please,' she says. 'And I don't mean thumping Pete, or anything. What I mean is, you handled a nasty situation, then got back to being yourself. It can take some people years of practice to do that.'

'Explain what you mean.' He lights the gas under the kettle and turns to face her. 'Are you talking about yourself?'

Laurie nods. 'I guess so. That struggle you've just faced, keeping yourself looking cool on the surface when your legs are trembling so much you wonder how you're still standing, I had a real problem with it.'

She tells him about the anxiety she felt when she first started working at the PRU, about children who'd had every shred of morality knocked out of them, so they faced the world without fear of anyone or anything.

There were days when the thought of trying to contain a child who was determined to challenge every moment was too much to bear, and she'd stopped at the front door of the building and tried to phone her boss with excuses about why she wasn't coming in.

She always did go in though, in the end. Eventually she got better at not absorbing the constant stream of hatred spewing from damaged children.

'So, you're talking about when your body panics and you can't control it,' he says. 'When you can't get any breath, and your thinking blurs and your guts threaten to explode.'

Laurie snorts softly. 'That, exactly. It's anxiety and it's toxic.'

'I thought it was just me, being weak.' His voice trembles as he turns back to his tea making. 'Stupid, aren't I?'

Lately, she's been thinking that he seems to cope remarkably well for someone who's been shut away from the world for so long. Now, she realises what the gaps in his understanding might mean. She slips her arms around his waist and leans against his back. He smells of laundry powder and softly scented soap, and she can feel his shoulder blades against her cheek.

'You're far from stupid. I'd say you were very intelligent, actually. The way you've kept yourself together all these years. I would have crumbled. I could hardly cope with the way my mother treated me, and that was just one person. But you don't have to put up with it any longer.' She slides herself underneath his arms so that she's facing him. 'You've got me, now.'

They rest against each other for a moment, and Laurie wonders what he's thinking. This is a guy who's had hardly any physical contact in his life. How will their relationship develop?

'Can I ask you a question?' Ed cuts across her thoughts.

She leans away from him and looks up at his face. 'Course.'

'What happens to me when you do go back to London?'

It's a question she can't answer. She's spent the past few days thinking about driving away from Chapel Field and back to her other life. She never gets any further than waving goodbye at the gates of Diamond Hall.

'That's something we need to talk about.' It's all she can think of to say.

He steps away from her and lifts one of the mugs of tea from the countertop, mumbling something about checking in on Elissa. Laurie watches him go. He must take the lead on any decisions about what happens between them; she can adapt. London feels a million miles away at the moment. Maybe she won't ever go back.

While Ed looks in on his sister, Laurie takes her tea to the sofa and pulls her phone from the pocket of her jeans. She's tucked the business card he gave her into the back of the case. It has the email address of the art dealership which bought Richard Diamond's paintings. She types it into the message box of her own account, then attaches the photo she took of his last canvas. When Ed comes back, she'll ask him to add a few words of greeting, then send the email out and see what happens. He has a studio of his own in one of the upstairs rooms; he's told her that much, but she's never seen any of his own work. His father's painting is deeply affecting but she's not sure she likes it, so would be happy to get rid of it and return any profits where they're owed.

Why her mother had the painting is a mystery, but she's sure if she asks Gina's nan about it there'll be some clue. Perhaps Alina Diamond gave it to her mother in a gesture of friendship. They were friends, that much is clear, though Janet Helm had never once mentioned it. Laurie had to take some of the blame for that; she and her mother hardly spoke.

'She's taken herself to the toilet and got her nightdress back on,' Ed says as he appears again. 'I think the visit tired her out. She seems happy, though. She's in bed, flicking through one of the books I read to her.' Laurie pats the sofa, and he comes to sit beside her. 'Sorry I put you on the spot, before.'

'Don't worry about it,' she says, with a shake of her head.

Ed lets out a long sigh and runs both hands over the back of his neck. 'You leaving isn't my main worry. It's what Pete O'Connor said that's bothering me the most. Well, the two things he said, actually.'

'The threat of social services?'

'Yes. What did he mean exactly?'

Laurie must be careful of giving the wrong advice. That Ed has put his sister at risk by keeping her hidden away she knows only too well. If Gina and her colleagues found nothing worth raising, he's probably safe, though she can't be certain.

'People do get in touch with what Pete called "social services" if they think someone is at risk and it's being kept hidden. It's usually to do with child protection, but not always.' She takes Ed's hand. 'It's also something I've heard used as a threat, not by anyone with intelligence, though. The services in question can usually tell the difference.'

Ed lays his other hand over hers. 'I know I've done the wrong thing as far as Elissa is concerned, but I've always had her well-being uppermost in my mind. Gina and the other ladies didn't seem worried.'

'Exactly. Pete's full of crap, but he always has been. How he landed Gina is beyond me.'

Her comment makes Ed laugh. 'He's got it in for me though, hasn't he? I'm pretty sure I heard him blaming me for what happened to that Marcus Butcher kid.'

'He was angry, but a lot of people haven't forgotten your dad banging on the hearse that day. Sorry, but there it is.'

'If we're using anger as an excuse, my dad was angry, too.'

Ed spits out the words with a force that makes Laurie wonder if she's said too much. 'When he saw what your friends had done to my face, I thought he was going to kill someone right there and then. There's always been a niggle. Lodged in the back of my mind, but it's there. Did he have something to do with Marcus Butcher's death?'

An awkward moment unravels between them. Things that happened so long ago have no business flaring up in the present moment, threatening to take away its purity.

'Let's not go there, Ed,' she says. 'Whether he did or didn't, we can't make any changes to what happened back then. I can only tell you again, I want to be with you.' She pauses. 'The best way to leave the past behind is to get away from Chapel Field. Come to London with me when I go back. Bring your sister, too. You can make a different life for yourself, and I'll help you to do it.'

Ed

Now that Laurie's gone, the full weight of the day's events hits Ed as hard as if he were being kicked in the face by Pete O'Connor all over again. Elissa is sleeping, so he's covered her with an eiderdown and left her to it. Their evening ritual usually includes reading and some television, hot drinks, and toast. Missing out on it has left him feeling lonelier than he has for a long time. Having Laurie in his life is making things complicated, and now she's asked him to go to London with her, and he doesn't think she means for a short visit. He would have to sell Diamond Hall. Impossible.

He is standing at the back door of the house, looking at the sky above the wood. The light is fading, amber to dark blue right above him and the moon is a vivid disc of white. It means the tides will be at their highest; and he can taste the sea. This is his reality. Not kisses and warm hugs and private jokes. If he hasn't been happy in his life, he's at least been at peace. Now it feels like every one of his ideas, all his emotions have been dumped in the middle of the sea for gulls and fishes to squabble over.

Laurie has pushed him into selling her mother's painting. If she'd wanted to do him a favour, she could have given it back. That way he'd have at least one thing to remind him of his father. The money would come in handy, but selling something given as a gift doesn't sit right with him. She's intent on finding out how her mother came to have it. She'd even asked if he wanted to meet Gina O'Connor's grandmother. He said no to that straight away. Shaking up his ideas of Diamond family life before he was born isn't something he wants to do.

He closes the door behind him and walks past the scruffy patch of kitchen-garden to the edge of the wood. The fence on the boundary of the Diamond Hall land is just visible from here. It cost him a ridiculous amount of money to have it put up, but it represents safety. Laurie is stripping that away from him. He feels something for her, and if he never saw her again, he would struggle. She's stirred him up, that's for sure. Pete O'Connor and all the other heckling, ignorant villagers have been on the periphery of Ed's life for a long time. It's been difficult, but predictable. Laurie's return has made everyone uneasy, like she's picked the scab from a wound that won't heal, and now it's open and oozing again. When he thinks about the way she slips her arms around him and makes him feel like the most important person in the world, his knees nearly give way: this is what she does to him.

Chapter 20

September 2018

Laurie

It's one of those mornings that come in early September, when summer makes a brief return, with its heat and its bright sky. There's a subtle scent of fading in the air, of turned earth and burned wood. Laurie would love to share it with Ed. Instead, she's on the street outside her mother's house waiting for Gina to pick her up. They are off to visit Olivia.

When no car arrives, Laurie starts to wonder if she's got the wrong day. Or perhaps Gina has forgotten their arrangement. Either way, Laurie needs this visit: she has questions.

The peaceful atmosphere is suddenly disturbed by a terrific and continuous roar. A bright blue car zooms up to where she's waiting. In the front passenger seat is Gina, and the driver is a young man Laurie doesn't recognise.

'Morning,' Gina calls as she winds down her window. 'We're getting the royal treatment: Reece is taking us.'

The young man cranes to look and waves a hand. He is dark-haired and thickset and is the image of Pete. Laurie smiles a hello and pulls open the nearside back door. She's hardly settled when Reece revs the engine again and they are away.

Gina starts to chatter about her son being only seventeen yet passing his driving test, about him needing all the practice he can get and about the car his father has purchased for him. This car. It's done a lot of miles, apparently, but was a bargain because it'd been looked after. Pete did work as a mechanic, once, when they'd been in their teens, so Laurie should trust his judgement; she feels anything but safe with his son. They speed along the promenade in a way that makes her want to ask him if he will stop and let her walk instead. She remembers how it had been to drive with Marcus Butcher when he was the same age. A healthy dose of fear was absent from his technique, too.

When they arrive at Abbot's View, Laurie's stomach is squeezing at her breakfast and threatening to make it reappear. She scrambles from the back seat and is grateful to feel the tarmac of the car park beneath her feet. Some deep breaths steady her nerves.

Gina stays in the car with her son for a few moments, then climbs out and bangs a hand on the roof as he gets ready to shoot away.

'Sorry about that,' she says as he pulls out of the gates. 'We can get the bus back if you like.'

'No, it's fine.' Laurie stretches her eyes. 'I like to live dangerously.'

Gina laughs at that, and links arms as they make their way into the building.

Olivia is in one of the lounges, practising with her walking frame. When she sees them, she drops herself into a red velour armchair and lets out a long sigh.

'You pair are a sight for sore eyes,' she says. 'They've been making me do circuits of the room with this damn thing. I'm to try outside on my own next.' She rolls her eyes. 'As if.'

'That's brilliant, Nan.' Gina kisses the top of her head.

'I see you've brought Janet again.' Olivia eyes Laurie.

'Not Janet, Nan, Laurie.'

'Yes. Sorry.' She peers at Laurie. 'Not that you look anything like your mother. I just got the name wrong. Take after your dad, do you?'

Laurie can only smile at this comment. She's never had the slightest idea who her father was. On her birth certificate it simply says *father unknown*; a Janet Helm special.

'Gina looks just like her mum,' Olivia is saying. 'Not that our Alison was much of one. I brought our Gina up, you know. She's been more of a daughter than bloody Alison's been, if you'll pardon my French.' She winks. 'Fetch us a cuppa, love.'

Olivia has the ability to make Laurie feel like a shy schoolgirl standing in front of a probing teacher. When she moves to fetch the tea, Gina jumps in and says she'll do it.

'I've brought some photos to show you,' Laurie says as she sits down.

'Oh, yes?'

'Gina and I have been up to Diamond Hall this week, talking to Ed. He gave me these to show you.' She pulls the photographs from the pocket of her handbag. 'I reckon that's you. Right there.' The wedding photograph is on the top of the pile. Laurie points to the youngish woman Gina identified as her nan. Olivia holds it as close to her face as she can.

'So it is. Blimey. I'd forgotten how good-looking Ritchie Diamond was, even with his funny eye. A right ladies' man. Though he scared the life out of me.' She turns the photo towards the light. 'And that's our Emily, right next to me, there.'

'Your sister? I think Gina mentioned her. Where is she now?'

Olivia hands the photograph back. 'She's in a little bungalow on the other end of the island. I don't see her much, but we keep in touch with cards and the like. Her husband died very young. Really sad, it was. See she's standing with that Jen in the photo. I wasn't keen on her.'

'Which one's Jen?'

Olivia snorts loudly. 'Her that's letting it all hang out.' She takes the photo again. 'Yes, that's her. Look at her dress. You're not supposed to outshine a bride, are you?'

Laurie hasn't been to a wedding, so she wouldn't know. When she says this, Olivia tilts her head quizzically.

'Not been to a wedding? Don't be daft.'

'I haven't, really,' says Laurie.

'Haven't what?' Gina is back with a tray of tea and biscuits. She puts it down on a small side-table and kneels in front of Olivia. 'What haven't you done?'

Olivia tuts. 'This one says she hasn't been to a wedding.' She looks at Laurie. 'Don't your friends believe in getting married?'

Laurie shrugs and picks up a cup and saucer from the tray. 'Sugar?'

They settle into a familiar pattern of chat and laughter. Olivia entertains them with tales of who's chasing after whom amongst the ranks of the support workers, while Gina tries to put faces to names. When she does, the two of them laugh even louder. Their closeness suddenly feels excluding, and Laurie wonders if she should leave them to it. She flicks through the photographs again and thinks about her mother; the one she never sat with and giggled over shared confidences. She was an attractive woman, there's no denying it. Though it's not how Laurie remembers her. Would she have caught the eye of Richard Diamond? Is that why she had one of his paintings in her possession? The idea feels repulsive. Her mother and Ed's father having a fling? She shudders.

'Are you okay, Laurie?' Gina has tuned in to her discomfort.

She turns to Olivia. 'Poor girl had to suffer our Reece's driving this morning. He might have passed his test, Nan, but I wouldn't call him competent. Yet.'

Olivia dunks a biscuit in her tea. 'I'd love to see him. Can you get him to pop in sometime. It's ages since we've had a good chin-wag. He reminds me so much of our Bob.'

Who? Laurie mouths.

Gina huffs and folds her arms. 'She's on about *Darling Robert*. Her brother, who left the family when he was still a young man. He can do no wrong.' She shrugs. 'Course he can't, when he's not here. It's not him looking after Nan in her old age, is it? FaceTiming hardly counts.'

'I am here, you know,' Olivia hisses. 'Talk about me later.' She reaches for the photo again. 'Bob didn't come to the wedding, did he? Not a friend of the Diamonds. But he was at that God-awful party.' Her expression darkens. 'When Alina died. Poor, poor girl.'

They sit together in silence. Laurie wants to ask about Alina, but she can see Olivia is upset. What would Ed think about her trying to prise information about his mother from this elderly lady? She knows exactly what he would think.

'Are we going for a stroll around the gardens today?' she asks instead, and Olivia brightens instantly.

'If you girls are up to it,' she says.

Gina jumps up from her seat. 'Course we are. Will you be needing your walker?' When Olivia shakes her head, she adds, 'Great stuff. Let's find you a jacket.'

In the furthest reaches of Abbot's View garden is an enormous horse chestnut tree. The five-fingered leaves are just starting to change colour and crisp at their edges. One or two, a dying ochre colour now, have fallen onto the lawn, along with their exploded, prickly fruits. Laurie picks up one of the glossy brown nuts and shows it to Olivia, who is clinging on to Gina's arm and tilting her face towards the sun.

'When we were kids, we'd have fought you for that beauty.' Olivia laughs. 'Not the same today, is it. They have mobile phones and cars and no fun at all. We had to make our own entertainment.'

Gina raises her eyebrows. 'Don't start with that again, Nan. Every generation has its plusses and minuses. My boys have had to put up with a lot that never crossed your minds, way back when.'

'Like what,' Olivia huffs. 'You spoil them three. I've said it before, and I'll say it again.' There is no malice in her tone, and Laurie smiles.

'I wish I had family,' she says, 'to always be moaning at me and keeping me in line. I feel like I've never had any.' She hesitates, then adds, 'I don't have any.'

They sit together on Olivia's favourite bench, while she tells them about her own family, stretching as far back as she can remember. Gina holds her hand and pats it from time to time, and Laurie gazes out across the garden and tries to clear her mind of anything but the beauty of the morning. Her thoughts drift for a while, then she's jolted back to reality by Olivia's shrill voice saying her name.

'Laurie? Are you listening? I asked what happened to your dad.'

Gina is trying to shush her, but Olivia is batting her away.

'Oh, sorry.' Laurie turns to face her. 'I think I dozed off there for a moment. I never knew my dad. Mum never told me anything about him or who he was. I sometimes wonder if she knew.'

'She knew,' Olivia mutters.

Gina holds up her hand. 'Stop. You're just being nosy now, Nan. This is what my mum objects to.'

'Among other things.' Olivia's tiny body has become tense and she's trying to get herself up from the bench. 'Past is best left where it was, if you ask me.'

'It's you that loves talking about it,' Gina spits out her words, then explodes with laughter. 'You daft mare. Every time we talk about the bloody old days, we end up falling out.' She grins at Olivia. 'Don't we?'

'We do.' Olivia shivers, and Gina starts to fuss over getting her back inside. Laurie walks behind them, feeling excluded again. It's not often she thinks about the father who never existed, yet he's come up for a second time. She wants to ask Olivia if she knows anything about him, but the moment has passed.

Now, she has a desperate need to see Ed again. In her London life, she has colleagues and friends but no one just for herself, no one she wants to spend the ends of days with, sitting together and sharing news and laughing at the world outside their private bubble. It's not something she's ever wanted before, or needed. The thought surprises her.

Back inside the building, a savoury smell is wafting along the corridors. There is the sound of metallic baking dishes and cutlery clanging together.

Laurie has drunk far too many cups of tea this morning and will have to use the toilet before she can even contemplate going back in the car with Reece. They get Olivia settled in the drawing room, and pull a blanket over her legs.

'Lunch smells good, Nana,' Gina says. 'Do they let guests stay?'

Olivia looks confused. 'No?'

'I was kidding.' She turns to Laurie. 'Ready?'

'Can I use the loo first? Do you think they'd mind?'

Olivia points a finger upwards. Gina explains that they keep the downstairs facilities for the older residents, and encourage more mobile visitors to use those on the first floor. Laurie nods and is about to set off towards the stairs when Olivia calls after her.

'Mind how you go, lass, on them stairs. You don't want to fall, like poor bloody Alina Diamond.'

June 1979
Richard Diamond

Richard Diamond frowned through the window at the perfect square of pastel-blue sky, then ran a hand over his face. It smelled of baby-powder and turps. He needed to get this painting finished but he could hear Janet and Jen bickering again, out in the yard. Closing the window would help, but he liked to keep track of what was going on, though they made him feel like the prize in some invisible but infinitely tangible tug-o-war. He could probably do with a break anyway. He was missing the babies.

Downstairs, he rinsed his hands in the kitchen sink then pushed his way through the half-open back door and into the heat of the day. Janet was hanging nappies along the length of plastic rope he'd rigged up in an area of the garden that wasn't too shaded. He let his gaze linger on the place where her skirt had ridden up as she stretched, then went over to the twin-pram. Eduardo was sitting up, supported by a pillow and strapped in with a soft leather harness, but Elissa laid flat and still, shaded by a lacy white canopy. Both babies smiled as he leaned towards them.

'She's not right, that little girl,' hissed Jen from where she sat, cigarette in one hand, coffee mug in the other. 'I keep saying it, and every time, I'm shouted down.'

Janet picked up the empty washing basket and turned to face them. 'You are not shouted down,' she snapped. 'The babies are only six months old. Plenty of time for them to develop their own traits.'

'And you'd know this because–'

'Meaning?'

'You've had babies, have you?' Jen blew a smoke ring into the morning sunshine. 'Miss Janet *virginal* Helm.'

'You're a right one–' Janet stormed towards the outhouse door and yanked it open. 'Are you going to let her speak to me like that, Ritch?' She flung the basket inside and slammed the door again. 'I can always leave the two of you to flounder on your own.'

Richard held up both hands, a palm facing each woman. 'Stop. The pair of you. I'm well aware Elissa isn't as she should be. And I'm grateful to both of you for sticking by me.' Under his breath, he added, 'Unlike others I could mention.' He felt Jen slide an arm around his waist. He let her in, smelling the aura of cigarettes and musky perfume that always surrounded her. 'If you remember, the health visitor told us the babies had a traumatic birth and we should expect some complications.' His voice trembled. This wasn't something he wanted to be reminded of: Alina kept alive long enough for the babies to be delivered; the sickening shock when she'd passed, holding his hand.

'Exactly.' Janet flashed a look at Jen. 'Now, I'm going to make these two a bottle before I go. Any objections?'

'None whatsoever.' Jen stubbed out her cigarette with the toe of her sandal. 'Where're you off to, anyway?'

'Just meeting a friend. Not that it's any of your business.'

Richard let out an exaggerated sigh. These women had helped him so much since Alina died, he couldn't be angry at them. For the first weeks after, he could hardly even look at the twins, let alone care for them. Between Janet and Jen, his new family had been given everything they needed, but the women were never kind to each other.

His wife hadn't had much of a bond with Jen, but she and Janet had been inseparable since the wedding. The wedding. Had it really only been a year ago since he'd come back to Diamond Hall? He'd lived a whole lifetime in those twelve months, and every one of his plans had been transformed. His father hadn't lived for long in the nursing home. Though he hadn't been close to Lenny in any real sense of the word, grieving for a parent held a particular kind of agony. Nothing like losing a wife, but painful just the same.

The tantalising picture he'd painted for himself of a life with Alina and the twins, money flowing in from his art and adoration tracking him as he moved amongst the villagers, it was gone. What the dregs looked like was anyone's guess; what they felt like was survival.

He freed himself from Jen's embrace and walked over to the pram. Eddie lifted his arms, wanting to be picked up, while Elissa just smiled. Once he'd checked each baby's nappy, sliding two fingers in between the towelling and rubber pants, he clicked off the brake and began to wheel them backwards and forwards over the hard-baked mud.

'She's seeing someone, you know.' Jen tilted her head in the direction of the kitchen. 'What've you got to say about that?'

'Enough!' Richard rounded on her as Eddie began to scream. 'Look what's happened now.' He unclipped the baby harness and lifted his son from the pram, jiggling and shushing. 'I've told you before, Jen. We're all free-agents. I need to focus on my children, and you two–'

'Us two what?' Janet came out from the kitchen carrying a plastic jug of water with bottles of baby-feed bobbing about on the surface. A pair of bibs hung over her shoulder, one pink and one blue.

'Jen was just saying how much you two love a good night out. I think you should get one organised. Go over to town and have a blow-out, this weekend. You deserve it. Between looking after me and your own work, you never have any fun.'

'You trying to get rid of us?' Jen peered at him, holding out her arms for Eddie. She sat down on one of the kitchen chairs they'd dragged outside, and perched him on her knee, stroking his dark, silky hair. Janet held a bottle to her cheek for a moment, then passed it over.

'Ritch is right, Jen. We do need to get our lives back. Why don't we go over to the labour club on Saturday night? It'd be a giggle.'

'You can go.' Jen let Eddie lean back against her arm and held the teat of the bottle to his lips. He latched on immediately. 'I'll be here, helping with these cutey-pies.' She drew out these last words in such a comic way, Ritchie couldn't help but laugh. This wasn't like Jen at all; the fussing over his babies was mainly done by Janet.

'Go,' he said. 'I can cope by myself; you know I can.'

Janet bunched up her blonde hair and leaned over the pram to lift Elissa. Her skirt slid upwards over her thighs. He couldn't tear his eyes away. 'Leave her, Janet. Ed feeds better if he's not distracted. I'll walk you down to the end of the drive then I'll be back to feed Ellie.'

Jen glowered at them both but said nothing.

'I'll just get my bag.' Janet flicked back her hair and skipped into the house.

Richard winked at Jen. 'Won't be long.'

As they walked, Janet slipped her arm through his and chattered about how he should cut back the thickly tangled trees and plant some borders. Roses, perhaps. Or some of that fancy lavender so the children could pick it and sniff it when they were toddling.

'Your children deserve a nice life,' she said, suddenly wistful.

'And that's what they will have. You will be part of it, if I have my way.'

Janet smiled sadly. 'Being a mother isn't something I'd be good at. I didn't have the best of role-models. My gran brought me up. If you can call it that. She had a hard edge to her, and I don't think she liked me much. Children need kindness as well as firm boundaries, don't they?'

'They do.' He liked this woman. While she could be caustic in her treatment of Jen and anyone else she didn't agree with, there was a gentle streak in her that sent his blood zinging to certain areas of his body. He could do with some softness in his life. It hadn't taken long for the hard faces of Chapel Field to be turned on him once again. He knew exactly what they were saying. That he'd somehow been responsible for Alina's death, that he might even have pushed her down the stairs. Which was ridiculous since he was nowhere near at the time. He'd explained this to the police when they'd performed a perfunctory investigation in the days after that awful party.

'So, I'll see you tomorrow evening, shall I?' Janet was asking. 'Rikki? Will you be all right until then?'

All right? How did that feel? The hollow pull of grief was shrinking from his body, it was true. But something more embarrassing was replacing it. Desire. For Janet Helm.

'You know fine well I'll be all right.' His smile dropped. 'It's what goes on out here that bothers me more.' He gestured towards the street beyond the gates of the house. 'They've started crossing the road to avoid me. Just like before.'

'It'll settle down,' Janet replied. 'They'll find someone else to gossip about soon enough. Me, probably. You know what they're like.'

He understood perfectly well what *they* were like. Their reasons? He had no idea. When he'd left Chapel Field, at nineteen years of age, hunched by the weight of other people's misunderstanding, he'd promised himself he wouldn't return. His mother had never forgiven him for that, and his father had died in a nursing home, hardly remembering he was a Diamond at all. They were ordinary people, with ordinary problems. He couldn't begin to understand why they attracted so much hatred, but he knew one thing: what they gave out, he could easily return, in spades.

'Why you, Janet? Why would they gossip about you? Salt of the village, aren't you?' He lifted a hand to her cheek and tucked some of her hair behind her ear. When her eyes locked with his, he wanted to kiss her. She moved away quickly.

'Twenty-odd and still not married. They hate it.'

He grabbed her wrist. 'Not their business, is it?' Before he could stop himself, he'd planted a kiss on the soft skin of her palm.

For a moment, she didn't react. Then she pulled her hand from his grasp and stepped back. 'I've got to go,' she muttered. 'I'll see you Saturday.'

He watched her walk away, watched the blonde hair swing at her waist, and stared at the bare legs between her tiny skirt and flat shoes. Then he turned and stomped back up the drive to Diamond Hall, his need pulsing through every part of his body.

Neither Jen nor the babies were in the front yard when he reached the house. The pram was empty. He rushed through the porch and into the hallway. The low hum of her voice was coming from the lounge.

'*Shhh,*' she mouthed as he crashed through the doorway. She was leaning over Elissa's carrycot and gently tucking a knitted blanket. 'They've both been a dream. A few guzzles of milk each and they were spark out. It's the fresh air.' She made a gesture that reminded him of praying, then pointed towards the hallway. 'Let's go.'

Richard took her hand and dragged her away from the lounge. She shuffled along behind him in her clunky sandals. Once he'd closed the door, he swung her around to face him.

'I want you,' he murmured, pressing her against the wall with the full length of his body. He lifted her dress, and she slid her arms around his neck and smiled.

'Have me, then,' she whispered.

Chapter 21

September 2018

Laurie

It's a strange feeling, having Ed and Elissa in her car. Laurie keeps catching glimpses of them in her rear-view mirror. Ed is smiling through gritted teeth and Elissa is simply smiling.

'Are you two okay?' she calls as she drives across the jarring surface of the road bridge. Ed tells her they are. He adds nothing else. The care-centre, where they've spent most of the day, has provided a canvas wheelchair, a commode and some special carpet slippers, all for the exclusive use of his sister. None of which he is happy about.

'They were really nice, the staff at the centre. Weren't they?' Laurie tries again to engage Ed. No answer comes. She sighs. The idea of his sister spending one day every week at the place has got him rattled. He doesn't need any respite from her, he says, and he made the same point over and over as they'd been shown round. He hadn't been impressed with the way Elissa fitted in perfectly, locking her eyes on some of the other residents, rather than on him.

'What do you fancy for tea? I'll cook, if you like.' Laurie hasn't offered this before, but she's trying anything to hook him.

'Stop,' he hisses at last. 'Just stop, will you. I don't want to talk.'

They drive the rest of the way in silence. When she swings the car through the open gates of Diamond Hall, Laurie suddenly gets a sense of how it must feel to carry the weight of what Ed has on his shoulders. He's lived in the gloom of this place for almost forty years with no one to share his burden. He must feel the shadow of his mother's death in every dark corner and half-whispered story. There are so many things she wants to ask him, though each will feel like a fish-hook caught under the skin: painful whichever way it's tugged.

She parks the car as close to the house as she can.

'I'll help you get Elissa settled then I'll go,' she says as she holds open the rear door.

Ed swings his long legs out first then ducks and steps into the afternoon shadows. 'Thanks,' he breathes. 'And I'm sorry.'

'For what?'

'For being so moody. It's terror, actually. Sheer terror.'

Laurie runs a hand along his arm. 'I get that. Your fears, I mean.' They both help Elissa from the car. 'But you're doing exactly the right thing for this one, Ed. You really are.'

'Sometimes I worry about my decisions, that's all.' He takes Elissa's arm and leads her to the porch. She's a little unsteady on her feet today, and Laurie wonders why she hasn't noticed this before. When she mentions it to Ed, he explains how it's his sister's way of showing she's tired. This is how much he's in-tune with her needs.

'Cup of tea and toast in bed, then?' Laurie says, then in answer to Ed's wry smile she adds, 'Elissa, not you.'

'I was thinking more of *us*.' He grins, and she feels a flush of heat spread across her cheeks. 'Sorry, that was crass.'

'Crass or not, I like the sound of it.' She giggles. And there is some truth in what she's saying. There is also the smallest thread of doubt, a loop that's pulled its way out of the main fabric and threatens to spoil the whole piece. If her mother did have a fling with Richard Diamond, could Laurie have been the result?

While Ed gets his sister washed and settled in her bed, Laurie rummages around in the kitchen, lighting the grill on the cooker for toast and filling the kettle. Everything is clean and fully functional, though it all belongs to the world of the nineties.

If she can raise some money from the sale of her mother's painting, it will help towards some overdue modernisations on Diamond Hall. She now thinks Ed won't come with her to London, given his reaction when she'd mentioned it. Which is probably for the best.

If they do turn out to be related, she will support her new-found family in a sisterly way from the safety of 300 miles away. Being in the vicinity of Ed, with his darkly attractive looks and his naïve manner, is provoking what she thinks might be completely inappropriate responses. She wants to kiss him, over and over, and see where it leads.

Later, they sit together on the sofa and talk about Elissa's care plan. She will go into day-care for one day every week and specialist nurses will visit Diamond Hall on a fortnightly basis to check on her welfare. When Ed needs to shop or carry out other errands, he can request a visit from support workers for an agreed length of time.

'I really want this for her,' Ed says. He is gripping Laurie's hand and jiggling his knees. 'But it scares me. She can never tell me if I'm doing the right thing or if she's happy. I can usually guess, as you know, but what if I'm wrong?'

'I'd say you can read your sister like a book,' Laurie tells him.

She's aware that things are moving fast for him. They need to. Especially if people like Pete O'Connor are intent on bringing up old grudges without any hint of understanding what's happening in the here-and-now. She runs a hand across Ed's shoulders. There is a tautness to the muscle and bone there and she tries to rub it out a little. 'Don't worry so much. Go with your gut.'

'What does that mean?'

Laurie leans her head against his shoulder. 'It means trust your feelings rather than what people are telling you is the right thing. Did you see how Elissa reacted at the centre today?'

He nods.

'What is that telling you?'

'That she loved it.' He puts his face in his hands. 'Oh, what am I doing? Help me, Laurie. I really want a better life for Ellie as well as for me. Do you think it's possible?'

'It's more than possible,' Laurie says, jumping up from her seat. 'And it's going to start with me cooking you a proper meal. Then we'll talk about this art dealer's visit and what *you're* going to do with the money.'

Ed

While she stays with Elissa, Laurie's made him walk to the shop and buy a bottle of wine. It's not something he'd drink himself, but she says it will make an occasion of the cheese omelettes she's going to cook. He's not exactly sure what she means, but he knows one thing: if he doesn't act on his feelings for her soon, he's going to explode. Which cuts him down to the size of an adolescent schoolboy.

It's a quiet evening. There's a light breeze tinged with the tang of seaweed and bonfire smoke. Ed pulls his jacket around him and zips it up. Summer is definitely over.

He passes one or two villagers on his way along the main road. They don't speak, but they don't cross over to avoid him, either. He is ready with a smile if any catch his eye. None do. In the shop, there's only a very young girl behind the counter, though she serves him the wine, so she must be eighteen. She's pretty but wearing a lot of make-up. Her eyebrows seem to be painted on and when she taps at the screen of the till, he can't take his eyes off her long hot-pink nails. She even gives him a muttered *thank you*, and his immediate thought is that she doesn't know he's a Diamond. Or she's not a Chapel Field girl at all. Then he berates himself all the way back along the road.

Laurie would tell him to stop being so down on himself, and she is right. He's just a normal guy, walking to the shop on an early autumn evening, seeking out a bottle of wine to have with his meal. Then Pete O'Connor appears, striding towards him like he owns the world.

Ed puts his head down and his collar up. What had Laurie said? *Go with your gut.* His gut is screaming at him to get past this guy as quickly as possible, without any interaction; he's trying to listen to it. Then Pete starts pouring out his malice and Ed can't help but take notice.

There are accusations: Ed's a nutter, a bully, a danger to women; he needs to leave Pete's wife alone; he's tricked Laurie by some wicked means, using sex, he thinks he hears; he and his family are offcomers and always have been. And the strangest thing he flings, with his chest puffed out so it almost touches Ed's, is that Richard Diamond tampered with the brakes on Marcus Butcher's car and that's why he died.

When Pete has exhausted every possibility and seems to have used all the air in his lungs, he steps away and squints at Ed in a way that is very familiar. An edgy silence hangs between them. Ed wants to pull the bottle of wine from inside his jacket and wrap it around Pete's head. That's what his gut is telling him now.

He chooses not to listen, chooses instead to step past the other man and saunter along the street as though nothing from the last few minutes even happened. He's expecting a blow across his shoulders at the very least, but the only thing he gets is the word *dickhead*, hurled from the safety of ten metres.

All the way back to Diamond Hall, Ed argues with himself about how he should have handled Pete. In the moment when they'd been eye to eye, something had passed between them that couldn't be spoken. He scouts around in his brain for words that could be applied but can come up with nothing. Which seems strange when there are plenty of words to describe Pete, and he is sure Laurie will add a few more that he's never heard. Though it was a long time ago, Ed has never forgotten his father's dying claim that he'd somehow got rid of Marcus Butcher. Was he speaking the truth? And how would Pete O'Connor know, anyway? Ed can't let those thoughts cloud his vision of the future. It wouldn't change anything: the Diamonds were always to blame.

The house smells of fried onions and Ed's stomach makes a loud gurgle in response. Laurie is standing in front of the cooker, shaking his old flat pan. She tells him Elissa is fast asleep after sharing a picture book.

He must look a bit rattled because she straight away asks him what has happened. When he explains about Pete O'Connor, she only sighs, then says Ed needs to meet with him, face to face, and get to the bottom of their differences.

That makes a total of two people she wants Ed to meet that he'd rather not, though Laurie had been right about meeting the health workers, so she's probably right about this, too. He wants to tell her about his decision not to go to London, but it will have to be at another time, because she's sliding omelettes onto plates and asking him if he has any glasses. He doesn't.

Instead, they sip their wine from coffee mugs and clink them together in celebration. Of what, he isn't quite sure. He only knows that when they've eaten their meal, he's not giving her the chance to stand at the sink again. He doesn't want to waste a minute of Elissa's sleeping time.

When Laurie finally stands up to lift their plates from the table, they have chatted about so many things, Ed's head is thick with dates and times and names, so many names.

She's mentioned his mother without actually asking anything about her. He can't give information he hasn't got. Laurie is wearing a white blouse with tiny red flowers embroidered around the neckline and red buttons. More than anything, he wants to open those buttons. Her hair is knotted at the base of her neck, and he wants to pull it free. He hates himself for these feelings, but it doesn't stop him from sliding out of his seat and coming up behind her. He puts both hands on her waist and turns her to face him.

She reaches out at first, grasping his head and the back of his neck. When he thinks she's going to kiss him, she suddenly pulls away. Then there are excuses about having to get home and not feeling comfortable with his sister next door. Ed can do nothing more than agree with her and stand awkwardly until she's gone.

Chapter 22

September 2018

Laurie

W hen the art dealer arrives from his gallery, he and Laurie sit together in the sparsely furnished living room of her mother's house. He'd knocked on the front door, all sharp navy-blue suit and leather portfolio, and Laurie had let him in and tried to be welcoming; he'd refused her offer of coffee or anything else, and is now perched nervously, waiting for Ed to arrive, and sipping from a bottle of Evian. He looks no older than some of her pupils at the PRU.

In truth, she wonders if Ed will appear at all. It's the first trial day of respite care for Elissa, when a minibus will take her to the centre and deliver her back at teatime, and she knows he wasn't looking forward to it. Then there's the problem of her reaction when he'd tried to kiss her the other evening. She wanted him to, but she can't stop thinking about Richard Diamond and her mother.

There's a knock on the front door, and Ed is standing there. His hair is loose across his shoulders and he's wearing a shirt she's never seen before.

'Hi. I wasn't sure you were coming.' Laurie steps aside to let him in. When she looks up at him, he leans in for a kiss and she can't help but return the gesture.

'Yeah. Sorry. Watching the bus drive away with Ellie shook me up. I almost ran after it and dragged her back out again. Then I stood on the porch for ages, wondering what to do next. Stupid, aren't I.' He points in the direction of the lounge. 'Is he here yet?'

'He is.' Laurie leads him through. 'Dwane Hutt. This is Ed Diamond.'

The man jumps up from his seat and holds out his hand. 'You're an honoured client, you know.' Dwane giggles. 'I don't usually travel this far north.'

Laurie smiles at Ed's confusion.

'And it's my father you've been dealing with,' Dwane continues. 'He wasn't up to coming here himself. I'm quite enjoying the trip, actually. I'm staying at The Duke. Do you know it?'

Laurie steps in to cover for Ed. 'Yes, it's really nice. What do you think of the island?'

Dwane holds his hands to his heart. 'Love it. Living on an actual island. How cool is that.' He looks at Ed. 'I've read about the place in Richard Diamond's bio, but never thought for one minute I'd visit.'

'Dad had a bio? Who knew.'

Dwane whips a mobile phone from his pocket and starts scrolling through. After a few moments he holds the screen so Ed and Laurie can see it.

'There,' he says. 'I guess the photo's really old. How long is it since he passed?'

Laurie stares at the photograph of Richard Diamond. Her last memories of the guy are from the time when he gate-crashed Marcus Butcher's funeral; there is no sign of that mania

217

here. Richard is looking away from the camera, a slight smile across his lips and his hair cropped close to his head, with a longer fringe, a style she recognises from the archive of eighties pop-stars.

'It's more than twenty years,' Ed is saying. 'I'm not sure how old he was in that photo. Where did it come from?'

'I scanned it in, when all our artist's bios went digital. I think he must have sent the original when my dad first took him on. He's got quite a following, you know. Collectors adore his work.' He puts his phone away. 'And I'm a big fan, too.'

Laurie leads them up the stairs and into the room where she's stored the items of her mother's that were for keeping. The plan had been to take them back to London and resume her life with only these few things as a reminder of Chapel Field. How her plan will play out now, she has no idea.

When she kneels in front of the canvas and pulls back its coverings, Dwane Hutt gasps.

'Like it?' she asks.

'Like it? For goodness' sake, it's wonderful.' He steps towards her. 'May I?'

She and Ed move to the window of the room while Dwane clears a space around the canvas and spends ten minutes viewing it from all angles and running his hand gently over the surface texture. It is an arresting blend of colour and shape, and Laurie can imagine Richard Diamond in his studio, smudging and scraping paint, time and again, before he is happy with it. If he ever was. Perhaps he gave it to her mother because he didn't like it.

'May I take a few photographs?' Dwane is asking. 'It's just that there are some features on this piece I haven't seen before. I'm too excited to wait until I get it back to the gallery. I want Dad to see right now.' He looks at Ed. 'Sorry, I meant, *if* I can take it back to the gallery. I already have a reserve on it that I can offer you. Without anyone else seeing it.'

'Of what?' Ed is frowning his surprise.

'Twenty.'

'Twenty what?'

Laurie elbows him. 'Ed,' she hisses. 'Twenty thousand.'

Dwane's eyes flit between the two of them. 'Is that not enough? I have the resources to–'

'It's enough,' Ed stammers. 'Thank you.'

Dwane makes a beckoning motion with his hand. 'Look at this,' he says, pointing to a corner of the painting. 'It's a Richard Diamond signature with a difference. Give me your hand.'

Ed crouches and lets his fingertips be guided across the surface. Laurie wonders what on earth is going on. She's already stunned by the amount of money the canvas is worth. Why her mother had just stashed it is something she'll never understand.

'It's a bit like Braille,' Dwane is saying. 'There's the R, and the D. Do you feel that? And there's another letter, too. It's a J. With a heart around it. If he gifted this to your mother, Laurie, I'd say he had a very good reason for doing so.' He winks. 'This will bump up the price. You can be sure of that.'

While Dwane begins snapping photos with his mobile phone, Laurie walks back downstairs with Ed. Neither of them says anything. If Richard Diamond felt enough love for Janet Helm to gift her this painting, it's not hard to imagine what else might have happened between them. Though it spells the end of anything romantic between her and Ed, it would create a family for them both. It's not what Laurie wants. Her feelings for Ed are anything but platonic; she's starting to care deeply about him, and there's more to come.

'Do you really believe this thing about your mum and my dad?' Ed says as they sit down in the lounge. He takes her hand. 'People hate the Diamonds. They always have. Why would your mum risk having a fling with him? And it must have been after my mum died, anyway. They lived in Spain right up until me and Ellie were born, I think. Dad always wanted to go back.'

'I'm not sure what I believe.' Laurie sighs. 'We don't look anything alike. But I know my mother liked men. She was always bringing them back to the house. It was pretty awful.'

Ed leans forward and puts his head in his hands. Laurie wants to slide an arm around his shoulder and hug him, but she doesn't trust herself.

'Did she not tell you about your father?' he asks. 'Give him a name or bring him to life?'

'No. Never.'

Dwane comes down the stairs and clatters into the room. He talks to them about taking the painting in his van, and about writing cheques. Laurie tries to pay attention, but Ed sits in silence. There must be a way of finding out about the relationship between their parents, but she can't think while Dwane is chattering.

'I'll leave you alone then, if there's nothing else,' he says, finally. 'Shall I post the provenance out for you to sign, Mr Diamond? That's the usual arrangement, isn't it?'

Ed gets up and holds out his hand. They shake, then walk towards the hallway. Laurie follows them. While Dwane and Ed bring the painting carefully down the stairs, she opens the front door and the garden gate and waits for them on the street.

It's a blustery morning, sharp with the tang of the sea. If she does go back to London, she'll have to drop the village habit of knowing the times and heights of the tide. As it is, she's thinking that if she and Ed want to visit the beach this afternoon, they'll have to wait until at least three o'clock, or there'll be no shingle path to use.

Once Dwane drives away, Laurie walks towards the house again, expecting Ed to follow. He doesn't. Instead, he puts some distance between them and mutters something about needing to get back to Diamond Hall.

'Have a cup of tea at least,' she pleads. 'There are things we need to talk about. Not least, Pete O'Connor.'

He shakes his head and won't meet her gaze.

'Ed? What's wrong?'

He shrugs and turns away from her, pushes his hands into his pockets and lopes off down the street.

When she can't settle, Laurie decides to take the short walk to Gina and Pete's house. If he's there, she can confront him about his verbal attack on Ed. And if he's not, she can relay it to his wife. Either way, she could do with talking to someone, whether it's a rant or not. She swings her handbag over her shoulder, slips her feet into a pair of trainers and locks the front door behind her.

Gina is in the garden when she arrives, kneeling by a border of decaying marigolds, trowel in hand.

'Hi there, sweet,' she calls as Laurie pushes open the gate. 'I'm glad you're here. It gives me the perfect excuse to stop for a minute.' She gets to her feet, pushing against her back and groaning. 'It's called *nurses' back*. We all get it, in the end.'

'A bit like *teachers' shoulder*.' Laurie laughs, though she hasn't written on a whiteboard for many years. PRU pupils have rarely got that level of concentration. iPads are more their style.

'Oh, yes. And Pete's got *mechanics' knuckle* from his years on the tools.' Gina huffs. 'What are we like? None of us are anywhere near fifty yet.' She prises off her shoes on the corner of the doorstep, and leads Laurie into the house.

'All on your own?' she asks, cocking her head. 'No Pete?'

'No?' Gina peers at her. 'Why? What's he done now?'

Laurie wishes she'd had another reason for visiting Gina. The woman is always so pleasant and welcoming. Her husband is about to be shredded.

'He's had a bit of an altercation with Ed. Again.'

'You can't have a *bit* of an altercation, Laurie.' Gina pats the sofa. 'Sit down and tell me exactly what happened.'

The thing Gina objects to most, when Laurie's finished giving her the list of Pete's accusations, is that Ed is a danger to women.

'Where's he got that from?' She frowns then tries to rub it away. 'Honestly, Laurie. His reactions to Ed Diamond are unbelievable.' She lets out a bitter laugh. 'I blame the mother.'

'What do you mean?'

'Pete's mother. She's a bloody awful woman. We don't see her, and she's never met her grandchildren. Which is a blessing, in my opinion, after the way she messed with Pete's head. I'm pretty sure his hatred of the Diamonds comes directly from her. Tea?' She gets up and wanders towards the kitchen.

Laurie follows. 'Come on. You can't leave it like that. What's your theory?'

Gina fills the kettle and sets it to boil, then sits beside Laurie on one of the kitchen stools. 'Well,' she whispers. 'And you mustn't tell Ed or Pete any of this—'

Laurie holds a finger to her lips, while Gina shines a light into every dark corner of Pete's life before they met. Some of the story is very familiar: Laurie remembers the swaggering, sarcastic teen who'd relished the chance to wade in when Ed was attacked.

What she didn't know, until now, is that Pete's mother had been even less capable than her own, of living up to that title. She'd fed him every bit of her personal hatred of the Diamonds, until it was part of his own story.

'Why was *she* so down on the Diamonds?' Laurie is

fascinated and horrified in equal measure. 'Everyone seems to be taking their cue from everyone else but can never say what the real problem is.'

Gina is standing at the kitchen counter, stirring two mugs and lifting teabags into the sink. 'You said Pete called Ed an *offcomer*? That must have come from his mother. The chip on her shoulder was actually a log, if you get my meaning. It didn't help that she was Irish, so struggled to fit in here, anyway. *Small-town* mentality.' She passes Laurie her tea. 'You want a biscuit? I do.'

When they are settled at the kitchen table, Laurie starts to wonder if she's being fobbed off with regards to Pete's behaviour. He's an adult. While she can excuse his adolescent wish to show off in front of Marcus Butcher, those days are long gone. She turns to Gina. 'Whatever his mother told him about the Diamonds, Pete needs to back off from Ed. He's got enough going on in his life. And Ed can't be held responsible for whatever Richard did. It's not fair.'

'I agree with you, sweet. I really do.' Gina nibbles at her biscuit. 'But my Pete is a very insecure man, believe it or not. He puts on a tough-guy front, but deep down, he's terrified of me leaving him, or anything happening to the kids. His mother caused him to be like that. Bloody cow. And she convinced him the biggest threat to his safety was Richard and Ed Diamond. I'm glad she can't do any more damage to him. I keep her well away from my family.'

'Where is she now?' Laurie wants to change the subject, but she's enjoying the dirt being dished on someone else.

Gina puts down her tea and walks over to one of the kitchen cupboards.

'I have this,' she says as she rummages under cookery books and pulls out a container. When she brings it to the table, Laurie can see it's a metal box with a tight-fitting lid and covered in a painted floral design. 'It's where I keep all those important things that have no other place: addresses, old Christmas cards with people's names, orders of service from funerals–' She looks at Laurie. 'You know the kind of thing.'

'I do.'

She pulls out a photograph and slides it across the table. 'That's her. Immy O'Connor. There's the last address she gave me written on the back. Pete doesn't know I've got it. He wouldn't care, anyway. I thought I'd better keep it, for emergencies. You never know, do you?'

Laurie picks up the photo. It's one of those grainy, square types, with a wide white border. She brings it close to her face so she can see the woman and the baby she is holding.

'Is that Pete. In her arms, I mean?'

'Yes, it's Pete. Cute there, isn't he?'

'He is.' Something connects in Laurie's memory, like the opposite poles of a pair of magnets: she's seen this woman before. From her handbag, she pulls the bundle of photos from Ed's house, then flicks through them until she finds the one of Richard and Alina Diamond's wedding.

And there is Pete's mother. Standing a row behind the bride and groom, same sardonic smile and bright hair. Immy O'Connor, the woman Olivia had named as Jen, and arch-enemy of the Diamonds, was a guest at their wedding.

Ed

Ed is finding it hard to believe his father was having an affair with anyone, let alone Laurie's mother. Though he'd rarely talked about Alina, Richard Diamond holds a revered place in Ed's memory as a devoted husband and family man, as much as

224

a talented artist. And that's another joke. The way his father's last piece of work has been sold off without Ed having much of a chance to see it or think about it. When he'd sold the others over the years, there had been plenty of time to look at them and commit them to memory, and it had been his choice to sell them; they'd belonged to him. Somehow, he feels cheated. Of the painting, of his father and of having Laurie. He understands there are ways to find out if any blood relationship exists between them; he's read about DNA testing. What he doesn't want to do is leave any trace of himself that could be linked to the Castella family. It could leave Elissa vulnerable, Laurie, even. There are no guarantees, either, no certainties. Explaining his fears might be difficult, but he is going to try.

He needs to find some space between the thoughts buzzing around inside his head, trapped like wasps, and flinging themselves against the casing of his skull. The look in Laurie's eyes when he walked away just now, he'd hated it, but what could he do? When he gets back to Diamond Hall, he is going to search the place from top to bottom and find something that proves she's not his sister. That thought sends him running for cover.

Inside the house it is settled and quiet. Elissa hardly causes a noise or stir, but her absence is a tangible thing. It makes him want to weep.

He storms up the stairs, tripping twice over his feet, and pushes his way into one of the bedrooms. Though he's been through it many times in the past, he pulls open drawers and cupboards, boxes of books and old suitcases. The contents haven't changed. He checks his own bedroom, his studio, the tiny loft space and even the hidden places in the bathroom. Everything is as he knows it will be. Running Diamond Hall by himself for the past twenty years has left him with a detailed understanding of the place. Everything of significance is stored in the box he's already shown Laurie. Its contents won't give him what he wants. He charges downstairs and checks anyway.

When every piece of paper, every receipt and bill and certificate are spread across the kitchen table, Ed realises there is nothing more he can do. Neither he nor Laurie will ever be able to get past the fact that they could have shared Richard Diamond as their father.

There is something special about Laurie. He knew it when they'd first met, on that awful date-night, and he'd still felt it when they'd found each other again, just a few short weeks ago. She makes him laugh at himself without it hurting, and she's gentle in the way she treats the world, though she must be made of steel, to do the job she does. Then there's the physical attraction: could these feelings be simply because they're tied by blood? He's not convinced. There must be proof. When he looks again at everything that defines his world, sliding across the surface of the table, he knows there isn't. With his fist balled, he sweeps it all onto the floor and storms from the kitchen.

He's outside in an instant and running down the driveway of Diamond Hall. He wants Elissa. She's his stability, even though she can offer him no emotional support. So he's going to run along the promenade and across the bridge and into town, and he's going to be with her. The staff at the centre said he could come anytime, that it might be good for him to see what went on.

Without thinking too much about what he's doing, Ed jogs along the main road and down the slope that leads out of the village.

As soon as he reaches the promenade, there is the water. It is as high as it can be without overflowing the pavement. It's a sunny afternoon, bright and breezy and full of the smell of the tide. If any villagers notice him, he doesn't feel the impact, he just keeps running.

Memories of another day come flooding back. When he'd sprinted along the crowded promenade, searching for his father; when the glass-sided hearse had pulled up; when Richard Diamond had made a spectacle of himself to the point where Ed had wanted to knock him unconscious and carry him away.

There is a woman coming towards him, with four small yappy dogs and they're all barking and tangling themselves around their leads. He slows his pace, but the dogs don't quieten. There's not much traffic so he thinks about crossing over. He's aware of a car's roar, somewhere to his left. He hesitates. The dogs don't let up and now they're close enough that he can tell their snapping and snarling is directed at him. One breaks free. It follows him into the road. When he steps back onto the pavement again, the dog keeps going. Then a car appears, bright blue and in full throttle. The driver must have spotted the dog, because he brakes and swerves at the same time. Ed hears the shrieking of rubber against the road, and watches in total horror as the car catches a stone bench, flips in the air and nosedives straight into the water.

Everywhere is quiet for a moment. Then the barking starts up again, and the woman is screaming and pulling her phone from her pocket. From nowhere, people are running towards them, but Ed can only stare at the car, which seems to be caught on the mudflats underneath the tide, nose down and sinking. The part of his brain which usually urges caution, has retreated. He's left with a kind of numb reaction, and it forces him to take off his plimsolls and jump into the water.

At first, it isn't deep. He can feel the soft slip of mud under his feet. Behind him, people are calling but he shuts them out. He can only focus on the windows of the car, half-submerged, and the driver, who is still seated and doesn't appear to be moving. The current is strong, even here. Ed can feel himself being dragged away from where he wants to be. The water is as high as his neck now, and he knows he will have to swim the last bit, but he needs to reach the car. If it goes down any further there will be no chance of getting the doors open.

He treads water and slams his palm against the driver-side window. A boy looks back at him from inside the car. He's in the driver's seat so he must be older than he looks.

Ed pulls at the handle of the door, and it opens a little, then water starts to rush in. The boy is kicking and pushing but the gap is far too narrow for him to climb through.

Neither of them can shift the door, and Ed's jeans are dragging him down. The boy is crying for his mother. There are probably a few seconds left before the car fills with water, and it won't matter a jot that people are calling to him from the roadside, or that sirens are sounding in the distance. It will be too late.

He swims around the side of the car and reaches the handle of the hatchback. It turns and the door pings open with enough force to clear the waterline. Just. Ed calls to the boy, tells him to calm down, over and over, and to try and get himself through the body of the car. The boy doesn't move.

Ed unbuttons his jeans and tries to kick them off. Then with every last bit of his strength, and with the waistband of the trousers still caught around his ankle, he propels himself into the boot of the car enough to reach out to the boy. He takes the proffered hand and allows himself to be coaxed out through the boot and into the open sea.

It isn't far to the shore, but the boy clings hard. Ed has to do the swimming and finally the wading, for them both. A crowd has gathered, and an ambulance and fire engine screech out their arrival.

Ed supports the boy, and they stagger from the edge of the now visible line of mudflat and onto the pavement. People take charge then, and someone wraps a coat around Ed's shoulders.

They lead him to the open back-doors of the ambulance. The boy is already inside. His face is pale, and he is shivering terribly. One of the paramedics is rubbing his arms, while the other is shaking out what looks like a silver blanket.

Then Laurie is there, and she is hugging Ed, and Gina O'Connor is pushing him out of the way. She is speaking to the boy in a high-pitched tone: *Reece, Reece*, she is saying, and squeezing him and calling him her baby. Ed doesn't register anything except Laurie's embrace. It's all that holds meaning.

Chapter 23

September 2018

Laurie

'Do you think she's warm enough?'

Ed reaches a hand across his sister's shoulder and hitches up the blanket she's got over her knees.

Laurie places the flats of her fingers against Elissa's cheek. 'She's fine. It's hardly the depth of winter, is it?' In truth, Ed has been fussing over his sister's health even more since Reece's accident. That it's shaken him, she understands only too well.

When Gina received the phone call, just as Laurie was leaving, the bottom dropped out of the poor woman's world. They'd sprinted through the village and on to the promenade, to be faced with emergency vehicles and crowds of people, and the sight of Reece's bright blue car, half-submerged at the edge of the tide. When Gina saw her son in the back of an ambulance, alive but ashen-faced and dripping with seawater, she'd shrieked so much Laurie thought she was having a panic attack.

Then she'd seen Ed. People were looking after him, draping him with coats and trying to rub him dry, and he was standing, hunched and shivering, and letting them.

Some of the emotion Gina must have been feeling shot its way through her own body. She ran to Ed, shoving everyone else away, and he collapsed into her.

He'd cried then, held her tightly and cried and she could say nothing, but the whole experience has left him so raw, she hardly dares touch him.

'I don't like to think of her suffering, that's all.' Ed pushes against the handles of the wheelchair and levers it over a slight rise in the pavement.

'She's not suffering. Look at her. She's loving being outside.'

They are heading to Pete and Gina's house, responding to an invite that was given several days ago, and which Ed has struggled with. Laurie has persuaded him, finally. If Pete O'Connor has any sense, there will be a grovelling apology the like of which Ed has never seen.

There's a creep of cold in the air, and a wet mist has come in from the retreating tide. Ed is wearing a coat she hasn't seen before. It's a kind of rain-mac, long and green and very dated. She wonders where he buys his clothes, if any of them once belonged to his father. When she says as much, his expressions slides.

'This is why I could never come and live with you in London,' he mutters. 'Fitting in is hard enough here. Can you imagine me, swinging down Carnaby Street in my old gear. People would think I was an advertisement for *vintage*.'

'What do you know about Carnaby Street?' Laurie ventures a smile. 'It's a dump, if truth be told.' She has already picked up on his trepidation about leaving Chapel Field. She never really believed he would, but she won't leave him behind. Which is presenting her with a problem she can't solve. 'It'd be much better for Elissa to live in a city. The facilities would be out of this world, and I'd make sure you fitted in.' She wants to touch him, but stops herself. 'If Pete O'Connor doesn't do everything he can to help your acceptance in the village, he'll have me to answer to. And Gina. Whatever happens in the future.'

'I know all this.' Ed sighs. 'You've said it many times. It doesn't help how I'm feeling. It's like everything I've based my life on – and Elissa's – is gone. I don't feel good at all.'

'Are you sure you're not just ill. Properly ill. You got a good soaking the other day, and you must have swallowed some of that water. You should have let them check you out properly.'

'It's not that. Physically, I'm okay. But we've talked about how anxiety feels and I'm pretty sure it's got me in its grip.'

Laurie hitches her handbag higher on her shoulder and leans across to take the handles of the wheelchair. 'Let me,' she says. 'You gather yourself. We're almost there.'

Ed steps aside, then runs a hand across his face. He leans over Elissa again, checking her temperature by putting his fingers between her collar and the skin of her neck. She smiles up at him, and Laurie slows their pace enough to let them stay like this until they reach the O'Connor's.

Gina is at the front door immediately. 'Hi, sweets,' she croons, then, 'They're here,' over her shoulder.

Ed and Laurie lift Elissa's wheelchair up the steps and into the hallway. It's warm with the smell of coffee and something baked. Gina beckons them into the lounge and when Ed hesitates, she tells him not to be so daft.

Pete is standing by the fireplace. He looks deflated. When he catches sight of Elissa, his face caves in on itself and he begins to cry. Not loud sobbing or attention-seeking weeping, but a gentle pulse of breath and tears that makes him cover his face with one hand so that Gina has to hug him for a moment.

'This is Elissa,' she says when he's recovered, 'and she's been hiding in Diamond Hall all this time.' Then she kneels in front of the wheelchair. 'Let's get your coat off and give you a cup of coffee.'

Elissa's smile grows and it sets Pete off all over again.

Gina takes their coats and hangs them over the banister, then gestures for Laurie and Ed to sit down.

'No. Wait.' Pete steps towards Ed. 'I want to shake your hand first, Diamond. I mean Ed.'

'Diamond's fine, O'Connor,' Ed says, and Laurie falls for him a little bit more. He takes Pete's proffered hand, and they lock eyes.

'Look, you saved my lad. I'm not going to forget that. I've been an arse. My wife would say that's not news to her. But I apologise, okay. For the past, for now and for everything in between.'

Ed steps away again and Laurie wonders what he is thinking, but Pete hasn't finished. 'I know it'll be hard for you to accept what I'm saying, Ed. I'd struggle, if it were me.' He swallows, as though he's gasping for a drink. 'There'll be no more of that pathetic stuff I've done over the years. I promise you. And time enough for mulling over my reasons.' He turns to Gina. 'But now, get us a coffee, love. I'm gagging.'

This last comment slices across the tension in the room, cutting a hole just big enough for them all to escape. Laurie laughs lightly and Ed does the same. Then he asks after Reece, and the conversation is freed up completely. He's in bed, apparently, not because he's still shaken up, but because he's a teenager with a few days free of college, and nothing to do but sleep. The car is a write-off and he'll be lucky to get a replacement, after the scare he gave everyone.

The police have been in touch, and Reece has had a minor caution and the suggestion of a probationary driving course. Which he doesn't want but which Gina has said is a prerequisite of ever getting behind the wheel again. By the time she comes back in with a tray of coffee and a plate of what look like home-made cookies, they are joking about Ed losing his trousers, and Pete is holding Elissa's hand.

'There's a lot of stuff gone on that Pete will never be able to put right, Ed,' she says as she passes him a mug of coffee. 'But I hope we can all start again from this moment onwards. The feud between your family and the village is something I've never understood.'

Laurie wants to point out that a feud needs two sides who are fighting each other. She doesn't. Instead she brings up the subject of Richard Diamond's wedding photo. The one with the mysterious woman named Jen, the one who she's sure is Pete's mother.

'You probably haven't had the chance, after what's happened,' she says, 'but could Pete shed any light on who this Jen is. In the photo I showed you?'

Gina stares at her.

'I mean, would it be okay to show him the photo I've got of Ed's dad's wedding.' She turns to Pete, then adds, 'We're trying to identify people. Let's see who you can spot.'

When she pulls the photo from her handbag, Pete looks at Ed. 'Is this okay, fella?' he says. 'One minute we're saying to leave the past alone, and the next we're dredging it up.'

A flush of heat spreads across Laurie's cheeks. Pete has it exactly right, but Ed is saying it is fine and tucking into Gina's biscuits, so she passes the photograph across.

'Well,' Pete says, scratching at his chin. 'This is bloody yonks ago and I'm rubbish with faces.' He peers closer. 'But I'm guessing the guy with the buttonhole and cheesy grin is Richard Diamond. So the attractive woman with the dark hair must be his wife. Right? Is that our Olivia? Christ, it is. I know she worked for Ritchie Diamond for a bit. Those other three women all look the same to me.'

'My mum's in the photo,' Laurie tells him, but he's stopped listening.

'Jeez,' he is saying. 'That one there, with her boobs hanging out. It looks like my bloody mother.'

Ed

Sitting in a room with another man, sharing anecdotes and coffee, feels strange to Ed. It's the first time for almost twenty years he's done it. Pete O'Connor's apology seems to have come from the heart, and he's made an instant connection with Elissa, which adds to his credentials. Now, he's saying his mother was at Richard Diamond's wedding. Perhaps she was a friend of Alina's. Ed knows nothing about her, so he can't comment. Instead, he sits and listens to tales of this Imogen O'Connor and the terrible impact she had on Pete's life. She'd reinvented herself as *Jen*, it seems, while trying to hide her embarrassment at being the great-granddaughter of an Irish *navvy*. Ed has no idea what this is, but from what Pete is saying, it's very like another word he's heard in connection with the Diamonds: *offcomer*. Though he's not sure why that would be a problem.

One thing coming over clearly from Pete's story is the way Immy O'Connor coloured his thoughts about Ed's family. Her hatred was a physical thing, he said, that pressed down on Pete's shoulders and clogged up his thinking. She'd been the one who insisted Elissa wasn't alive anymore, that she'd died when she was very young.

When Pete had become free of his mother, at eighteen years old, he didn't feel the slightest tinge of sadness. He'd never been able to shake off her resentment of the Diamonds, though; it was too deeply ingrained. Laurie stops Pete at this point and asks for details, but he can't give any, except to repeat how much his mother had despised them. Yet here he is, stroking Elissa's hand and holding her coffee mug steady.

Ed can feel a pulse of anger starting up in his belly. It's a small beat but he knows it will push certain questions up to the back of his throat and out through his mouth. Is this the place for them? He's not sure, and he can hardly whisper to Laurie about it.

Before he can think any further, he has asked Pete about the night of the beating, when Ed had curled up in a protective ball and Pete had kicked at his face anyway.

Pete's head goes down and he hides behind his hands. The friendly atmosphere zips itself back up. His sister continues to smile.

After a few minutes, Pete tells them he was half in love with the boy named Marcus Butcher and would have done anything for him. Then he begins to sob again and says he didn't mean to kill him.

Gina kneels at his side and slides an arm around his shoulder. She explains about how Pete, thinking he was doing Marcus a favour, put a new set of brakes into his old rust-bucket of a car in the days leading up to his crash. It was never mentioned, so he kept it quiet: everyone knew what a crazy driver Marcus was, and this was the verdict at the inquest. Pete only told her a few years ago, she says, and this is why he's carried so much worry around about his friend's death.

Ed jumps up from his seat. He needs to be away from this situation. Only a few days ago, he'd heard Pete O'Connor accuse his own father of being responsible for Marcus Butcher's death. Now here he is, practically owning up to it himself. He is stupid to trust any words that tumble from this guy's mouth; he's a liar. Then Laurie is holding on to his arm and saying she just wants a few moments with him outside and nodding across to

Gina. Pete is still crying quietly, trying to cover it with his hands. Ed doesn't want Elissa to feel the tautness in the room, so he steps into the hallway with Laurie.

Before he can say anything, she presses him against the wall and reaches her arms around his neck and kisses him like she's going to devour him whole. He can do nothing but respond. When she pulls away and he looks to her for an answer, she tells him she is proud of him, and she loves him, and she doesn't care what went on between her mother and his father.

He believes every word of what she's saying, and he so wants this to be the end of things, but he knows it can't be. When she suggests they go back into the lounge and retrieve Elissa, he is happy to agree. Whatever the outcome of his relationship with Pete O'Connor, it doesn't matter. Being back at Diamond Hall with his sister and Laurie is all he wants.

Pete has managed to calm himself. He is helping Elissa on with her coat. Gina is crashing about in the kitchen, then she comes back into the room, saying something about confessions and having one of her own. There is a photograph in her hand, and she tells Pete his mother sent it a few years ago; that her address is on the back. He frowns out a mild anger, but Ed can see he doesn't have much left of any emotion; the guy looks wrung out.

Laurie wanted to do all the talking, so he listens as she turns to Pete and almost demands they visit his mother and get the last shreds of truth about Richard Diamond and his family. Pete lets out a long sigh and agrees.

Diamond Hall, October 1979
Richard Diamond

Richard Diamond put his hands over his ears as though the gesture could cancel out what Jen had told him. Pregnant? They'd only been together a handful of times, though he'd never asked if it was *safe*. That was the woman's responsibility. He hadn't wanted her anyway, yet here she was, sitting on his sofa and crying and asking him what they were going to do. They? There was no *they*.

'I can't believe you've been so stupid,' he shouted, above the sobbing. 'I've already got two babies. I don't need any more.'

Janet was putting the twins down for their nap. She was on leave from work as she hadn't been well, though he suspected it was because she'd become involved with someone. She hardly came to Diamond Hall anymore.

'Keep your voice down.' Jen tilted her head in the direction of upstairs. 'This is none of her business, and you'll panic the babies if you're not careful.' She wiped the palm of her hand across her nostrils. 'Like it or not, Ritch, I've got a baby on the way, and it's yours.'

Richard needed to think about this. How far along she was, he had no idea. The first time he'd had sex with her it had been summer; she'd been wearing a tiny floral dress and a pair of sandals. It must have been four months ago. Did that mean it was too late to get rid of the thing? He was hardly going to let himself think of it as a baby, not like the two sweet things Alina had given him.

'When's it due?'

Jen narrowed her eyes at him. 'It? That's horrible. You mean when is our baby due?'

'That. Yes. When?'

'I must have fallen pregnant almost straight away.' She

giggled through her tears. 'You're so virile. The midwife's given me a rough date of mid-March. I'm probably eighteen weeks gone.'

There was a self-importance in her tone which made Richard want to throttle her. Did she have no idea what a baby would do to them?

'Does that mean it's too late to get rid?'

'What?' Jen stared up at him from her seat. 'What are you saying?'

Richard lifted one shoulder then turned himself away from her gaze. He wasn't going to let himself become trapped.

'Ritch. Answer me.' Jen's voice had risen to a shriek. 'Are you saying you want me to get a termination? An abortion? Oh, my God.'

'What's the alternative?' he spat. 'You moving in here with me and us playing happy families? I don't think so.'

'Why not? Your other children need a mother. Let's face it, however much you'd like it to be Janet Helm, that's not going to happen.' She was up, out of her seat now, and wagging her finger like he was an errant schoolboy. Well, he wasn't. This woman had no right to try and get control of his life. Using a baby to do that was the worst thing possible.

'Leave Janet out of it,' he cried. 'At least she'd never deliberately get herself pregnant to snare a man. Unlike some I could mention.'

Jen stormed over to him then, and before he realised quite what was happening, she'd punched him in the side of the face, hard enough to make him see small pinpricks of light for a moment.

'Who knew everything that's said about you is the truth, Richard Diamond? Who knew?'

He rubbed the side of his face, more from shock than actual pain. At this moment, he didn't care what people were saying, didn't care that he was treating this woman with contempt, he just wanted her out of his sight. If she didn't go, he would not be able to control his actions. Anger was rising in him as quickly as if it were the tide flooding a pool, and it was scaring him.

Then Janet walked into the room. 'What the hell is going on?' she breathed. 'I've struggled to get the kids settled.' She looked at Jen. 'What are you screeching about, lady?'

'Ask him.' Jen stomped towards the front door. 'But watch your back, you silly bitch, or you'll be next.' Then she slammed her way out leaving Richard to wonder what her next move would be. As far as he knew, she had no father or mother to be chasing him up for support. If he didn't see her again, he wouldn't care.

'Well?' Janet was shaking his elbow. 'Something's not right here, Ritch. Tell me.' She led him to the sofa, and they sat down together.

'Jen's expecting,' he muttered. 'My baby.'

Janet sighed. 'You idiot. Didn't you use protection?'

'God, Janet. That's so crass. Why does it even matter now, anyway. Didn't you hear me? Jen's pregnant.'

'If I'm crass, you're nasty, Richard Diamond.' She wasn't shouting and he really wanted her to shout. Then he could prove to himself how much women were always the issue: women and their needy, wheedling ways. She got up from the sofa and moved towards the door.

'You're on your own with this.' She staggered slightly. 'I've got enough problems, without taking on anyone else's.'

What was he doing? If Janet Helm walked out of his life, he really was on his own. He could manage the twins himself, that wasn't the problem. She was his last contact in the village, his last platform for acceptance and inclusion. If he lost that, he might as well shut the front door of Diamond Hall and become a recluse. If he wasn't one already. He needed to change tack.

'Don't go, Janet,' he pleaded. 'I've made a complete muck-up of this situation and you're the only one I've got to help me out of it.'

Janet leaned against the door frame and put a hand to her forehead. 'God, Ritch. You're one on your own, you really are. I don't need this.'

'Please, Janet.'

'Look,' she said. 'You can't just dump a pregnant woman. You'd be leaving a child with no support. Imagine if that had been Ed or Ellie. Alina just left on her own, with no money or anything. Jen's baby is your son or daughter. You owe her.'

'I don't love her.'

Janet screamed. He heard it as a high-pitched and exasperated yell. 'What the hell has love got to do with it? You've created a child. Own it.'

There was a bitterness to her tone. A jagged edge. It brought Richard down to earth with a gigantic thud. He felt it judder his bones and pierce his brain. Janet was right; the child he'd created with Jen, a woman he'd hardly got to know, should not have to pay the price for their stupidity.

'What should I do? I've hardly any real money. It goes out as fast as it comes in. Shall I go after her and explain that?'

Janet shook her head. 'No. Don't go after her. She looked so angry; it'd probably make things worse. You're going to have to come up with a means of supporting her and the child. Any ideas?'

Richard let out a loud huff. 'I don't even know where she lives. I couldn't get money to her even if I had any. Where does she live?' He had a couple of new paintings on the go. They usually went for a tidy sum. If she sold one privately, she could probably get even more. He would send Jen a painting. Perhaps more than one. Janet could get it to her, and he could avoid another scene.

'I'm not sure where Jen lives, but I can find out. You need to speak to her again, once both of you have calmed down.' When he shook his head, Janet continued. 'Don't be like that. You must have fancied her; you had sex. Are you telling me you just *used* her?' She twisted up her top lip. 'Ritch? Can you imagine what Alina would have thought about that?'

'Leave my wife out of this.'

'Sorry. I shouldn't have mentioned her. But you know I'm right.' Janet lifted her coat from the back of an armchair. 'And now, I've got to go. I'll get back to you with Jen's address, and I don't mind delivering the painting, as long as you speak to her first. Okay?'

When Richard moved with Janet to the front door, it was all he could do not to throw his arms around her. There was a frailness to her appearance he hadn't noticed before and it made him want her even more. Alina had been her friend. It was obvious she'd never betray that fact. He watched as she slid her slim arms into her raincoat, then pulled the belt tightly around her waist. As she slung her handbag over her shoulder, she turned to him.

'I meant to say. I'm having to leave my flat, the one over the shop. Don't ask me to tell you why. I'll be in touch with my new address. Hopefully, I'm moving into the village. That'll make things easier, won't it.' She reached up and kissed him lightly on the cheek, then she opened the front door and left.

Richard stood in the porch and watched her go. He took a deep breath and let it trickle out again slowly through his nostrils. He didn't need this kind of upset.

Why he'd ever got involved with Jen, he didn't know. Missing Alina wasn't an excuse, and neither was Janet's rejection. In truth, whenever things didn't go his way, he got angry.

The anger could always be dampened down by grabbing at

something, anything, whether he wanted it or not. For some people it was cigarettes or alcohol; for him it was the frisson of a liaison. It needed to stop. He wasn't a bad man. If he gained control of himself, he might feel better about life in general.

The first thing for him to do was talk with Jen and map out a way through their stupidity. She was bound to visit Diamond Hall again; she loved Ed and Ellie almost as much as he did.

He would find a way to support her financially, and work out a plan for merging the life of his new child with the ones he already had. There could never be a relationship with her, though. It wouldn't be fair to lead her down that path again. If he was going to be with anyone, it would be Janet Helm.

Chapter 24

October 2018

Laurie

There had been another time when Laurie travelled in a car with Pete O'Connor, anxiety bubbling away in her stomach and numbing her thoughts. This time, she's in control, and she has Ed sitting alongside.

They are on the road to Keswick. It had been a shock for Pete to discover his estranged mother lived no more than forty miles away, and when Gina had offered to look after Elissa for the day, Ed had surprised Laurie by agreeing to take the trip with them. He'd wanted to see The Lakes his whole life, he'd said, though his agitated behaviour this morning had convinced her he was about to change his mind.

Craggy screes and slopes of sparse grassland zoom by. Ed has his window open, and his nose in the air. It's a beautiful morning, billowing blue and fresh, with only the first fade of autumnal decay fringing the green. Each time they pass a body of water – Windermere, Rydal, Grasmere – Ed wants to stop. He has instead, to be satisfied with the promise of a walk down to the edge of Derwentwater after their visit to Immy O'Connor.

'Who'd have thought my mother lived up here,' Pete says, from the back seat. 'The last I knew, she'd moved off the island and into town.'

'When was that?' Laurie catches his eye in the rear-view mirror.

'Just short of twenty years ago, I think. I dossed on Jamie's couch for a while; remember him? His parents weren't too keen on my oily overalls, so I didn't stay long.'

'I do remember Jamie. Do you still see him?'

'No. Did you keep in touch with that Ruth? The one who had a fling with Marcus?'

Laurie flashes him a warning; there is to be no talk of Marcus Butcher today. 'She went to Canada. We did Christmas cards for a few years, but it fizzled out when I got my house in London.'

'Oh, yeah. I forgot you sold out to the south. How will that work when... you know... when you go back?'

Laurie hadn't thought Ed was listening, but when Pete says this, he leans in from the window and looks at her.

'If,' she says and puts her hand on his.

As they reach the highest peak of the main road, the town of Keswick comes into view, sprawled out in a valley ahead of them and blurred with the mist of a chilly morning. Ed gasps, but Pete has spied the coffee shack in a lay-by up ahead and is directing Laurie to stop.

'If my mother's anything like I remember, she won't offer us *hospitality*. If she's there at all. Gina says she's had that photo and address for a few years. Anything could have happened. There's no other trace of the woman, as far as we can see, and I wasn't having my kids search her out on their social media. That grandma's dead, as far as they know.'

Laurie pulls the car into the lay-by, and Ed is outside in an instant, tucking his scarf into the collar of his anorak, and inhaling deeply through his nose. She can't help but smile: she's not seen him expressing pure, untainted happiness. When Pete brings three tall cardboard cups of fragrant coffee, she thinks Ed might explode with the joy of it.

'Thanks. So many firsts today,' is all he says.

They reach the main car park of the town and Pete buys a ticket. Then they wander into a shopping area, Laurie with her arm through Ed's and Pete striding ahead.

'Not as many tourists as I thought there'd be,' he says, eyeing up the cafés and mountaineering shops. 'I've no idea where I'm going but Google said Derwent Street is just off the main thoroughfare.' He nods towards a huge slate-built clock tower. 'This way, I think.'

He's right. They've walked no longer than a couple of minutes when they arrive at a quiet side street lined with terraces of white-washed cottages. They remind Laurie of the tiny homes on the outskirts of Chapel Field. Ed is saying very little, but his face tells her a story; he is fascinated by every aspect of this Lakeland market town.

'Here's number nineteen.' Pete has stopped outside a smart house with a black door and newly-painted sash windows. A square of slate on the wall has the number carved out in white, and a tiny shamrock in the corner. 'God, I think I'm going to lose my nerve.'

Suddenly, Ed pushes himself in front of them. 'Leave it to me,' he says. 'I've no vested interest and I'm that full of caffeine and adrenaline, no one could defeat me now.'

They all laugh at this, then he lifts the knocker, and they wait. No answer comes. Ed tries again while Pete peers through the ground floor window. When they are about to walk away, the door opens. A small woman is standing there.

She has the leathery complexion of a smoker and short, brassy-blonde hair.

'Sorry. I was out back.' It's a jagged voice with an unmistakable Irish accent. None of them speak while she runs her gaze from one to the other. Then she whispers *my God* in a way that makes Laurie feel like she's been caught playing *knock-a-door-run*.

'Mother. Long time, no see.' Pete is still half hidden behind Ed and it's him the woman is staring at.

'Jesus! You've nearly given me a heart attack.'

Ed smiles and holds out his hand. 'Ed Diamond. I'm a friend of your son. And this is Laurie Helm.'

'Eduardo Diamond? Never.'

Laurie watches the woman's face. If she had to summarise the emotions she saw in that moment, she'd say fear and love, in equal proportions.

'What do you want with me?' she continues. 'There's not bad news, is there?'

'You could ask us in, Mother.' Pete pushes himself forward. 'There's no bad news, but we'd like to talk. If that's okay?'

Imogen O'Connor doesn't move for a moment, and Laurie thinks she might close the door again. Then she sighs and pulls it back. 'In you come then. But I'm expecting Stu back in a half-hour and he'll be wanting his dinner.'

As they follow her into a tiny living room, Pete asks who Stu is and finds out his mother has a long-term boyfriend: he knows nothing about her son.

'He's not the family type,' she says by way of an explanation and Laurie feels some sympathy for Pete. He's only suffering this woman's coldness because of her. So she's not going to prolong it.

A brown corduroy corner-sofa dominates the room and faces an unlit wood-burner. The ceiling is low enough that Ed and Pete must stoop. They sit down and Imogen stands in front of the fireplace, arms folded and waiting.

'I knew you when you was a baby,' she says to Ed, 'but don't you be telling me anything about *him*, because I don't want to know.'

'You knew me as a baby too, Mother. Have you forgotten?' Pete's tone is scathing, and Ed shoots him a look. Laurie thinks it says *be quiet.*

'If you mean my father, Richard Diamond,' Ed continues, 'I do want to talk about him, actually. He's dead, just in case you didn't know.'

'Course I bloody know,' Imogen snaps.

'But my sister isn't. Elissa? Remember her?'

Ed pins Imogen's gaze with raised eyebrows. Laurie hears a slight huff from Pete, and she puts her hand on his knee to steady him. 'Hold it,' she whispers.

'What would you be talking about?' Imogen hisses. 'That little girl never made it past one year old.'

'Well, that's weird, because I've met her, Mother.' Pete explodes. He jumps up from his seat and steps towards her. 'There were a lot of other things you told me about the Diamonds that weren't true, weren't there?'

'Meaning what, exactly?' She reaches up and pushes against his chest. 'And you can stop throwing your weight around. I'm your mother, in case you'd forgotten. I know you.'

It's at this point Ed stands up and slides an arm around Pete's shoulder. Laurie wonders what he is doing. It dawns on her just as Ed begins to speak.

'Are you seeing the resemblance now, Mrs O'Connor? Who do we remind you of?'

Imogen puts her hands against the side of her head and begins to mutter *no, no, no*, over and over.

'And how is it you've found out?' she asks, when her breathing calms.

Pete is shaking his head; he's clearly the last one in the room to work out what is happening.

'As soon as I met Pete again, I suspected,' says Ed. 'But when he connected with my sister, it was obvious. He looks exactly like my dad in the few photos I've got of him as a young man.' He turns to Laurie. 'Show her the wedding one.'

She pulls it from her handbag and holds it out to a stunned-looking Imogen, who shakes her head and turns away.

'I vowed never to look at Ritchie Diamond again, and I'm sticking to it,' she spits. 'He ruined my life, that fella. And I hear he ruined a lot of others.'

Pete grabs both her arms, forcing her to face him. 'So I guess *I* ruined your life, too, did I? Nice one, Mother. Real nice one.' He lets her go again and she starts to wail. It's not the kind of crying that tugs on heartstrings and garners sympathy. It's a high-pitched sham and it makes Pete put his hands over his ears.

'Be quiet, you silly cow,' he shouts. 'You're going to go into that kitchen and make us all a cup of tea, then we're going to listen to what happened between you and... my father. And there's not going to be another fucking lie in any of it.' He takes hold of Ed's elbow and pulls him onto the sofa. 'Go on, *Mother*. What are you waiting for?'

Imogen scuttles through a door at the back of the living room. Laurie wonders if the woman will try and telephone for help. She's been rumbled, and this long-term boyfriend probably doesn't know the half of it. Pete and Ed sit side by side, shoulders rigid and hands clasped between their knees. Ed gives her a wink and she knows he's okay. Pete is grinding his teeth together so that his jawline looks completely different, and much more like Ed's. How has she never seen the resemblance before? It's subtle, but it's there, especially in their height and physique. Perhaps it was Jen O'Connor that Richard Diamond loved and not Janet Helm. It's possible. If the painting was meant for Jen, why did Laurie's mother have it? Does this whole fiasco mean her mother was not in Richard Diamond's eye-line at all?

When Imogen comes back carrying a tray of hot drinks, her hands are shaking. Under her lined and lightly tanned complexion there is a pallor that wasn't there before. Laurie feels some sympathy at last.

'Let me take that,' she says. 'Us turning up has been a shock, I imagine. We've all had to give ourselves a long hard look in the past few weeks. Me especially. I was rotten to Ed when we were kids. He didn't deserve it.'

She puts the tray on the floor in front of them and starts to pass out their drinks. Imogen perches on the edge of a small fireside chair and moves a cushion so that she can hug it.

'I know he was your dad, Eddie, but Ritchie Diamond was nothing but mean to me. He told me to get rid of my baby. Can you believe that? I'm talking about our Peter.' Her bottom lip trembles and she sucks it in.

'Well, you didn't.' Pete holds out his hands. 'Ta-da. I'm still here. So you'd better start from the beginning of the story and not leave anything out. Our *Eddie* has a particularly good instinct for lies.'

Imogen tells them about how she'd been drawn into the tight-knit friendship group of Alina and Richard Diamond, how she and Laurie's mother had vied for his attention, even while his wife was still alive. Alina hadn't even realised, so ready was she to believe the best of everyone.

They'd argued on the night she'd fallen down the stairs because Richard and Imogen had shared a drunken kiss and she'd seen. The guilt she'd felt afterwards made her keep going back to Diamond Hall to help with the twin babies. Richard's babies. He'd been so good with them, Imogen fell for him even more.

He was only interested in Janet Helm. Finally, Jen had broken him down and they started having sex, but when there were consequences, he flipped and called her stupid and told her to get rid of the baby. She'd refused and walked away from the situation, though she knew it would be a struggle to bring up a child on her own. She'd seen Janet Helm once or twice after that, and been told that Ritchie was going to send money. None came.

'Was he still seeing my mother at that point?' Laurie can hardly contain herself.

'I'm not sure he was *seeing* your mother, as you put it. Richard Diamond wasn't the type to be *seeing* someone. I know that, to my cost. But she must have been in contact with him for a while, bloody cow. She would walk past me in the street and shout across that Ritch was going to look after me because she'd told him to. I wasn't nice back to her, as you can imagine.' She tuts and Laurie laughs.

'My mother won't have liked that,' she says. 'Did you ever get any money from Richard?'

Imogen shakes her head. 'He didn't know where I lived, anyway. And she never said money, as such. Just that he was going to look after me.'

'The painting.' Ed's drink catches in the back of his throat. 'The painting was for *Jen.*'

'And my mother must have been trusted to pass it on, but she never did.' Laurie puts a hand to her forehead. 'Oh, my goodness.'

'What is it that you're saying?' Imogen is running her eyes between Ed and Laurie and chewing her nails in a way that makes Pete tell her to have a cigarette. She lights up with only a cursory *do you mind*, then starts again about the painting.

Laurie explains what she found amongst her mother's belongings and how it was probably meant for Jen, to help her pay for the baby.

'What use would that have been,' she huffs, smoke trailing out after her words. 'A bloody painting.'

'Richard Diamond's work was worth a lot of money. Is still worth a lot of money. I guess he meant for you to sell the painting privately. It would have given you a decent sum.' Laurie can hear a patronising tone in her voice. Imogen is right. What use would a painting have been to a woman struggling to buy things for her new baby. 'It's worth at least twenty-thousand pounds,' she says, and the tautness in the room shifts.

Imogen stretches her eyes. 'What the–'

'So. My father was thinking about you, after all.' Ed puts his mug back on the tray, then stands up. 'And we need to be going. I've got my sister waiting for me. Remember her? But there's something I want to say before we go.' He hesitates and catches Laurie's eye. She nods lightly. 'Whatever the reasons my family were treated so badly by the people of Chapel Field, you played your part. You knew where we lived. You could have come anytime and sorted out your grievances with my father. You chose to slander him behind his back. Just like everyone else did. It killed him, in the end, but it's not going to kill me or Elissa.'

Pete stands up and hugs him, then turns to Imogen. 'Bye, Mother. You've three grandchildren you've never seen, but hey-ho. Your choice, as always.'

He pulls open the front door and steps outside. Ed says a quiet goodbye then follows him.

Sorry, mouths Laurie, but she's not feeling it. Especially when Imogen calls after them that she'll be waiting for the money from the sale of the painting.

Ed

Pete wants them to find a pub and steady their nerves with drink; Ed's don't need steadying. There is a tantalising glimpse of water in the distance. That's where he wants to be. Pete is happy to be left at a pub while Ed and Laurie take a walk. When Pete says he'll catch up with them later, then adds *bro* to the end of the sentence, he hugs him again.

Ed thinks back to the evening when they'd stood chest to chest in the street while obscenities were exchanged. It was like staring into his father's face when he was in the fullest throes of anger. Ed has family, now. So does Elissa.

He's happy to send the proceeds from selling the painting, to Pete's mother. It's what should have happened all those years ago.

What Ed can't fathom is why his father had been chasing other women so soon after the death of his mother. Especially when he had two babies to look after.

His earliest solid memories of Richard Diamond came from when Ed was five years old and allowed into the *studio* for the very first time. This was what his father had called the upstairs room where he painted and sculpted. He'd talked to Ed about colours and brushes and clay, and there was no hint of anything but the devoted father and inspired creator.

That Richard had a temper, Ed had found out not long after this, when he'd taken it upon himself to have a go at painting in the studio and ruined an expensive canvas.

Perhaps it was simply living at Diamond Hall his father had found so unsettling. The place might be their home and the only one the Diamonds had ever known, but Ed feels like a different person, walking through this market town with Laurie, breathing in the scent of open water and mountains. There is an atmosphere of gloom surrounding the house, even on the sunniest days. He often feels it as a darkness behind his eyes and along his shoulders.

Could he bring himself to leave? For love, maybe, and it's what Laurie has promised him. Something doesn't feel right about it, though she's holding his hand as they walk. She's hardly saying anything.

At the edge of town, they duck through an underpass decorated with bright mosaics depicting the local landscape. Ed runs a hand across these murals and thinks about how much his father would have loved them. He'd spent the last seventeen years of his life holed up in Diamond Hall, watching out for people who might be gossiping about him; no life for a person of his father's talent. It must have felt crushing. Is Ed destined for the same?

Laurie leads him through a beautifully groomed and ornate public park and then they reach the lake. It stretches in front of him with its teal-and-silver surface, choppy from the wind and startling in its position at the foot of towering fells. He lets go of her hand and runs to the edge, picking up loose pieces of slate from the beach as he goes. Then he is skimming them and breathing in the freedom of the place. For the first time in his life, Ed thinks he could live away from Diamond Hall and Chapel Field, and when he says this to Laurie, she smiles. But she won't meet his eye.

Chapel Field, Christmas 1979
Janet Helm

Janet's stomach heaved and the red vitamin tablet appeared again, along with a gush of pale green bile. She leaned against the toilet for a moment longer then hauled herself up. Almost every morning for the last five months she'd been taken like this: a taste of metal at the back of her tongue then a flood of nausea that made her think she was dying. Once her stomach was empty, she felt well again, but the flesh was dropping off her like she had an illness. Now, the solid mass of her lower belly pushed out from her pelvis enough for it to be noticeable.

The floor on the landing didn't have carpet. She'd been in the house for three months and the small pot of money that had been her savings was long gone, most of it spent on making the place habitable for her and the tiny human being who would come into her life in the spring. She walked carefully downstairs, one hand on her bump and the other holding an armful of washing for the tub. She'd been lucky with the things people donated for her new home: a metal bedframe, a wooden cot, the twin-tub and a plug-in electric fire so she didn't have to start messing about with coal deliveries.

Her boss at the dressmakers hadn't been quite so kind: his gift had been a shrug of his shoulders and the comment that he didn't employ *unmarried mothers*. As if she'd ever have considered marrying Bob Johnson. He was nice enough, in a puppy-dog kind of way, and he had a gorgeous smile, but he was so serious, wanting to study and go to university. She'd been after some fun. There wasn't going to be any now though, was there.

This move back to the island was supposed to have brought her closer to friends and family. That was the hearts-and-flowers version. In truth, her gran was the only family she'd really had ties with, and she was long gone.

As for friends: Alina might be dead, but she was still a tangible presence, wedged between herself and Richard Diamond. Then there was Jen O'Connor. Janet loved Ritchie with all her heart, but those feelings could go nowhere. Especially now, when she was expecting another man's child.

A loud thumping on the front door jolted her away from these negative thoughts. This was probably the man come to take a new gas meter reading. She dropped the washing onto the kitchen counter and went through to the hall.

When she pulled back the door, there was Richard Diamond. Balanced between the toes of his boots and his hands was a large parcel wrapped in brown paper. She peered past him for a sight of the twins.

'They're with our Ron,' he said. 'In case you were wondering. He's down for Christmas with his *boyfriend*, so I thought I'd pop by and see how things were. Can I come in for a bit?'

Janet pulled back the door, keeping one eye on the parcel.

'What are you saying *boyfriend* like that for? It's up to Ronnie what he does with his life, I would have thought.' She watched as he staggered past. 'And what on earth's in there?'

'It's a painting for Jen. You did say I could leave it with you. I don't think she'd appreciate me turning up on her doorstep, even if I did know where she lived.'

He leant the parcel against a wall at the foot of the stairs, then started to unbutton his overcoat. Janet met his gaze. Her heart jumped. She offered him coffee and he smiled an acceptance. In the kitchen, he pulled out a stool and sat down.

'I've missed you up at the house, Janet. Are you avoiding me?'

Janet flicked on the kettle and turned to face him, bunching up her pinafore so that her bump was visible.

'Jeez,' he gasped. 'You never said.'

'How could I? What with the Jen situation and everything. It's my problem to deal with.'

'Who's the lucky guy?' Richard was smirking in a way that

made Janet want to slap his face. Everything was about sex to him.

'There was no luck involved, believe me. And it's over now, anyway.' She ran a hand across her bump. 'It's easy for the fellas. They can walk away whenever they want to.'

Richard snapped his gaze to hers. 'I haven't walked away.'

'You were going to.'

He let out a loud huff and shook his head. 'Look. I said I would look after Jen and I'm trying to. If you could give her the painting or tell her you've got it, that would help. But I'm really here to see you, Janet. I've missed you.'

Janet turned her back and carried on making their drinks, but her thoughts were racing. Could there be a future for her with Richard and the twins? What would the gossips of Chapel Field make of it? Not that their opinion mattered. Diamond Hall was full of memories of Alina and what came after. A future with Richard Diamond would have to be made far away from here.

'And I've missed seeing the babies, Ritch.' She handed him a mug, then pulled out another stool and sat down. 'It's all right you saying you've missed me, and I appreciate it, I really do.' She sighed. 'But I can't be with you, no matter what I feel. It wouldn't be good for any of us.'

'Why not?'

'Because of Jen, for one thing. Imagine how she'd be if she saw the two of us together, playing at happy families. It's exactly what she wanted but couldn't have. And anyway–'

Richard interrupted with a loud huff. 'What you mean is, you don't want to live with the Diamond *taint* for the rest of your life. Give me a bit of honesty, at least.'

Janet heard a quiver of emotion in his voice. It made her want to slide her arms around his shoulders. She mustn't give in. 'I am being honest. My feelings for you aren't strong enough to shore up the consequences of us being together. Sorry, Ritch, but there it is.'

'I don't believe you,' he whispered. 'I won't believe you.' He slammed the mug onto the table between them and knelt in front of her, taking her hands in his. 'You love me, I know you do.'

'No. And even if I did, it wouldn't be enough.' Janet stared at the man in front of her, with his dark hair and pained expression, and almost gave in. Then she thought of Jen and the way the woman had screeched at her when they'd passed in the street. It couldn't have been good for her own baby, that level of stress. More than anything, Janet wanted a healthy outcome for all their children. Which meant setting herself free from Richard Diamond.

Now, he was getting to his feet and looming over her. 'You're making a mistake, Janet,' he was saying. 'And you won't be welcome at the house if you don't want me. Ed and Ellie and me come as a package. All of us, or none.' There was a hardness to his expression, and one she'd seen before. In that moment she knew she'd made the right decision. There was no love for her in this guy; it was all about convenience, and now he was trying his hand at blackmail.

'Fair enough,' she spat. 'And I'll try and do your dirty little delivery to Jen, but I can't guarantee it. That bloody painting looks heavy. Taking it to her yourself would be a better option. She does live in Chapel Field, you know. It wouldn't be *too* inconvenient.'

Richard was already moving out of the kitchen. She could hear him in the hallway, slipping on his coat and opening the front door.

'See you around, Janet,' he called, then he was gone.

Chapter 25

October 2018

Laurie

By the time she's finished packing, there are tears streaming down Laurie's cheeks. She dabs at them with a piece of kitchen paper, then stuffs it in the pocket of her jeans. Leaving Ed and Elissa hasn't been an easy decision, and she's decided to keep her mother's house on, so there's a base for any future stays in Chapel Field. Her job and her London life can't be ignored any longer; she's needed elsewhere.

Despite many conversations with Ed, they'd never managed to return to the ease they felt around one another before mention of Richard Diamond and Janet Helm's affair. If there ever was one. It's the not knowing that's caused problems. Ed can't bring himself to take a DNA test, though Laurie is keen. He has tried to explain his reluctance; she has tried to understand.

Now that Gina is on Ed and Elissa's case, now they're *family*, Laurie has every confidence in their future, but she loves Ed, and she wants him and it's bringing her down. The sooner she can get some perspective on the situation, the better. She's said her goodbyes: they were messy and teary and incredibly sad.

It's raining again, and there's a gloom outside that feels like evening. Laurie pulls up the hood of her anorak and runs to her car. Ed's scarf is still on the passenger seat, and the sight of it gives her a feeling of profound loss. She picks it up and holds it to her nose, inhaling his scent.

It carries her back to their last conversation, the one where they'd almost agreed to forget about the past. Then Ed mentioned babies and things had spiralled again. Laurie wants children one day, wants the chance to be the kind of parent she never had. She wants Ed to be the father of those children. If she found out for sure that he mustn't be, it could destroy them both. Perhaps it is better to live in ignorance. Either way, there is not much she can do. He has refused to take the test.

As she drives along the promenade and across the bridge into town, Laurie tries to blank out the look on Ed's face as she'd walked away last night. Though she'd promised to be back within a few weeks, he wasn't convinced. He hadn't tried to persuade her to stay. Instead, he'd set his expression into a tight-mouthed grin that didn't match the tears streaming down his cheeks. Now, she was taking the main route out of town, and joining the traffic heading up to the motorway.

The journey takes her more than six hours, and she doesn't have even one break. There will be safety waiting at her flat, she's sure. Memories. A life with no connection to Chapel Field. Then her bond with Ed and Elissa will take on a more realistic size; she'll be able to manage its fraying.

When she arrives back in London, there's a hold-up on the dual-carriageway leading to her suburb. The traffic grinds to a halt and Laurie feels a bubble of anxiety in her stomach. Having time alone with nothing to think about is the last thing she wants. Tomorrow morning, she'll be back at the PRU and everything it stands for: demands, physicality, paperwork, sport, food, love and hate. It's exactly what she needs.

Ed's scarf is still on the passenger seat and his presence looms as much as if he were sitting there wearing it. Her shoulders sag, her face falls in on itself and she can do nothing but sob so loudly it's terrifying. Then her mobile phone rings. It's Gina.

Laurie almost declines the call. It can only be about Ed. Perhaps he's not coping. Or maybe he is. Either way, the woman feels like family now, and there's also the possibility she really is. In the end, as the traffic is still static, she presses the green button on the screen and waits for the other woman to speak.

On the previous evening, Gina tells her, Olivia had been taken ill; a stroke, the doctors thought, and she'd died a couple of hours ago. Laurie can only listen, and hold on to her tears and promise she will be back for the funeral. Which will mean another emotional return to Chapel Field, when she's hardly had time to process the first.

It's almost eleven o'clock when she finally makes it to the car park of her building. She doesn't even try to unpack, can only crawl up the one flight of stairs to her front door, have a brief look around, then pull on a musty smelling pair of pyjamas and fall into bed.

Ed

Elissa is asleep now, and Ed knows he should get up from where he has been lying, along the edge of her bed. It's more than twenty-four hours since he'd waved Laurie off, and she'd promised to come back in a few weeks. He's not sure she will. They both understood that being together could be more difficult than being apart, in the long term. He pictures her in the London flat she's talked about so often, cooking or reading or getting ready for work. That he's not in the picture almost cuts him in two, gives him a pain across his body like nothing he's felt before. If it's love, he'd rather not have it, though it's not the same as the panic he feels whenever his sister is out of sight.

The bedroom is so quiet. Through the French windows he can see the dark outline of the sea-wood and the silvery edges of raincloud backlit by the moon. Will he be able to get up tomorrow and live his life as usual, caring for Elissa and keeping them both alive? He's not sure. Gina was supposed to call in on him this evening, but she didn't turn up. Perhaps she won't now that Laurie's gone. The past couple of months feel like a dream. A beautiful one, so that waking up to reality is brutal.

There have been times, when he's laid with his sister to help her drift off, that he's thought about how easy it would be to end both their lives. Would anyone miss them? But it would mean he never saw Laurie again, though, and for that reason alone, he thinks he will have to carry on.

Chapter 26

October 2018

Laurie

I f there is such a thing as *rubbing someone's nose in it*, this is how Laurie feels as she walks towards Gina and Pete's house. It's barely been two weeks since she'd said goodbye to Ed, and a visit to Diamond Hall isn't going to help either of them. She can hardly come back here and not see him, and she wants to; more than anything, she wants to.

It's a damp October day, with a sky the colour of paper and just as flat. Behind her eyes, Laurie can feel the grittiness of fatigue. She'd driven in late last night, travelling once work had finished. Her boss had used words that suggested he understood her need for another absence, but his expression told her something else. So, she's going to say her goodbyes to Olivia, then be back on the road this evening.

A number of people are gathered outside the house, and there's a dark blue limousine waiting, with black-and-white cones holding the space for another. Gina waves when she spots Laurie, then steps towards her, arms outstretched. 'Thanks so much for coming, sweet,' she says.

Laurie lets herself be hugged, feeling the tension in Gina's body through the thick wool of her coat. 'Course I was going to come. I'm so sorry for your loss.' Pete is standing amongst the crowd, and it takes her back to the day of Marcus Butcher's funeral. How young they'd been, and how much they'd all been dealing with. The dislike she'd had for this man, when he'd been living with the same issues and difficulties is something she won't forget. It's making her overcompensate now. She hugs him in a way that he resists at first, then she feels him relax into her embrace.

'Loz,' he says, teeth chattering. 'How are things with you? Gone back to being a bloody southerner, have you?'

She grins up at him and notices the lilac smudges under his eyes and the patchy shaving-job. 'I'm not loving it like I should, Pete, if truth be known. There's a... drabness I haven't felt before. Is that wrong?'

He shakes his head. 'You're missing the sea-light, I guess.' He shrugs, then adds, 'And Ed. Am I right?'

'You are. How's he been?'

Gina comes over to stand with them. 'We need to get in the cars,' she says. 'Are you all right to come with me and Pete, Laurie? Mum's going in the limo with the boys, following the coffin.' She gestures towards the top of the street. 'It's here, now.'

Laurie hasn't met Gina's mother and can only assume she's the small woman with the frizz of grey hair who's standing with Reece and the other O'Connor boys. There's a hard edge to her face, otherwise she is the spitting image of Olivia.

As the hearse pulls alongside the pavement, voices are lowered and Laurie gasps at the beautiful floral displays visible through every window. People cling to their loved ones and bow their heads as they climb into their cars. All she can think of is how she wants to be holding Ed's hand and breathing in his clean paint and laundry powder smell.

While Pete drives them off the island, Laurie sits with Gina in the back of his car and watches the day flash by. People stare as the cortège passes, some stop and wait, some continue with their life, unaffected by the death of someone else's loved one. She's done this often enough herself: on the day of Marcus Butcher's funeral not one thought crossed her mind about his parents and what they'd lost.

'I've seen Ed a couple of times,' Gina is saying. 'Elissa is thriving. She loves being at the centre. I've learned enough about her now to know when she's happy. Ed seems relieved that someone else is as connected to her as he is.'

'Is he coping?' Laurie asks. Part of her wants Gina to say he's not. She wants to slap her own face for that reaction.

'It depends on what you're asking about. As I think you know.' She takes Laurie's hand. 'He's adapting to his new life in a way that reminds me of a puppy finding its feet. His enthusiasm knows no bounds and it's great to see, considering what's gone before. But–' She sighs. 'I know you two had a thing for each other, sweet. And it's killing him, not having you there. Is there no way–'

Laurie tries to blink away the tears forming along her lower lids. Explaining her fears won't be possible when they're still tangled up in the pit of her stomach along with her love.

Gina doesn't press her. Instead, she talks about Olivia and the way she'd been there, when Alison had not.

Laurie can relate to this. If there was ever a story to be told about the mothers of Chapel Field, *absent* might be a word used frequently. Gina has bucked the trend. For that, a lot of people are grateful. Laurie included.

When they pull up at the crematorium, a queue of people are waiting, huddled into their coats and chatting, but without the usual animation. To the side of the flat-roofed main building, a woman in a wheelchair is being lowered from a disability vehicle.

'That's Auntie Emily,' Gina whispers. 'I'm so glad she could make it.' She takes a deep breath then pulls on the door handle. 'Let's do this.' She puts a hand on Pete's shoulder. 'You okay, sweet?'

He nods. The three of them join Alison and the O'Connor boys while they wait for Olivia's coffin to be lifted from the back of the hearse. Then they walk together into the chapel and Laurie stops thinking about anything except the sharp little woman who is no longer with them.

The service lasts twenty minutes, and the celebrant is soon expressing the wishes of Olivia's family to join them at a local hotel for refreshments and the chance to reminisce about her life. It all seems so dignified. Laurie hasn't been to a funeral since Marcus Butcher's, and she can remember the weeping and crying out, the religious words dragging on and on, though no one seemed to be listening. Marcus hadn't had more than twenty years of his life; Olivia's had been eventful and full of love.

Gina and Pete and Alison stand together to greet people as they leave the chapel, and Laurie moves out of their way, hoping to get the chance to speak with this Auntie Emily, if only to say how much she admired Olivia, though she hadn't known her for very long. The woman is still in her wheelchair and is being pushed away from the crowd by an older man. He's wearing a navy-blue overcoat and has a mop of curling blond hair, threaded with grey.

'Hello,' she says as she catches up with them. 'Wasn't it a beautiful service. Olivia would have loved it.'

The man stops wheeling and turns to look at Laurie. And suddenly she's staring at her own face. It's her smile and her eyebrows and even her own slightly crooked nose. He clearly thinks the same because his jaw drops, and his eyes stretch wide.

'What on–' he stammers. 'My God. Who are you?'

When she tells him she's Laurie Helm, that Janet was her mother, his eyes stretch wide.

'This is our Bob, Laurie.' Emily is peering up at them both. 'Gina told me you were back in Chapel Field and had been to visit my sister. That was nice of you.'

But Laurie can't answer. She's pretty sure she has just come face to face with her father, for the first time in her life. Bob puts the brake on the wheelchair and then holds out his hand. 'I'd like to have a talk. If that's okay with you.'

Laurie nods, vaguely aware of Gina, who has moved away from the others and is walking towards them, raw faced but smiling.

'You've met then,' she says, tilting her head towards Bob. 'Let me take auntie and you two can chat.' She eyes Laurie. 'Funny how things come together, isn't it. From the first day I met you, I knew there was a familiarity. I've not had a lot to do with Bob, but a smile's not something you forget.' She leans her weight into the wheelchair and moves back towards her family.

For Laurie, the moment feels like she is standing on the edge of a cliff. The world behind her is lovely, but there is something infinitely more beautiful waiting if she can only allow herself to jump. She shuts her eyes and takes that step.

While she stands on the slopes of the cemetery, holding her coat around her, and looking out across the town, towards the coast, Bob explains everything. How he'd had a brief relationship with her mother, how she'd been in love with someone else and how she'd suddenly dropped him. He'd been heartbroken, wanting a future with Janet Helm, though she'd been a bit older. She'd blanked him. He hadn't told his family, had instead looked for a job away from the island and made it his business not to come back very often.

'I had no idea she was pregnant, I swear. You do believe me, don't you? I'd never have left her to cope on her own. I was with her through the summer of 1979, Laurie. I guess that fits with your birthday. Spring of 1980? Is that when you were born?'

'Spot on,' she says. 'Besides which, I'm the spit of you.' She runs a hand over her face. 'I'm finding this hard to take in, sorry. My mother and I never talked much. And she never mentioned you.'

'I'm not expecting anything, Laurie. I have a family of my own. Kids and a wife. We've just been presented with our first grandchild.'

Bob has a family. Laurie can't believe what she's hearing. There was a moment Ed and Pete shared, standing shoulder to shoulder in Immy O'Connor's living room and grinning, when she'd felt a twinge of jealousy. Not the full-blown, *I hate you, and hate myself more for being so envious*, kind of jealousy, but something. Discovering your family after having none. And now it's happening to her, she's not sure what's expected. Ed's come into her mind again, and there is only one thing she wants to do.

It doesn't take her long to give her excuses to Bob and persuade Pete to lend her his car. Then she's zooming up the drive of the cemetery and trying to keep herself breathing.

———

It's raining when Laurie pulls the car up the driveway of Diamond Hall, a fine rain, with a taste of the sea. The house is in darkness, and she wonders if Ed is even there; but where would he be, with Elissa, in weather like this? She tries flashing the headlights, but there's no response. Sounding the horn might scare Elissa, if she's here. Laurie turns up the collar of her coat and runs for the porch. If it's not open, she can always try the back door. Both are locked. It could be his day for taking his sister to the centre, but how would she know?

One of the last conversations she'd had with Ed involved her wanting him to have a mobile phone and him refusing to entertain the idea. It would be like being fitted with a tracking device, he'd said, and they'd laughed at that.

She decides to have a quick look through the French windows into Elissa's bedroom. If she's in there and asleep, Laurie will know Ed is in the house somewhere.

The chair by the window is empty and the room is unlit. It's hard to make anything out, but it could be that someone is lying on the bed. Or two people. Laurie knocks lightly with one knuckle, but nothing changes. She tries again and sees movement. Then Ed is at the windows and pulling them open.

'Laurie,' he breathes, then rubs a hand over his eyes. 'I've just got Ellie settled after her morning at the centre. What are you doing here? I thought–'

She pushes her way inside and closes the windows behind her. 'I wanted to see you,' she says. 'Something's happened.'

'Gina's grandma died: I already know.' He runs his fingertips over his eyes, then stares at her. 'When did you get back? I'm so glad you're here.'

'It's not about Gina's nan, Ed. I–' There are more words, but she can't say them because Ed has grabbed her and is holding on to her like his life depends on it, like he's a man about to fall into a deep hole and she's the only thing left to stop it happening. She can see Elissa, asleep on the bed, peaceful in the gloom, and she wants to ask why he didn't answer the door. Instead she frees herself slightly and peers up at him.

'Sorry. I've been standing out there for a while, and my coat's a bit wet. Can I take it off?'

Ed leads her out of Elissa's bedroom and into the darkness of the lounge. Laurie unbuttons her coat and lays it over the back of a chair.

'My dress is damp, too' she whispers. 'And you need to help me with it.'

Ed

Though Laurie is trying to tell him about meeting a man she considers to be her father, he can't focus.

Not when she's unbuttoning his shirt and running her hands upwards from his stomach to his chest, then across his shoulders. She's cold; he's not. Then she turns her back on him and is asking for help with her zip and he thinks he won't be able to give her what she wants; he's shaking too much. Somehow, she slips out of the thing, and it slides to the floor, leaving her standing in front of him in her underwear. He runs his hands along her collarbones and marvels at her softness. When she pulls him onto the sofa and kisses him, he thinks he might die from the sheer brilliance of the light shooting through his body.

He knows he shouldn't be doing this, knows they might be siblings, but he doesn't think he can help himself. Laurie must sense his hesitation because she stops kissing him and moves to sit in his lap. With her fingers over his lips, she explains to him about meeting a man at the funeral, who has the same face and features as her and a connection to Janet Helm that is undeniable. It takes a few moments for her words to crystalise into something he can understand. She has found her father, and it's not Richard Diamond.

There will be more of this story to come, he doesn't doubt. But it can wait. Right now, his attention is completely captured by the way Laurie has moved her thighs so that she's facing him, and is threading her fingers through his hair. He's caught in a beautiful and tantalising trap.

Chapter 27

November 2018

Laurie

The morning is clean and damp and filled with the smell of the tide. Ed clings to Laurie's hand like he'll never let her go, while she struggles to keep hold of the bouquet of shop-bought roses she's carrying. There's no warmth in the wintry sunshine but it's bright enough that Pete is wearing sunglasses and fussing with the peak of Elissa's cap.

'There you go, lovely girl,' he says as he starts to push the wheelchair again. 'She needs a pair of tinted glasses.' He directs this comment to Ed.

'Do you not think I've tried,' he groans. 'She just pulls them off again. This girl knows what she likes.'

Elissa smiles up at them all, and Laurie thinks her heart might explode. There have been further conversations with Bob Johnson, and she's found them meaningful and genuine: he is a professor of history and has travelled the world; he's studied and charted human pandemic infections; he's a clever man. Nothing Bob can offer compares to being able to plan for a future with Ed. Her London life can wait while she decides her next move,

272

though it's looking more and more likely that she will give up her job at the PRU and look for something nearer home. Ed has decided he wants rid of Diamond Hall once and for all.

'Ellie has some of the O'Connor stubbornness,' Pete is saying. 'Even if she's not one. If I'd ever had a daughter, that stubborn streak would have been magnified many times. Thanks, Miss Imogen O'Connor.'

Laurie thinks back to their meeting with his mother. When she compares her to Gina, that title shouldn't apply. *Mother*. It has to be earned, biology aside. Which is why she could never call Bob by anything other than his name. He'd had some interesting observations to make about the Diamond family, too. There had been a few parties at Diamond Hall, he told Laurie, and he was at the one when Alina fell to her death. He blamed the place. It's air of misery was nothing to do with who lived there.

The house should never have been built, he said, because the site was home to a fourteenth century plague pit. Ed's reaction, when she'd told him this, hadn't been what she'd expected. She'd seen relief in his eyes. It was like he'd been given a reason, finally, to explain his loathing of the place.

'We've all suffered at the hands of our parents,' Laurie says to Pete, 'but they were just trying to survive, like we all are. I'm glad I wasn't having to do it in other decades. Imagine not being able to have instant access to people's lives. It's how misunderstandings happen. I'm all for twenty-first century living.'

Ed splutters with laughter. 'That comment is for me, is it?' He smiles wryly. 'I'm not having a mobile phone, no matter how much you go on. You can teach me about the internet if you like, but that's it.'

Although he is making a joke of his previous way of living, Laurie knows how much he is struggling with the changes that have happened in the past few months. His issues around trust are understandable. So, when he'd suggested the three of them take Elissa and visit Marcus Butcher's grave, she'd shaken her head in disbelief. The only explanation he could give was that Marcus needed to be in on the end of their story; in some ways, he was the cause of it all.

They follow the sweep of the promenade, past a tiny café with two tables outside its blue-and-white frontage and the nutty scent of coffee filtering out through the open door. Just off the main road and up a steep slope are the gates of the island's church. Pete leans into the wheelchair and huffs his way to the top, while Ed and Laurie study the piece of paper they have, giving directions to Marcus's gravestone. The vicar had looked it up for them and emailed a map of the plots: another use of twenty-first century technology for Ed to moan about.

When they let themselves into the churchyard, Laurie and Pete talk about their memories of the place. Pete has been here many times, to attend weddings and baptisms and even the funeral of one of his colleagues. Laurie hasn't been inside the gates since she'd walked arm in arm with Ruth, trying to keep her upright while Marcus's coffin had been unloaded.

Ed isn't saying much. He's studying their map with an intensity Laurie can understand. They're about to search for the grave of a boy who'd never grown up with them but had somehow remained part of their lives.

They find Marcus's headstone in a quiet corner, shaded by an ancient yew tree. The dark-green marble is grubby and there are no flowers in the pots on the grave. Laurie tears open the plastic wrapping on her bouquet and starts to push rose stems into the holes.

'What happened to Marcus's parents?' she asks Pete, but he says nothing.

'Pete?' She looks up. He is staring across the graveyard,

towards the sea. He is crying. She lays the rose bouquet down and moves to stand beside him. He slides an arm around her shoulder, and she leans into him for a moment.

'Remember how Marcus used to stick up for me against your jibes,' she says. 'You were merciless, Pete, and he let you go so far, then he shredded you.'

Pete nods. 'We looked up to him though, didn't we. We had no dads, but there was always Butcher.' His voice breaks, and he slides a hand over his eyes. 'That's Chapel Field, isn't it. All our lives merged, like it or not. I wish—'

Ed puts the brake on Elissa's wheelchair then comes to stand beside them.

'No point in wishing,' he murmurs. 'I've never liked wishes. I used to read about them in books and they were always so—' He pauses for a moment and Laurie wonders what he is going to say. 'So wishy-washy. I want real things to happen, fights and love, and visits to wonderful places. And coffee. In cardboard cups. I loved that coffee.' He smiles at them both. 'You two have made those things happen for me, and I'm still struggling to believe it.'

Laurie wants to hug him. Here is a man who's been at the mercy of human misunderstanding for most of his life, yet he's come through. There's a grace about Ed Diamond, a humility, and she knows, with absolute certainty, there will never be another Diamond like him.

'You want coffee?' she says. 'I know just the place.'

THE END

275

Also by Paula Hillman

Seaview House

The Cottage

Blackthorn Wood

Acknowledgements

People local to Walney Island will recognise the name *Chapel Field*. It was an area of sea-wood, now given way to a small housing estate. The village in my story is fictional, but the premise of a chapel and plague grave will resonate with islanders. What I wanted to explore with this novel is how it might feel to live on the margins of conventionality, to be an *outsider*. Each time I've edited or proofread *Chapel Field,* I've experienced the emotionality that went into Ed's story, the claustrophobia of being trapped in a position caused by others. I hope my readers will become immersed in the same way.

As always, I am grateful to Bloodhound Books for the chance they took with my writing, and for the support and guidance I've had, editorially and personally. Thanks particularly to Betsy Reavley and Fred Freeman, and to Clare Law and Tara Lyons for their eagle-eyed support of my words. My daughter, Rosie Hillman, read *Chapel Field* in its early stages, and gave me timely advice; my husband adored the story from the start.

Chapel Field is dedicated to my local fan-base: those people who have stopped me in the street to chat about my writing, or have bought my books and messaged about new releases. And my heartfelt gratitude goes to Marianne… she knows why!

A note from the publisher

Thank you for reading this book. If you enjoyed it please do consider leaving a review on Amazon to help others find it too.

We hate typos. All of our books have been rigorously edited and proofread, but sometimes mistakes do slip through. If you have spotted a typo, please do let us know and we can get it amended within hours.

info@bloodhoundbooks.com

Made in United States
North Haven, CT
30 March 2024

50708605R00171